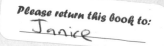
TEMPLAR'S WRATH

"I think the door is rigged," said Holliday. "I suggest that you stand aside."

"You're trying my patience, Colonel. I'll shoot you without a second thought."

"Just a suggestion," said Holliday.

Genrikhovich eyed him thoughtfully, then stepped to the left, the gun never faltering. Eddie did the same. Holliday tugged hard on the latch, then stepped rapidly aside. There was a deep, thrumming resonance from the corridor beyond the open doorway, followed by a groaning metallic whirring, like some sort of mechanical device being released. An instant later four immense arrows, each one at least five feet long, hurtled out of the doorway, their eight-inch-long iron points crashing through the mosaic tile on the floor and embedding themselves into whatever was underneath. The projectiles jutted out of the floor at a forty-five-degree angle about three feet from the open door. If Holliday had been standing in front of the door he would have been skewered like a shish kebab.

Also by Paul Christopher

RED
TEMPLAR

PAUL CHRISTOPHER

A SIGNET BOOK

SIGNET
Published by New American Library, a division of
Penguin Group (USA) Inc., 375 Hudson Street,
New York, New York 10014, USA
Penguin Group (Canada), 90 Eglinton Avenue East, Suite 700, Toronto,
Ontario M4P 2Y3, Canada (a division of Pearson Penguin Canada Inc.)
Penguin Books Ltd., 80 Strand, London WC2R 0RL, England
Penguin Ireland, 25 St. Stephen's Green, Dublin 2,
Ireland (a division of Penguin Books Ltd.)
Penguin Group (Australia), 250 Camberwell Road, Camberwell, Victoria 3124,
Australia (a division of Pearson Australia Group Pty. Ltd.)
Penguin Books India Pvt. Ltd., 11 Community Centre, Panchsheel Park,
New Delhi - 110 017, India
Penguin Group (NZ), 67 Apollo Drive, Rosedale, Auckland 0632,
New Zealand (a division of Pearson New Zealand Ltd.)
Penguin Books (South Africa) (Pty.) Ltd., 24 Sturdee Avenue,
Rosebank, Johannesburg 2196, South Africa

Penguin Books Ltd., Registered Offices:
80 Strand, London WC2R 0RL, England

First published by Signet, an imprint of New American Library,
a division of Penguin Group (USA) Inc.

First Printing, January 2012
10 9 8 7 6 5 4 3 2 1

*For Helder Rodrigues, roommate,
who started me thinking about a big man with a kind
heart, from the older gentleman.
And for fellow author
Simon Toyne,
who is just beginning the hellish journey.*

"There is no proletarian, not even a Communist, movement that has not operated in the interests of money, in the direction indicated by money, and for the time being permitted by money—and that without the idealists among its leaders having the slightest suspicion of the fact."

—Oswald Spengler, *The Decline of the West*

"Man has an invincible inclination to allow himself to be deceived."

—Friedrich Nietzsche, "On Truth and Lies in a Nonmoral Sense"

"La mediocridad se impone."

—Fermina Alfonso, *Cantante de Opera Cubana*

PROLOGUE

The bearded man stumbled out of the kitchen entrance of the enormous house, blood and vomit streaming from his open, gasping mouth. The snow was blinding and he beat at it furiously, desperately trying to see where he was going. The pain in his upper back was excruciating, and his right ear had been torn to shreds by Felix's second shot. The bearded man brushed a bloody hand across his face. His eyes were almost swollen shut from the beating he'd taken, but if he could only make it home, home to his little girl, Maria, he would be all right.

He heard muffled footsteps in the snow behind him, the footsteps of a running man. It had to be Rayner, Felix's sodomite friend from Oxford. Despite the awful pain welling up in his stomach and the blood draining from the stab wounds in his back, the bearded man increased his pace, his heaving lungs on fire, his bleary eyes searching for the steps that led down to the frozen canal. If he could cross to the other side he could disappear into the maze of streets and alleys and, if he was very lucky, reach safety.

He gritted his broken teeth and forced himself onward through the blizzard, silently cursing the cowards who would so savagely attack a man of God. He had never wanted anything more than to bring his knowledge and his powers to the world, but to them he was a danger: light to their darkness, good to their whispered evil, courage to their cowardice.

Somehow he managed to find the steps and staggered downward, his left hand gripping the cold metal railing. He risked a quick look back over his shoulder. There was no sign of Felix or his foppish, smooth-faced friend. His heart beat faster. There was hope! Of course there was hope, for wasn't he one of the chosen of God, with nothing less than the healing faith of the Xristos coursing through his hands? He had brought a sick and dying prince back to his mother's arms; there must be hope for him as well. Certainly Saint Seraphim would not abandon him now.

The bearded man reached the ice of the canal, then slipped and slid toward the bridge two hundred yards away, where he knew there was another set of steps. There would be lamplight on the bridge and perhaps even a policeman. Here and there the ice was black and thin, cracking beneath his feet. He skirted those areas, his eyes on the snow-shrouded span of the bridge.

The bearded man reached into the pocket of his dark, heavy coat and felt the heavy oval object deep in the fleece lining. . . . This, at least, he could keep from them, their foul crucible, their blasphemous secret. Such things were monumentally dangerous and could change the world if revealed by those without the understanding to deal with them. The proverb learned by the bearded man from his friend Spiridon Ivanovich still held true: "For upright men there are no laws," and if he was nothing else in this frozen hell of a city on the edge of the world, he was an upright man.

The terrible pain deep within his chest caught him by surprise. He stopped dead in his tracks and stared downward. There had already been bloodstains on his white cotton shirt from the beating and the stabbing, but this was something else. This was blood from a spigot splattering out in thick, gouting splashes, deep red heart's blood.

The bearded man looked up. Across a narrow patch of dark, thin ice he could see a figure with a large pistol in his hand. The man was slender, with a tweed overcoat over his uniform. Oswald Rayner, George Buchanan's man from the old Saltykov mansion on the Neva.

"Вы убили меня! You've killed me!" said the bearded man, his accent that of a peasant. He fell to his knees, his hands cupping the blood still streaming from his chest.

"Еще я не имею," said Rayner. "Not yet I haven't."

He raised the big Webley again, aimed it at the bearded man's face and pulled the trigger. A large circular hole was punched in the man's forehead and the back of his head turned into a fountain of blood, bone and brains spraying back for several yards along the ice-covered canal. "*Now* I've killed you," said the young lieutenant. He stuffed the Webley back into the pocket of his overcoat. The body of the bearded man sagged forward and then struck the ice. The ice cracked and then broke under the weight of the body. The remains of the bearded man slid instantly into the black, freezing water. The Mad Monk was gone at last.

Grigori Rasputin was dead, taking his secrets with him.

1

Lieutenant Colonel John Holliday (U.S. Army Rangers, retired) had spent half a lifetime in the military and had flown millions of miles in various airplanes without the slightest fear for his own safety. But now as he rode along in a Tupolev 154 airliner he was suddenly aware of the craft's appalling crash record, not to mention its NATO designation: *Careless.*

"Why did we have to take *this* particular flight, Eddie?" Holliday asked his companion. Eddie, whose full name was Edimburgo Vladimir Cabrera Alfonso, was an expatriate Cuban who had saved Holliday's life recently in the middle of an African revolution. The man was now accompanying him to Turkey, and perhaps on to Russia. They traveled at the request of a man named Victor Genrikhovich, who'd buttonholed them in the Khartoum International Airport. Genrikhovich, who only spoke Russian, looked like someone who'd just walked out of a Bowery flophouse, and claimed he was a curator at the Hermitage Museum in St. Petersburg.

Under most circumstances Holliday would have smiled, given the man a dollar and gone on his way, but this Bowery bum knew the name Helder Rodrigues and the Latin term *Ferrum Polaris*. Either the name or the Latin would have stopped Holliday in his tracks; both together were enough to get him onto a plane bound for Istanbul, even a decrepit old Soviet model belonging to a company called Assos Airways.

"Señor Genrikhovich said it would get us to Istanbul the most quickly," answered Eddie. The Cuban had been born barely a year after Fidel made his triumphant entrance into Havana in 1959, and spoke fluent Russian. He turned to Genrikhovich, who sat across the aisle eating his complimentary cheese sandwich, and spoke a few machine-gun phrases. Genrikhovich nodded and spoke briefly through a mouthful of half-chewed sandwich. Eddie turned back to Holliday. "Same as before. He says there is someone in Istanbul he wants us to meet. This man will explain everything."

"He has to tell us something. I'm on a plane to Turkey, for Christ's sake. Who are we meeting?" Holliday asked.

Another exchange between Eddie and Genrikhovich, and Eddie turned back to Holliday. "His name is Theodore Dimitrov. A monk."

A monk—at least that made a bit of sense, thought

Holliday. Helder Rodrigues had been a monk of sorts, guardian of Aos, Sword of the East, one of four swords taken out of the Holy Land by four different Templar Knights shortly after the fall of Acre in 1291, which effectively ended the Christian presence in the Holy Land.

Aos in turn was the perfect mate to the sword he and his cousin Peggy had discovered hidden in his uncle Henry's library at his home in Fredonia, New York: Hesperios, Sword of the West, the sword that had taken him and Peggy halfway around the world and back again and showed them a dark, underground universe of secrets that still plagued him.

And now this—Ferrum Polaris, Sword of the North. The third Damascus blade of the quartet supposedly made by Alberic, the mythical and magical dwarf blacksmith common to the mystical cultures of a dozen empires and nations. To Holliday it somehow seemed that the ghosts of those four Templar Knights from eight hundred years ago were haunting him, forcing him to discover their final secrets before their souls could finally rest.

The seat belt sign flashed on and the intercom crackled as the heavily accented voice of the pilot announced that they were making their final approach to Istanbul Atatürk Airport. Holliday sighed. He stared up at a loose, rattling rivet in the roof of the old aircraft and hoped for the best.

2

The Tupolev 154 landed without incident and eventually the three men made their way through customs and immigration. Genrikhovich's tattered Russian Federation passport, as well as Eddie's pale blue República de Cuba passport, raised a few eyebrows among the bored customs staff, especially since the two were in company with an American identified as a retired lieutenant colonel in the U.S. Army, but they were allowed to proceed.

They stepped out into the modern concourse and Genrikhovich immediately spoke to Eddie in Russian, casting worried glances in Holliday's direction every few moments. Finally he stopped talking and began scuttling down the concourse, heading for the car rental agencies.

"Now what?" Holliday asked as he and Eddie followed the Russian down the long, echoing corridor.

"The monk, it seems, is not in Istanbul. We must rent a car."

Holliday sighed wearily. "So where is he?" His patience with Genrikhovich was rapidly running thin.

"Bulgaria," said Eddie.

Holliday stopped in his tracks. "You're kidding me."

"I am afraid not, *mi coronel*," the Cuban answered. "The monk is in a place called Ahtopol. Our Russian friend says it is about a hundred and fifty kilometers from here. Perhaps ninety of your miles."

"You're sure there really *is* a monk?"

"According to tovarich Genrikhovich there is."

"So what was this about a restaurant in Istanbul?"

"Tovarich Genrikhovich is extremely hungry. He has not eaten since leaving St. Petersburg two days ago, except for the sandwiches on the aircraft."

Orange rubber between pieces of white cardboard. Holliday had taken one bite and stuffed the remainder of his into the seat's barf bag.

"In for a penny, in for a pound," said Holliday, setting out after Genrikhovich again.

"*¿Cómo? ¿Qué dijiste?*" Eddie asked quizzically.

"We're a day late and a dollar short—we've gone too far to back off now."

"Ah." Eddie nodded. "In Spanish we say, '*Faltan cinco para el peso.*'"

Genrikhovich stopped at the Terra Car booth at the far end of the terminal and had a discussion with the man behind the counter. They spoke in neither Russian nor Turkish as far as Holliday could tell. He asked Eddie, but the Cuban only shrugged. Finally Genrikhovich turned, chattered away to Eddie, and then turned and looked expectantly toward Holliday.

"It is difficult to rent a car that you can take across borders," explained Eddie, translating. "He needs your credit card to get approval."

The rental car turned out to be a Moskvich Aleko of roughly the same vintage as the Tupolev on which they'd flown into Turkey. Not only did Holliday have to pay the rental fee, insurance and security deposit; he had to drive as well, since he was the only one with an international driver's license.

With the car dealt with they went in search of food for Genrikhovich. His choice, bizarrely, was one of three Burger Kings at the airport, where he inhaled a Quad Stacker and fries. Holliday settled for a Whopper Jr., and Eddie begged off entirely, refusing to eat what he referred to as *la carne de la calle*—"street meat."

They finally set off, the four-cylinder sewing-machine engine in the Moskvich grinding and banging, barely making fifty miles an hour on the surprisingly good highway leading northeast. Within ten minutes of leaving the airport, Genrikhovich was groaning, his stomach gurgling, and he muttered, *"Prash-chayn-ya,"* every few seconds for the inevitable and gaseous results of a Quad Stacker on an empty stomach. Eddie rolled the window down and smiled, enjoying the early-fall scenery.

For the first hour the roads were smooth—modern

freeways with good signage, even if it was in an incomprehensible language. Foreign traffic signs never bothered Holliday, though; there were invariably rest stops and roadside food and lodging turn-ins where a traveler could always find someone willing to give directions, even if it was half in broken English and half in sign language. As a soldier, Holliday had done a lot of traveling, and in his opinion most people were proud of their country and proud of their innate hospitality—with the possible exception of the Asmat people of New Guinea, who would sooner eat you than feed you.

By the second hour they'd veered even farther north toward the coast, and the roads went from good to bad very quickly. Soon they were traveling on old concrete pavement that kept throwing up stones that sounded like machine-gun bullets whacking into the underbelly and the side panels of the car. Scrubby cedars and pines edged both sides of the two-lane road. By then Eddie had rolled up the window because of the dust and Genrikhovich's incessant *"prash-chayn-ya"* apologies for the state of his bowels. The noxious effect of a half pound of meat, four slices of rubbery cheese and six strips of fatty bacon had turned the air in the small, hot and noisy car into a fetid soup.

There turned out to be several border crossings. The first was a modern arrangement of buildings, flags and poles, which they got through with a minimum of fuss and lots of smiles. They quickly filled out visa forms and had their passports duly stamped, and Holliday used one of his credit cards to purchase a walletful of smallish pink and blue twenty-lev notes from the border post's ATM.

The second border crossing was a slightly tougher-looking but abandoned version of the first that dated back to perestroika. The last one, small, overgrown and choked with underbrush, was a plain, one-man hut with a broken barrier that was probably World War II vintage. It was the off-season, so there wasn't much traffic.

A few minutes later the two lanes became one, with a mysterious dotted white line where the shoulder should have been. Off to the right the Black Sea appeared, hazy in the distance. To Holliday it looked like every other ocean he had ever seen, and he'd seen a lot of them through the years. Maybe too many. He'd thought about that a lot since the horrors he'd witnessed recently, deep in the African jungle. Maybe it was time to quit. Maybe it was time to do what old soldiers were supposed to do, just fade away. It wasn't the first time the thought had crossed his mind in the last few years.

Dust or not, Holliday and Eddie rolled down their windows. In the backseat, Genrikhovich just moaned.

"You never talk to me about the ladies, *mi compadre*. You never talk about you make sex like other men," said Eddie.

Holliday burst out laughing. He turned toward Eddie, whose deep brown eyes were twinkling like an Irishman's. The big black Cuban was grinning. He reached out and poked a forefinger into Holliday's ribs.

"You not *un comepinga*, are you, a *maricón*?"

"No, not if that's what I'm pretty sure I think it means."

"You have a lady, a wife?"

"I did, a long time ago."

"Where is she now?"

"She died. Cancer. More than ten years ago now."

"*Mi mas sentido pesame, compadre*, but that is a long time, no?"

"Yes."

"You loved her very much, yes?"

"Yes, very much."

"Did you have children?"

"No, unfortunately. We both wanted them, but . . ."

"*Se agote el tiempo*—time ran out, yes?"

"Yes."

"I have many, little Eddie . . . Eduardo, not Edimburgo. *¡Alabado sea Dios!*, I would not do that to a child . . . Cleopatra, Estrella, Domingo, Miroslava . . ."

"Miroslava? Funny name for a Cuban."

"My mother, she had admiration for a famous Mexican actress, Miroslava Stern."

"There was such a person?"

"Of course, she is starred with Mel Ferrer in *The Brave Bulls*. It was the story of Luis Bello; 'the Swords-

13

man of Guerreras,' they call him. The greatest matador in all of Mexico. Very, how you say, *classico* with the ladies as well. He would say to one, *'Cada día te quiero más que ayer, y menos que mañana.'* 'I love you today, but not as much as I will tomorrow.' And they would fall into his arms. Ay, what a man was this!"

"Where are these children?"

"In Habana."

"And their mother?"

"Many mothers. One for each child, which is what I am saying to you. You need . . . *la variedad, ¿comprende?*"

"Variety?"

"*Sí*, variety, *la variedad*."

"So you're telling me I should get out more—is that it?"

"*¿Qué?*" Eddie responded, then smiled, nodding. "Yes, this is what I am saying."

"I'll think about it."

"That would be a start."

Holliday decided that it was time to change the subject. "Genrikhovich's asleep," he said, glancing in the rearview mirror. The Russian was snoring loudly.

"At least he is not making *peos* anymore." Eddie grinned, pinching his nostrils.

"Good point," said Holliday. "Maybe things are looking up."

Ahead of them Ahtopol appeared, a 1950s pastel vision of a Black Sea resort for high-ranking apparatchiks, government employees with enough money to rent an umbrella on the beach and a pink or yellow or blue little villa by the sea. A Marxist-Leninist paradise. The place was a ghost town, and from the highway they could see that all the beaches were empty. It was October and winter was in the wind.

3

The monastery of Saint Simeon the Plowman lay nestled in the hills above Ahtopol, surrounded by stands of birch and alder. Farther up the slopes spread the cool green of a pine forest that had once provided the lumber for the fishing fleets and trading ships that set out from Peronticus, as the Romans had once called the seaside town.

The monastery had the typical look of most Templar sites Holliday had seen, as much fortress as a place of religious enlightenment. A high stone wall surrounded a round church, its windows doubling as slits for archers. There was a refectory behind the church, presumably with the kitchens below, and a bleak-looking windowless chamber that was probably a charnel house for depositing the bones of monks who'd died here over the past eight hundred years.

Ranged around two sides of the fortress walls was a cloister with cells for the monks, and in the center of the cloister a courtyard with a well and a statue. For a monastery dedicated to Saint Simeon Stylites, the hermetic who set himself upon a stone column to deny himself temptation. Simeon himself would have been an appropriate subject for a sculpture, but instead there was a life-size figure of a horse and two riders, one of the most enduring symbols of the Templar Knights. The statue was in bronze green with age, the walls and church were local pale stone and the roofs were iron gray slate.

Holliday parked the rental car on the gravel beside the death house and woke up Genrikhovich, who still looked a little queasy. Leaving the doors and windows of the Moskvich open to give the vehicle a much-needed airing out, the three men entered the church. It was a simple room, with a single aisle lined with perhaps twenty benchlike pews on each side, the aisle leading to a plain stone altar with a rose window behind it with a rendition of the face of Christ. Each of the four petals of the rose contained the figure of a knight, the familiar Croix Rouge of the Templars on their body-length "kite" shields. Each knight wore a helm and hauberk of chain mail and carried a sword in his right hand. At the feet of each knight was a single word on a ribbon: Aos, Hesperios, Polaris, Octanis. The stars of east, west, north and south. It was certainly no coincidence. The four words were the names given to the four swords that carried the hidden and coded message out of Castle Pelerin and the Holy Land: *We are betrayed. The king and the Holy Father conspire against us. Let Sagittarius be the guardian's inspiration and pray that he be guided by the loins of the bear.*

Although the last part of the message remained obscure, its meaning lost in time, the first part was prophetic enough. King Philip IV of France, in the midst of a financially draining war with England, had already expelled the Jews from his country, seizing their assets, and by 1293 was conspiring with his chief political adviser, the Bishop of Bordeaux, Raymond Bertrand de Got, to assassinate the pope, then replace him with the bishop.

As pope, on Philip's order, de Got would dissolve the Templars and seize their enormous assets in France, thus simultaneously absolving Philip of responsibility for his equally enormous debts to the order. A simple enough plan on the face of it, but it took time to put all the pieces in place, giving the Templars an opportunity to discreetly move the greater part of their wealth out of France and Philip's clutches, as well as to infiltrate the royal court with well-placed spies. On Thursday, October 12, 1307, there were fifteen heavily loaded Templar ships in the harbor at La Rochelle, the last of the Templar fleet in France. The next day, when Philip's order to arrest the senior members of the order took effect, the ships had vanished. Their secrets vanished with them.

* * *

A monk in the plain working robes of a Russian Orthodox monk was on his knees in front of the altar with a bucket and a scrub brush, cleaning the stone floor as Holliday, Eddie and Genrikhovich entered the monastery chapel. Genrikhovich muttered something to Eddie, and the Cuban turned to Holliday, nodding toward the monk.

"That is the man, Theodore Dimitrov."

The monk stood as they approached, drying his hands unceremoniously on his water-stained robes. He was much younger than Holliday had expected, no more than thirty or so, slim, dark haired, with a long, narrow face and deep-set eyes as black as Eddie's skin. He nodded perfunctorily to Genrikhovich, then concentrated on Holliday.

"You are Holliday, the one who knew Brother Rodrigues?" His English had a faint British cast to it.

"Briefly," Holliday answered, surprised at the monk's abrupt question.

"You keep the book?"

The bloodstained notebook of names, contacts and coded account numbers given to him by the dying Rodrigues, the *codex mystericum* to nine hundred years of the ancient order's history.

"Yes."

"You keep it safely?"

"In a bank vault."

"You saw the rose window. You know its significance?"

"It marks the four swords that went out from Pelerin."

"Who made them?"

"Alberic Fecere," Holliday responded.

"What is the true meaning of the cross?"

"The four sides of the pyramid, the secret revealed."

"Which sword was yours?"

"Hesperios," said Holliday. "The Sword of the West."

"Which sword did Rodrigues have?"

"Aos, Sword of the East."

The monk nodded as though Holliday had passed a test of some kind.

"Come with me," said Dimitrov.

The monk led them to a narrow door to the left of the altar, which he opened with an iron key hanging from his belted cassock. Stone stairs led downward. The monk headed down and the others followed. The stairs led to the chapel crypt. It was a single, barrel-vaulted room lit by a lone clerestory window, which allowed in a bar of sunlight that fell upon the stone effigy of a knight set on a high granite plinth. Instead of a shield across his breast there was a sword. A motto was carved into the plinth, the letters worn with age and time: *Non nobis, non nobis, Domine Sed nomini tuo da gloriam. Not to us, not to us, O Lord, but to your name give glory.* Beneath the inscription was a circular seal—a double-headed eagle gripping a sword in its talons circumscribed by the inscription: *Magister Templaris in Rostov.*

The double-headed eagle, a heraldic device used by half the countries in Europe, including Bulgaria, and the central part of the Romanov crest.

"Who was he?" Holliday asked.

"Mikail Alexandreivich Nevsky, the last master of the 'Rus' Templars, an illegitimate child and grandson of Alexander Nevsky. He had no place in the hierarchy of his family even though he was a prince, so he joined the order."

"He carried one of the swords from Pelerin?"

Dimitrov nodded. "Polaris."

Sword of the North.

4

The monk brought them out of the crypt and led them to a small office in what had probably once been the sacristy of the little church. There was still a large vestment cupboard with beautifully carved and decorated doors against one wall and a table on which stood various gold chalices, patens, ciboria, aspergilla and other liturgical vessels.

There was a plain wooden desk and several chairs set around it. The monk sat behind the desk and gestured to his guests to seat themselves. The only artwork on the wall was a wood-and-gold-leaf-framed icon of Saint Simeon seated on his column. The walls, like the rest of the church, were bare stone.

Tired and more than a little annoyed at the game of hares and hounds he'd been lured into playing for the last ten hours or so, Holliday spoke first. "All right then, Brother Theodore, if that's what you call yourself, I've come a long way on the strength of a name and a Latin phrase. I'd much rather be sitting down to a nice rib-eye dinner at the Plaza right now, which was my previous intention, so let's see if my side trip to sunny Bulgaria was worth it or not."

The monk said nothing. He opened the drawer in the desk and withdrew a large manila envelope, pale with age. He slid it across the desk to Holliday, who opened it and removed a single photograph. It showed six men standing in the courtyard of the monastery, identifiable because of the statue. The six men stood in a semicircle examining a plain medieval short sword.

"Do you recognize any of the men in that photograph?" Dimitrov said. "My grandfather was prior then. He took the photograph from the shadows of the cloister. Had they seen him he would have undoubtedly been killed on the spot."

"I recognize three of them," said Holliday, his heart pounding. A photograph such as this one simply should not exist. "Averell Harriman, the U.S. ambassador to the Soviet Union, Lavrenti Beria, the head of what was then the NKVD, the Soviet secret police, and Molotov, Stalin's foreign minister. I don't know who the others are. The man in the business suit on the left looks vaguely familiar."

The monk spoke again. "That's because he's George Herbert Walker, grandfather to President George Herbert Walker Bush, and great-grandfather to President

George W. Bush. He was vice president of Harriman's Wall Street company."

"The other two?"

"The man with the long beard is Sergey Vladimirovich Simansky, better known as Alexis I, Russian Orthodox patriarch of Moscow and all the Russias. The slim man in the plain brown NKVD uniform with the sidearm is Molotov's aide, Vladimir Spiridonovich Putin."

"Putin's father?"

"Yes. The photograph was taken during the Yalta Conference in 1945. Harriman borrowed Roosevelt's C-54 *Sacred Cow* and they flew into Burgas Airport. It was less than a two-hour flight across the Black Sea. They weren't even missed at the conference."

"They came for the sword? Polaris?"

"Yes. The abbot, a corrupt man who it later turned out was a Nazi collaborator, gave it to them."

"But why on earth would they want it? How did they know it was here?"

"Putin's father had been with an NKVD sabotage squad during the war. He heard about the sword and the story behind it. He in turn told his father, and *his* father told Stalin."

"Putin's *grandfather* knew Stalin?" Holliday said, not quite believing it.

"Spiridon Putin was Stalin's cook," said Dimitrov. "The only man Stalin trusted to prepare his meals. Stalin even brought him to Yalta. Before that he cooked for

Lenin, and before that he was a cook for the czar's family."

"That's all very interesting, but it still doesn't explain why they wanted the sword, and it sure as hell doesn't explain why the U.S. ambassador to the Soviet Union and a Wall Street financier were interested, not to mention the Russian version of the pope at the time."

"My grandfather heard Molotov mention the Order of the *Sirin*," said the monk. "The *zhar-ptitsa*."

"The *pájaro de fuego . . .* the *fénix*," explained Eddie.

"The Order of the Phoenix?" Holliday asked.

"It dates back to the time of Yaroslav the Wise and the establishment of the Saint Sophia Cathedral in Kiev. To most Ukrainians, Yaroslav was a hero for making the Orthodox Church truly Russian with the appointment of a Russian metropolitan. To others and to history he was clearly a white supremacist. The charge of the Order of the Phoenix was to bring an all-white Russia and specifically the Ukraine to world domination."

"A Russian Ku Klux Klan," said Holliday.

"Far more meaningful than that," said the monk. "Imagine your Ku Klux Klan with the power of both the state and Church behind it. There are two hundred and twenty-eight million members of the Orthodox Church around the world, the large majority of them Russian— one hundred and twenty-five million, to be precise. It is a number to be reckoned with, Colonel Holliday, especially when it is effectively under the control of the *Si-rin*, the upper-echelon members of the Phoenix order."

"How many?" Holliday asked, startled.

"Two hundred and twenty-eight million, of which three-quarters of a million are American."

"That's a little hard to believe," said Holliday, his tone skeptical. "But even if it's true, it still doesn't explain why Harriman and Walker were there, especially with a monster like Beria."

"No, it doesn't."

Holliday thought for a moment. "Was Beria one of these *Sirin*?"

"Almost certainly." The monk nodded. "In fact, it hardly could have been otherwise. Beria joined the NKVD, or Cheka, as it was known then in 1921. The NKVD in its various incarnations virtually ran the order dating all the way back to the 1917 revolution. Perhaps even before."

"Before?"

"Before the NKVD there was the Okhrana, the czar's secret police, and secretly members of the order as well."

"It still doesn't make any sense. Why would they have been interested in the sword?"

Throughout Holliday's conversation with the monk, Eddie Cabrera had been keeping up a whispered running translation for Genrikhovich. At the mention of the sword, a word he clearly recognized in English, the

Hermitage curator began a frenzied stream of Russian. The man was clearly extremely upset. Finally he stopped and turned to Holliday, his eyes wide and his expression one that Holliday could only conclude was abject fear.

"What's he so frightened about?" Holliday asked.

"Yay-eech-a!" Genrikhovich blurted.

"The eggs," translated Eddie. "Something about eggs."

"What eggs?"

"Fabergé!" Genrikhovich said, obviously agitated. "*Yay-eech-a* Fabergé!"

Holliday's brow wrinkled. The priceless Fabergé eggs given to the wife of the czar each Easter. What connection could they possibly have to a compromising photograph taken during the Yalta Conference in 1945, where Churchill, Roosevelt and Stalin agreed to cut up Europe like a birthday cake, and a Templar sword lost to history in the first years of the fourteenth century?

5

Holliday held up a hand. "Okay, let's stop this right now. Back it up a little." He looked at Genrikhovich hard, then turned to his friend Eddie. "Ask him how he knew about Rodrigues, and how he knew we were going to be at the Khartoum airport when we were."

Eddie spun out a long, lilting line of Russian. Watching Eddie speak like a native was almost as strange as being in Dublin and hearing a waiter in a Chinese restaurant take your order in an Irish accent. Coming from a relentlessly upstate New York, blue-collar, Presbyterian background, Holliday was always astounded at people who could speak fluently in two languages, or in Eddie's case three: Spanish, English and Russian.

Genrikhovich's response was equally complicated and accompanied by various incomprehensible hand gestures. Dimitrov's name was mentioned several times. In the end it was a waste of time.

"I can answer for myself, Colonel Holliday," said the monk.

"Please do."

"Do you know the name Theodore Svetoslav?"

Holliday dug into his memory banks. The file drawer for Bulgarian history had very little in it, but it was just enough. "Wasn't he an emperor?"

"He was, between 1300 and 1313. I'm named after him, in fact, Theodore Svetoslav Dimitrov. My family traces back to his on both sides."

"I'm sure that's very impressive, but right now I'm not. What's the connection?"

"As well as being emperor, Theodore Svetoslav was also a friend to the Templars and they to him. At that time much of the old Pilgrim Road from the Holy Land ran through the emperor's territory. They fought with him in the Battle of Skafida in 1304, less than a hundred miles from here. A Templar saved the emperor's life at the bridge at the Battle of Skafida. A special Templar."

"Don't tell me—the Templar in your crypt."

"Mikail Alexandreivich Nevsky." The monk nodded. "From the bloodline of Mikhail Yaroslavich, also known as Michael of Tver or Michael the Saint."

"I'm not following," said Holliday.

"My grandfather was a member of the White Templars, as was his father before him and his father before him. As am I." There was a long moment of silence. Holliday knew what was required of him—it had been

29

one of the first things he'd learned from the notebook Rodrigues had given to him as he lay dying in that volcanic crater in the Azores.

"What do you seek?" Holliday asked.

"I seek what was lost," answered Dimitrov.

"And who lost it?"

"The king lost it."

"And where is the king?"

"Burning in hell," said Dimitrov with a smile. Holliday relaxed slightly. The exchange was almost a thousand years old, devised after the fall of the Templars so they could safely identify one another. The first time Holliday had used it was with Pierre Ducos, the fat little spider of a man who seemed to be at the center of the whole Templar web, living out his years in the little hilltop village of Domme in France.

"I never met Brother Rodrigues, but we corresponded. I was terribly saddened by his death. He was a good man."

"That he was," said Holliday, remembering the tall, dark man with the deep-set eyes.

"It was the first time I heard your name," said Dimitrov.

"From whom?" Holliday asked.

"Pierre Ducos," replied the monk.

"And he was the one who told you I was in Khartoum?"

"Yes. After *Gospodin Doktor* Genrikhovich contacted

me with his story. I thought I should inform you. I asked him where I might find you and he told me."

"And what is *Gospodin Doktor* Genrikhovich's story?"

"In a nutshell, *Gospodin* Genrikhovich says that the Fabergé eggs in the Kremlin Armoury collection are fakes. He also says that one of the eggs is the lost secret of secrets that allowed the *Sirin* to invisibly rule Russia for hundreds of years. According to Genrikhovich, if the secret were revealed it could destroy the world." Dimitrov paused and glanced at the Russian. He turned back to Holliday.

Holliday gave Genrikhovich a long, skeptical look. "And what secret is that?"

Genrikhovich began to babble wildly, throwing his arms around. He looked as though he were having an apoplectic fit, his eyes bugging out, sweat beading on his face and his entire body shaking.

"He does not want me to tell you, not yet, but I feel I must. The key will reveal, among other terrible things, the final location of the Apophasis Megale, the Great Declaration of Simon Magus. The declaration supposedly proves beyond any doubt that Jesus Christ was a mortal man who lived and died as all of us do. And according to Genrikhovich, there is even more that he does not know about."

Holliday took a breath. Simon Magus was the court magician of Emperor Nero, who could, with only the power of his mind, levitate and move objects at will.

Simon Magus, the man who virtually single-handedly invented the gnostic creed. Simon Magus, the man the Catholic Church called the King of Heretics and perhaps the devil himself. Simon Magus, whose very name gave the world the term 'simony': the crime of paying for the sacraments and holy offices. If the document was what it purported to be and the proof offered for Christ's 'humanness' by Simon Magus was established, it would rock both the Orthodox and Roman Catholic churches to their very foundations.

Incredible, thought Holliday.

"Katwazanyet, katwazanyet, Rasputin *katawaza-nyet!"* Genrikhovich blurted.

"He knew, he knew, Rasputin knew," Eddie translated.

"Rasputin was one of these *Sirin,* or whatever you call them?" asked Holliday.

"Genrikhovich thinks almost certainly." Dimitrov nodded. "So was Spiridon Ivanovich Putin, at that time a chef in the Winter Palace of the czars. It is a black conspiracy of terror that goes back a very long time. The secret now belongs to Vladamir Putin, Spiridon's grandson and presently the prime minister of Russia, the chairman of United Russia and chairman of the Council of Ministers of Russia and Belarus.

"In 2013 Putin will be legally allowed to run for the office of president, and there is no doubt at all that he will win. He controls the state and he controls the Church.

He has more power than Stalin ever did, and it grows with each passing day. From the dissolution of the Soviet Union in 1991 to Putin's rise after forcing Yeltsin to resign, Russia's place in the world faltered. Vladamir Putin wants to see Russia rise again, and with the *Sirin* and their deadly secrets he will succeed. Have you ever seen a gas and oil pipeline map of Russia? They could choke Europe to death in a minute."

"The rest of the world wouldn't allow it," said Holliday. "It's not like the old days."

"Give Putin a little time to strengthen the military and it *will be* the old days all over again," Dimitrov said. "Over the past few years he's allowed the Church to infiltrate every facet of daily life in Russia. He doesn't need the KGB or the FSB anymore—he has the priests. He's developed a cult of personality in Russia that is at least the equal of Stalin's. To most people Vladamir Putin *is* Russia."

"So what am I supposed to do about it?" Holliday said.

"Stop him," said Dimitrov.

"Don't be idiotic. I'm one man, a nobody."

"You're far from that, Colonel Holliday, and you know it. You have great power at your command, and great wealth. Use them if you have to, but however you do it, you must stop him. Stop the *Sirin* once and for all."

Sure, thought Holliday. That's me, Sancho Panza,

tilting at windmills. "Nice idea, but how do I practically go about taking on the dark lord of all the Russias?"

"Go with Genrikhovich to St. Petersburg. See what he has to show you. Begin at the beginning."

"I'm not sure I'm ready for this," said Holliday. "When you get right down to it, Brother Dimitrov, regardless of my admiration and respect for Helder Rodrigues, I've fought too many battles in too many wars and I'm getting a little too old for saving the world. Maybe this is where it should end."

There was a long silence. Finally the monk reached into the drawer of his desk and took out an old, butterscotch-colored molded leather holster with a snap flap. The leather had been cared for, but the holster was very old. It was also quite small. Dimitrov undid the flap and pulled out a short-barreled pistol. The black plastic grips were embossed with the TOZ logo of the famous Tula Arms Factory. Holliday had never seen one before, but he recognized it from the old weapon-recognition books he'd collected over the years. It was a Korovin .25-caliber automatic, a Russian-made civilian pistol and standard issue for the NKVD back in the early twenties and thirties. Because of the heavy-duty construction of the weapon, the rounds used tended to be loaded with almost twice the powder of a normal .25-caliber round, and the pistol was known for packing a punch almost equivalent to a much larger Browning .45.

"You may have no choice in the matter, Colonel," said Dimitrov, sliding the weapon across the desk toward Holliday. "Since I spoke with Ducos there have been a number of strangers in the area. The DS may have changed its name since the fall of the Soviet Union, but they still have the same look about them." The DS was the infamous Bulgarian State Security, KGB-trained and just as feared.

"You're being watched?" Holliday asked.

"Yes, and my telephone is surely tapped."

Holliday picked up the lethal-looking little pistol. "Why does a monk have a gun?"

"It belonged to my grandfather. After the war there was a great deal of looting. The monastery has several valuable icons and altarpieces."

"I wonder where your grandfather got it," said Holliday, a note of suspicion creeping into his voice. The priors of monasteries didn't generally pack weapons under their robes.

"He got it from an NKVD agent who thought he was an art collector. My grandfather killed him with his bare hands. He's buried in an unmarked grave in our little cemetery behind the wall." The monk smiled. "My grandfather was a man of many talents. He was a *yatak* during the war, a 'friend of the resistance,' right under the abbot's nose."

"Thanks for the offer," said Holliday, putting the gun back on the table and sliding it back to Dimitrov.

"But I wouldn't get it through the Turkish border, let alone through airport security."

Dimitrov shook his head and slid the pistol back to Holliday. "I would suggest that you not return to Turkey and continue north to Varna instead; it's less than a hundred kilometers, and the connections to St. Petersburg will be much better. When you get to Varna throw the weapon away, but while you are in my country it would make me feel better if you kept it."

Holliday picked up the pistol and popped out the magazine. He thumbed out a round. The spring was strong and the magazine well oiled. The round was a brand-new Fabrique Nationale hollow-point, the brass gleaming. "It's in good condition," Holliday observed.

"My grandfather told me that tools taken care of will in turn take care of you."

"My uncle Henry used to tell me the same thing, more or less," said Holliday. "He rescued Hesperios from Hitler's Berchtesgaden just after the war." Holliday slid the round back into the magazine, then snapped the magazine back into the grip.

"I have a feeling your uncle and my grandfather would have liked each other," Dimitrov said.

Holliday picked up the pocket pistol again and hefted it. At least a pound, maybe more. Heavy for such a small weapon. "You're sure?"

"Certain." Dimitrov nodded.

Holliday shrugged and slipped the pistol into the pocket of his jacket. "Okay," he said. "But I'm sure it'll be unnecessary."

"Better safe than sorry," replied the monk.

"My uncle said that, too." Holliday laughed, standing up. A hundred kilometers to Varna and then the trials and tribulations of buying visas and booking tickets would put them on a plane to St. Petersburg by late evening at best. It was time to go.

The monk was kneeling at the altar in the church when they came for him. He'd heard the squeak of the gate and the creak of the door as it opened, but he did not move from his knees; nor did he stop his prayer. Less than half an hour had passed since his conversation with the American. It was a relief to know that someone else would be taking up the quest that had begun so long ago. He finally ended his prayer:

Many are the scourges of the sinner,
But mercy shall encircle him that hopeth in the Lord.
Be glad in the Lord, and rejoice, ye righteous;
And glory, all ye that are upright of heart.

He stood and turned, his hands held together beneath his robes. There were two of them, one older with very short gray hair, his bad suit barely covering a bulging middle-aged paunch, and a younger one with dark oily hair who wore a brown leather coat.

The older one spoke. "You are Brother Theodore Dimitrov?"

"Yes."

"You know why we are here?"

"To torture me and force me to tell you things you wish to know."

The younger one snickered. "We have people in Sofia who do that."

"We're just here to accompany you, Brother Dimitrov. The best thing would be to come peacefully."

"I'm afraid I can't do that," answered Dimitrov.

"Yes, you can, priest," said the younger one. He took a weapon out from under his coat. It was a Veresk, an older Russian-made version of an Uzi, which explained the long coat.

"Put that away, Kostya," said the older one, taking out his own weapon from under his jacket, this one a much more discreet Yarygin nine-millimeter. He held it loosely in his hand. "Please, Brother Dimitrov. I would like to do this without any unpleasantness."

"I'm afraid I can't accommodate you," answered the monk. The younger one made a threatening gesture with the little submachine gun. The monk wondered for a brief moment which it would be. He decided on the older one. An object lesson for the young man in the leather coat. He took his hands out from between the bell-like sleeves of his robe. In his right hand he held the other weapon his father had taken from the NKVD agent just after the war. The Korovin .25 he'd given the American had been the NKVD agent's backup gun, worn in a concealed holster on the hip. The other weapon, worn in a shoulder holster, was a Tokarev TT-33, a rough knockoff of the classic Browning .45 and just as powerful. The monk pulled the trigger twice, hitting the older man in the chest and the belly. The older man looked surprised, vomited blood and slid to the floor. The one the older man had called Kostya lifted the Veresk and frantically squeezed the trigger. Nothing happened.

Dimitrov turned the old Tokarev on the boy in the coat and waited while he flipped off the safety. Killing the young man would serve only to prolong things. Eventually they'd find him, torture him, and in the end they would kill him anyway. Brother Theodore Dimitrov took the last long seconds to speak to his God, and then the church filled with the screams of the boy and the thunder of his weapon and then there was nothing.

6

"We have—*¿cómo se dice? una cola*—a tail?" Eddie said.

"We're being followed?" Holliday answered, startled. He looked in the rearview mirror of the stodgy old Moskvich he'd rented in Istanbul. There was no traffic behind them on the narrow coast road running along the rocky cliffs that dropped down to the Black Sea. To the left of the deserted old highway there was nothing but scrub forest and wooded hills.

"*Sí.*" Eddie nodded. "I have been watching." He spoke softly. In the backseat a less flatulent Genrikhovich was asleep again. "Three of them. A red BMW, an old KrAZ truck with a . . . thing on the front, and also there is something that looks like one of those old ZiL limousines El Comandante used to drive around in. Black and very big." The tall Cuban shrugged. "*No estoy seguro.* Maybe a Chaika."

"I don't see anything," said Holliday, checking the mirror again. The highway was still empty. The very fact that Eddie had seen three vehicles of any kind was reason enough for suspicion.

"They keep back most of the time and they . . . *¿cambiar de posición?*"

"Switch places?"

"*Sí*, that is what they do. Switch places to try to make it seem like they are not together. An old trick of the Seguridad del Estado in my country when they followed dissidents." He laughed quietly. "Three men, three different hats. *¡Muy estúpido!*"

Holliday looked in the mirror again. This time he saw the BMW. He wasn't much of a car buff, but it looked like one of the bigger models from the eighties or early nineties.

"Shit," said Holliday. Eddie checked the side mirror.

"*Sí.*" Eddie nodded. "*Una mierda grande.*"

Holliday dropped his foot down on the gas pedal. The Moskvich responded with a shudder and a grudging acceleration that took them up just barely past one hundred kilometers per hour. It wasn't going to be the car chase from *The French Connection*; that was for sure.

The big BMW accelerated until it was fifty yards from their rear bumper. The narrow highway began a sweeping series of easy S curves. On the left the wooded hills closed in, and on the right the ragged cliffs looked steeper. Holliday became acutely aware of the single 3-shaped guardrail bolted to wooden stumps that was the only thing between them and a long swan dive into the surf five hundred feet down.

There was a flicker of movement in the side mirror. The large black car Eddie had spotted was pulling out from behind the BMW and passing. It stayed in the other lane, surging forward, speeding past the Moskvich through the turn, ignoring the risk of oncoming traffic. It was a big, bullying ZiL, just as Eddie had thought. It pulled in front of them and took up a station fifty yards ahead, matching the BMW, which was still behind them. Holliday had seen two men in the car, both hard-faced men wearing black.

"It's a squeeze," he muttered, thinking about the third vehicle—the truck.

"*¿Qué?*" Eddie asked.

"They've got us boxed in," said Holliday. "The truck will come up and push us off the road and over the god-damn cliff."

"Goddamn," said Eddie, looking to his left at the rusty old guardrail.

"Goddamn right," said Holliday.

Right on cue a giant green truck appeared, rumbling up behind the red BMW on their tail. It was a monster, and the "thing on the front" Eddie had described was a double-bladed snowplow, one blade forward and the second blade angled to one side. The enormous vehicle sounded like a tank, big puffs of sooty exhaust bellowing out of the high stack that jutted over the cab.

"This is not good," said Holliday, his heart pounding like a trapped animal in his chest.

"Dame la pistola," said Eddie quickly, his voice urgent.

Behind them the truck downshifted and there was a bellowing roar as it pulled out into the left lane. "What?!"

"*¡Dame la pistola!* Give me the gun, *mi amigo!* And roll down your window, *por favor!*"

The noise and commotion woke up Genrikhovich in the backseat. He struggled sleepily into a sitting position. *"Shtaw?"* he mumbled, blinking. Holliday dug into his jacket, handed Eddie the gun, then rolled down the window. Eddie rolled down the window on the passenger side. The muscular Cuban put a meaty hand on the Russian's head and pushed him back down.

"Lazeet salyetch!" Eddie ordered. Genrikhovich acted predictably, fighting against Eddie, who forced him down again.

"Chto za huy?!" screamed the Russian, trying to pull himself up again. *"Chyort voz'mi!"*

Eddie twisted around in his seat. *"Lazeet salyetch, yob Tvoyu Mat!"* He let go with a left cross that caught Genrikhovich on the point of his chin, dropping him to the floor of the car. The massive truck pulled up beside the Moskvich. Eddie gave Holliday an evil grin, eyes flashing. *"Yo disparo; lo lleve a.* I shoot; you drive." Eddie began humming "Auld Lang Syne," the tune for his

Young Pioneers farewell campfire song. He flipped off the safety and pulled back the hammer of the pistol to full cock. The Cuban was definitely pissed.

The high-wheeled truck began to make its move, the giant gleaming side of the plow sliding toward the side of the Moskvich like a massive ax blade as the KrAZ turned in toward them. Ahead of the Moskvich the ZiL slowed, boxing them in tightly, while the BMW moved even closer behind them. At the last second Holliday made his move as well.

"Hang on!" he yelled to Eddie. With the snowplow blade less than a foot away, raised at eye level, Holliday simultaneously jammed his foot down on the brake pedal, twisted the wheel toward the flimsy guardrail and dragged up on the handbrake between the two front seats.

It was a classic bootlegger's turn, but done on a front-wheel-drive vehicle. The rear wheels locked, the back end slewed out and the front end ricocheted off the guardrail with a tearing clang as the front bumper tore away. Instead of doing a complete one-eighty turn, the Moskvich turned broadside to the BMW, offering Eddie a sight line through the car's windshield. He raised the heavy little Korovin .25 and pumped half the clip at the car behind them. The windshield shattered and the BMW spun out, then hit the ditch on the far side of the road, flipping over twice, then flipping right-side up again, the roof crumpled between the doorposts.

"¡Aprende a manejar, aweonao!" Eddie whooped happily.

The snowplow truck, taken by surprise, kept swinging into where the Moskvich had been a second before. Air brakes screaming, the driver tried to stop the sideways motion of the giant vehicle, but inertia had its way with the steel beast, and the side blade of the plow hooked the rear end of the ZiL, slammed into the guardrail and sliced through it like a knife through soft cheese.

The twenty-two-ton behemoth and the four-ton ZiL rocketed out over the cliff, seemed to hang against the bright blue sea and the sky for a split second, and then disappeared. An eternity later there was a muted, thundering crash and the sound of an explosion. The Moskvich screeched to a halt.

There was silence except for the distant pounding of the surf and the soft rustling of wind in the trees. It was almost peaceful. There was a twenty-foot gap in the guardrail and another ten feet on either side of the hole that sagged out over the cliff, the stumps torn out of the ground and the galvanized steel twisted into corkscrews.

"¡Hala!" Eddie whispered, staring. *"¡Ay, coño!"*

Holliday looked back over his shoulder. Genrikhovich was groaning on the floor. "Let's check on the BMW." He left the car engine running, pushed open the door and stepped out onto the road. Eddie followed.

Holliday stopped suddenly, swaying for a second, holding on to the open door of the Moskvich as a wave of nausea swept over him. His face was suddenly slippery with flop sweat, his heart was still jumping behind his ribs like a jackrabbit and he could hear his pulse hammering in his ears. He knew it was just the adrenaline rush, but he also knew that thirty seconds ago he'd been staring death in the face and it wasn't looking good. A herd of buffalo stampeding over his grave. For a moment he thought he was going to puke all over his shoes. He closed his eyes and shook off the nausea.

Eddie came up beside him. He had a worried look on his face, staring at his friend. "*¿Estás bien*, Doc?"

"I'm okay."

"Is crazy all this, no?"

"Is crazy *mucho, compadre*," answered Holliday. He let go of the car door, the ground solid beneath his feet again.

He and Eddie crossed the road to the ditch and peered inside the BMW. The two men were both dead. The driver had the jagged end of the steering column through his chest, and the man on the passenger side looked as though his head had gone into the dashboard and then rebounded against the roof. His face had been pulped into gravy, and his skull was crushed like an egg, the whole mess held together by a bag of flesh and sitting at an odd angle on his neck. There was blood and tissue everywhere. If one of Eddie's shots had found its mark, it was going to take a coroner a bit of time to find it.

"You missed," said Holliday.

"Mis disculpas, Coronel." The Cuban grinned.

Holliday reached in carefully through the shattered window and flipped back the passenger's jacket. There was an empty shoulder holster on the left. The weapon, a big Stechkin APS, was clutched in his right hand. Holliday leaned in farther and pried it from the man's fingers, then handed it back to Eddie. He reached back in and slipped his hand into the inner pocket of the man's jacket and took out the man's wallet. He eased it back through the window, then flipped it open. There was a red plastic ID case inside. He flipped the case open. Inside was a card with a plastic shield with an eagle and a sword on it, and a picture presumably showing what the dead man had looked like up until a few minutes ago. The cover of the ID case had three Cyrillic letters stamped in gold on the cover:

ФСБ

Holliday handed the case to Eddie. "Those Bulgarian State Security types Dimitrov mentioned?"

"Much worse, I'm afraid, my friend. These men are not Bulgarian at all. The letters are FSB, and they stand for Federal'naya Sluzhba Bezopasnosti Rossiyskoy Federatsii."

There was a keening, moaning sound from behind them, like one of Scrooge's terrible, desperate spirits in *A Christmas Carol*. Eddie and Holliday turned. A bleary-looking, ashen-faced Genrikhovich had managed to drag himself out of the Moskvich and stagger across the empty road. He stood just behind them, his lank gray hair plastered sweatily across his cheeks. He looked over Holliday's shoulder, swaying back and forth, staring goggle-eyed and horrified at the ID case in Eddie's hand. He began to shake his head wildly back and forth, wailing loudly.

"KGB!" Genrikhovich screamed. "KGB!"

7

In the late afternoon they stopped in a place called Golden Sands, a resort town about fifteen miles outside the city of Varna. Like most off-season summer destinations, there was an empty, abandoned air to the town, the neon signs on the strip bars and the sex stores dark, the soft-ice-cream stands boarded up for the season and almost no traffic, pedestrian or otherwise.

They found a hotel called the Grifid Arabella that was still open for business, booked a suite and put an exhausted Genrikhovich to bed. The Russian had become apoplectic at discovering that they'd been involved with the deaths of the secret police thugs they'd left in the ditch, and it had taken them more than an hour to calm him down with a combination of violent threats from Eddie and reassurances from Holliday.

All three restaurants in the high-rise hotel were closed, but they eventually found a place on the main street of the town called the Happy Bar and Grill that looked like it was part of a chain. The logo showed a smiling man, in a tall white hat and a mustache, who looked remarkably like Chef Boyardee from the spaghetti cans, and the interior decor was a combination maritime/rock-and-roll theme, with neon guitars, real saxophones and ships in bottles.

The Happy menu offered everything from sushi to skewers to something dreadful-looking called "Happy Bits," which appeared to be crinkle-cut home fries and chicken nuggets covered in a congealed grayish gravy that gleamed in the harsh overhead lighting. They also offered something suspiciously called "Krispy Loins," which Holliday didn't even want to think about. Virtually everything on the menu was served with an ice-cream scoop of potato salad and sour cream.

"Genrikhovich would love this place," commented Holliday. He ordered a "Slavic Salad" and a chicken skewer from the pleasant, English-speaking waiter, whose name was Viktor. Eddie ordered the same thing.

"Let him sleep," said the Cuban. "I've had enough of his *peos* for one day."

"Agreed." Holliday nodded. Their food arrived quickly and they began to eat. Slavic Salad turned out to be a mixture of peeled tomatoes, roasted peppers, garlic, black pepper, olives, olive oil, cottage cheese, yogurt and fresh parsley, and it wasn't half-bad.

"They will have discovered those men by now," said Eddie, looking suspiciously at the lump of cottage cheese in the middle of his colorful paper plate. He took a small taste on the end of his fork, made a face and nodded. *"Ah, es requesón."* He speared a piece of tomato on the end of his plastic fork and chewed thoughtfully. "They will be watching the airport, I think."

"Train station and bus station as well." Holliday nodded. "Not to mention the fact that neither you nor I have visas for entering Russia."

"If we stay here they will find us sooner or later. They will check the Turkish border crossing, I think. I am the very handsome man, I am sure, but I am also very black, and I don't think they would be seeing too many *pasaportes* from Cuba."

"So what do we do?"

Eddie shrugged. "There must be places where the border is easier to cross."

"Into Serbia, maybe, but not into Russia."

Viktor the waiter shimmered up and asked them if they needed anything else . . . fresh-squeezed pomegranate and tangerine juice, perhaps, dessert, coffee, anything . . .

Holliday took out his wallet and counted out ten twenty-lev notes and set them on the table. By his calculations two hundred leva was about a hundred and fifty bucks. Viktor didn't even blink. He swept up the bills, folded them neatly and tucked them into the pocket of his black-and-red vest.

"*Dobar wecher!* What I can do for the *gospoda* to-day?"

Holliday smiled pleasantly. "My friend and I are looking for a bit of an adventure," he said. Viktor's left eyebrow crept up and he glanced toward Eddie, but he remained silent.

"What kind adventure the *gospoda* look for? Small-type adventure, bigging adventure, or very serious adventure?"

"Very serious," answered Holliday.

Viktor stared at the spot where the money had been. Holliday took out ten more bills. Viktor didn't look happy. Holliday laid out an additional ten. At that point they disappeared into Viktor's vest pocket again.

"You look for what adventure, exact?"

"We were thinking there must be an adventurous way to get into Russia."

"Definite, sure." Viktor nodded, giving his patented stare down at the table again.

"Two hundred more when you give us directions."

"Easy," said Viktor, grinning. "My friends, we do it all the time. Easy-peasy."

"How?" Holliday asked.

"The ferry."

"There is no ferry."

"Not people ferry, ferry for the trains. Hero of Sevastopol. Leave tonight, nine o'clock, thirteen hours after, *pssht!* You have achieved Russia at port of Illichivsk."

"Where is Illichivsk?"

"Maybe ten mile Odessa. Very nearby. I have girl there. Marinoska. Blondie-type girl. Nice."

"I'm sure she is, Viktor. How do we get on the ferry?"

"Two hundred leva, I show you, another five hundred, I take you there."

"To the ferry?"

"No, no." Viktor grinned. "I take you Illichivsk and then Odessa to meet with Marinoska. Viktor give the best service in Varna, no doubt!"

"Okay," said Holliday. "When do we leave?"

"Seven thirty o'clock. You have car, of course?"

"Of course."

"In parking lot of hotel then," said Viktor. "Seven thirty o'clock we meet. I bring food and some nice beers. You pay me then. We have good time, okay?"

"It's a deal," said Holliday.

The ferry terminal at the port of Varna was south of the main port and the naval base. After the fall of the Soviet Union, trade between Bulgaria and the Ukraine had collapsed, but UKR ferries had recently revived the trade in moving railcars back and forth between Varna and Odessa.

There was a crane arrangement where the wider-gauge bogies on the Russian cars were switched to the narrower European gauge, a large multitrack holding facility for waiting railcars, and a dock and hydraulic ramp system capable of handling two ships at a time, usually one just arrived and one just leaving.

Each four-hundred-foot-long ship was capable of taking a total of one hundred and eight freight cars on the main deck and the two decks below. The trick was to know which cars were going on the top deck and which were going below, and to make sure you didn't try to hop a freight car that had just been unloaded. Empty freight cars were easy to spot, since they weren't padlocked. Incoming cars were chalked with the capital letter Б, for Bulgaria, and outgoing were marked with a Ю, for Ukraine. Tonight it was Hero of Sevastopol outgoing and Hero of Pleven incoming.

Viktor told them all of this on the twenty-minute drive from the Golden Sands to the outskirts of the ferry terminal, a pool of sickly yellow sodium lights in the dusky October evening. Holliday and Eddie had brought Genrikhovich a taco plate from the Happy Bar and Grill, a late-night dinner they knew might have the same kind of repercussions as the Burger King Quad Stacker, but the old man had to eat something, and an open freight car was much airier than a cramped little Moskvich.

Viktor turned out to be a full-service guide on their "very serious" adventure, turning up at the Grifid Arabella's parking lot right on time and bringing four sleeping bags and a knapsack full of sandwiches, apples, two pomegranates, eight bottles of Zagorka beer and two rolls of toilet paper.

"Do they patrol the rail yard?" Holliday asked as they abandoned the rental halfway down a gravel side road.

"Sometimes. They have dogs but I have never been caught."

"I do not like dogs," said Eddie.

"Shtaw?" Genrikhovich said nervously.

"Saabaka," translated Eddie. *"Awchen Gnevny Saabaka."*

Genrikhovich went pale but he kept his mouth shut.

"What did you say to him?" Holliday asked.

"I told him there were dogs. *Very* big dogs," said Eddie.

"You sure that was the right thing to do?"

"It will keep him . . . *¿paralizado por el miedo?*"

"Paralyzed with fear?"

"Sí, we will be much happier." Eddie grinned. "Your Cuban is getting *muy bueno.*"

"Muchas gracias, mi compañero," answered Holliday, bowing gravely forward.

"¡Ay, coño!" Eddie laughed. "Soon I take you back to my family in Habana." He clamped a hand on Genrikhovich's narrow shoulder as Viktor the waiter led the way down between the railway tracks. Viktor found the appropriate chalk marking on one of the cars and rolled back the door. The Bulgarian boosted himself

up, then helped Holliday and Eddie up. Genrikhovich came last.

The interior of the empty boxcar was half-solid and half-slatted. The lingering smell suggested that some kind of root vegetable like rutabagas had been the last cargo. Viktor rumbled the door shut and set up the bedrolls in one corner of the car, and they all settled in. Holliday had one of the bottles of beer Viktor offered and then lay down on his bedroll.

Ten minutes after finishing the beer he was fast asleep. He woke once to the thumping and banging as the boxcar was loaded onto the ferry, and woke briefly again, feeling the odd, almost comforting sensation of being rocked on the sea. He fell asleep again and didn't wake until the ship docked at the Ukrainian port city of Illichivsk at noon the following day. For the first time in twenty years Lieutenant Colonel John "Doc" Holliday, United States Army Ranger (retired), was back in what had once been enemy territory.

8

"You will need documents," said Viktor. He nodded toward Genrikhovich. "Even him." They were sitting in a dive called the Celantano Pizzeria in Illichivsk, eating slices. The glass-fronted fast-food joint had square panels of fluorescent lighting, plastic brick to waist height, and lime green roughly plastered walls above.

"What kind of documents?" Holliday asked, feeling his wallet getting thinner by the minute. They'd already visited an ATM and he'd stocked up on two hundred twenty-griven notes, which, at ten grivna to the dollar, were the equivalent of twenty bucks, and which seemed to be the most common banknote in use.

"The Russian will need an internal passport as well as an international one and a residency card."

"My friend and I?"

"New passports. *Gospodin* Eddie is too . . . obvious as a Cuban," said Viktor.

"What do you suggest?" Holliday asked

"Argentina, Venezuela. Best would be American. Spic, yes?"

"Puerto Rican?"

"Yes. You, too, must be American, of course, unless you like to be Canadian. Canada is very easy."

"I'll stick with my own country for now."

"Okay, yes, easy-peasy, you know." Victor nodded, sucking a straw stuck in a bottle of livid green Fanta passion fruit and orange Taste of Africa.

"Are these forged documents or real?" Holliday asked.

"Oh, very genuine."

"How do you get them?"

"Not me, oh, no, I have no way of knowing this, really, but I have a friend. . . ."

"I thought you might." Holliday nodded.

"His name is Gennadi. Good friend."

"Where does he live?"

"Odessa. Not far, twenty minutes on bus. *Pssht!* We are there."

"Easy-peasy," Holliday said.

"Right," said Viktor, speaking around the straw. His tongue was as green as the walls.

Holliday wondered how far they were from Chernobyl. "Easy-peasy."

Gennadi Bondarenko lived in an old yellow stucco building in the Privoz district of Odessa, close to the railway station. In the old days the apartment would probably have been shared by at least three families, but now it was just Bondarenko and his voluptuous girl-friend, whose name was Natasha.

There was a large living room/kitchen/dining room with a huge round caramel-colored velvet couch that could have slept two couples comfortably, expensive-looking Persian carpets, an eating island that jutted out between two massive windows covered in drooping vel-vet curtains the same color as the couch, and a refrig-erator in one corner and a strange gas-powered hot plate that sat on the kitchen counters with its big pro-pane supply right beside it.

Built-in nineteenth-century cupboards and shelves covered the walls, which were painted a uniform sallow cream color. One area of open wall six feet wide and eight feet high had been painted flat white, for some unknown reason.

Outside the bustling street seemed to be a combina-tion farmer's market, tailgate junk sale and pickup stroll for hookers. According to Gennadi, the party went on twenty-four/seven and drew no ethnic or religious bor-ders. Jews, Asians, locals and anyone else sold whatever people wanted. Gennadi specialized in selling docu-ments.

Bondarenko had been born on the Lower East Side of New York in the old Ukrainian part of the city and spent most of the first fifteen years of his life in a fourth-floor walk-up on Second Avenue. In 1999, his grand-parents from Odessa had died, leaving the family farm to his parents. The parents went home, and with nothing else to do the young teenage Gennadi had been forced to go along with them.

Now he was what his mother and father called a charter member of the Solntsevskaya Bratva, the Brotherhood, a colloquial term for the Russian-Ukrainian-Georgian crime family run by the Solntsevskaya gang out of Moscow. Bondarenko denied it, but the tattoos of crowned skulls and ornate stars that covered both arms told a different story. Now in his late twenties, Bondarenko was lean, with a shaved head, hooked nose and dark, suspicious eyes.

"Five thousand dollars U.S. for everything," he said, sprawled on the big couch smoking an evil-smelling Veraya cigarette. Natasha was curled up beside him, a vision swelling out of bulging silver hot pants and a red Victoria's Secret push-up bra. She was either sleeping off a drunk or stoned out of her mind. Bondarenko used her large, upthrust hip as an armrest.

"I don't have that kind of cash on me," said Holliday. "I'd have to go to a bank. Besides, I'd like to see what I'm getting first."

"Not a problem, bro," said the Ukrainian thug. "I take Visa, MasterCard, Carte Bleue."

Using Natasha's ample rear end to brace himself, Bondarenko levered himself off the big couch and disappeared from the room. When he returned he had a fistful of various passports. He sat down on a bar stool at the eating island and spread them out. Holliday picked one up at random. It was a genuine U.K. passport in the name of Simon Toyne, London resident at 20 Cheyne Walk. Holliday knew London well enough to know that Simon had big bucks; Cheyne Walk was for big-time high rollers, often in the music or the writing game. Dante Gabriel Rossetti, the English poet, had once lived there, as had Henry James, George Eliot and Mick Jagger. Holliday wondered what Simon did to make his pile, and also wondered how the rich man with the twinkling dark eyes and the slightly unnatural-looking silver hair had come to lose his passport in Odessa.

"U.K. is better for your Cuban pal than Puerto Rico. Lots of blacks in England these days. He speak any African?"

"Nenda kajitombe, mkundu," said Eddie with a smile.

"I'm not even going to ask," said Bondarenko. He picked up another passport, this one American. It belonged to a man named Michael Enright, a professorial-looking man about Holliday's age, half-bald, with a silver-gray goatee and a pair of thick Harry Potter spectacles that made him look a little silly. Both the U.K. and U.S. passports were definitely genuine.

"Where do you get them?"

"I've got pickpockets at the train stations. Odessa, Kiev, Moscow, St. Petersburg. Airports, too. I buy them wholesale: two hundred per. Kids work the whole railway system like Gypsies. It's the only kind of work they can find these days."

"How do you work all the electronics and the biometrics?"

"I toss out biometric ones, just keep the older ones. I've got a laminator in the back and a heat delaminator as well. I print out your picture on ultrathin Mylar and drop it in over the existing one. We leave everything else the same, name, age and all that."

"All right," said Holliday.

"Let's see your plastic."

Holliday reached into his wallet and took out the Carte Bleue card that he'd found in the safety-deposit box after reading Helder Rodrigues's bloodstained notebook. He never got printed statements, and apparently the account it drew against was infinitely large. He handed the card to Bondarenko. "How long is this going to take?"

"No time at all. Half an hour or so. I'll take your pictures and get right at it."

"All right," said Holliday.

Bondarenko stood up and then paused, a thoughtful expression on his face. "Where are you guys going?"

"Do you have to know that?"

"No, but it's better if you don't fly. The cops here are

pretty uptight about airport security after all these crazy suicide bombings."

Holliday thought about the Korovin .25 and the Stechkin APS he and Eddie were still carrying.

"What do you suggest?"

"Train. The cops at all the stations are usually local *militsiya*. Slobs. Except for Moscow, maybe. Everyone travels by train. You'll fit in better." He glanced at Eddie again. "If that's possible," he added.

"Okay." Holliday nodded.

"While I'm doing the documents you should go down to the market and get some luggage, backpacks or something." Bondarenko crossed the room, opened a cupboard and returned with a Nikon D3X. Now Holliday knew what the blank white space on the wall was for.

"Since you're being so helpful, Gennadi, maybe you can get something else for us," said Holliday.

"Yeah?"

"Ammunition. Twenty-five-caliber hollow-point and nine-millimeter Parabellum."

Bondarenko gave Holliday a long, thoughtful look and nodded slowly. "Sure, I could do that, but if the *militsiya* or the OMON catch you, you never met me, okay?" The OMON were special police units stationed in every district. They were the Russian equivalent of an American SWAT team.

"Okay," agreed Holliday.

"How much you want?"

Holliday thought about it for a second. The Stechkin on full auto went through bullets like popcorn. "Five hundred of the nine and a hundred of the twenty-five."

"I can do that," said Bondarenko. He paused again. "Just in case you and your friends are going through Belarus I'll throw in the transit visas for nothing—it's just a stamp."

"Thanks," answered Holliday. "If that's everything, why don't you get your credit card swiper and we'll let you get to work."

"No problem," said the Ukrainian with a pleasant smile. "I can do it myself."

"No, you can't," said Holliday. And he wasn't smiling at all.

At six thirty-one that evening the three men carrying the passports and transit visas of Michael Enright, Simon Toyne and Andre Belekonev left the city of Odessa on Russian Railways train number twenty, the Pivdenny Express fast train to St. Petersburg. Thirty-four hours later, they arrived in the city of the czars.

Less than twelve hours after their departure, Gennadi Bondarenko and his girlfriend, Natasha Bohuslava Shtokalo, were found brutally murdered and their apartment ransacked. Bondarenko had been tortured savagely before he'd been killed by a bullet to the back of the head, and *gaspazha* Shtokalo had been raped a number of times before receiving the same treatment.

In a statement to the press, Odessa colonel of *militsiya* Yuriy Fedorovych Kravchenko stated that Gennadi Bondarenko was a well-known member of the criminal establishment and the murders were clearly gang related. In addition, robbery might well have been a motive, since there was some evidence that Bondarenko dealt in large amounts of cash. There had also been rumors that Bondarenko might have been soliciting for *gaspazha* Shtokalo's services as a prostitute, although that had not as yet been confirmed.

When queried, Colonel of *Militsiya* Kravchenko said that neither he nor his lead investigators had any expectations of making any arrests in the near future; nor did he care. The prosecutor's office had no interest in going forward with the investigation and he didn't either. As the policeman bluntly put it: "The deaths of these two people simply means that there are two fewer criminals on the streets of the Odessa Oblast."

9

Genrikhovich lived in an old five-room apartment in a nineteenth-century stucco building on Nevsky Prospekt not far from the train station and the Hermitage. By old-fashioned Soviet standards it was lavish, sharing a bathroom and toilet with only one other apartment and having a kitchen of its own.

The apartment had apparently been assigned to his grandfather by the local party committee shortly after the revolution. His grandfather, curator of the Hermitage's Treasure Gallery, raised Genrikhovich's father there, and he in turn passed it along to his son.

Genrikhovich's wife had fled for greener pastures after the fall of the USSR in 1991, and Genrikhovich had lived alone in the apartment ever since. The furniture was of the large, dark, Victorian variety, the chairs old, worn and comfortable, the lamps fringed. There were books everywhere, and where there weren't books there were paintings, mostly small and gilt framed, some with their own little lamps and virtually all of them horticultural or seascapes.

Genrikhovich excused himself and left the apartment to use the toilet facilities. Holliday wandered around the living room while Eddie sank gratefully into a plump, overupholstered chair.

Holliday checked out the bookcase and frowned. Like the paintings, many of the books were about horticulture and the sea. Erskine Childers's *The Riddle of the Sands*; *Aero-Hydrodynamics and the Performance of Sailing Yachts* by Fabio Fossati; *Illustrated Custom Boatbuilding* by Bruce Roberts-Goodson; *The Gardens at Kew*; *The Gardener's Essential Gertrude Jekyll*; *Botanica's Trees & Shrubs*; *The No-Work Garden* by somebody named Bob Flowerdew, which had to be a pseudonym; *David Austin's English Roses*; the bookcase was packed with them.

He stepped over to what was obviously Genrikhovich's "comfy chair," a Russian version of a La-Z-Boy recliner with a perfectly placed reading lamp and a side table stacked with books and magazines.

Holliday looked at the titles: *WoodenBoat, Hortus, The Marine Quarterly*. On top of the pile was a paperback called *Black Fish* by Sam Llewellyn, a sailing thriller. Holliday seemed to recall that he'd read some of Llewellyn's early historical novels and quite liked them.

"I smell a rat," said Holliday.

"*¡Una rata!*" Eddie said, jumping up out of his chair.

"*¿Adónde va?*" He whirled around frantically. "*¡Odio las ratas!*"

"The books and the magazines," said Holliday. "They're all in English. I thought Genrikhovich didn't speak any English."

"*¿No hay ratas?*" Eddie said, confused. "There is no rat?"

Genrikhovich came back into the room. "I'm sorry to have deceived you, Colonel Holliday," the Russian said, his English tinged with a slight Oxford plumminess. "I assure you that it was entirely necessary, given the circumstances."

"Sorry isn't good enough," snapped Holliday angrily, turning to face the Russian. "I'm in a shitload of trouble with the secret police because of you. People are dead because of you, Mr. Genrikhovich, and now I find out you've been lying to me."

"It's Dr. Genrikhovich, Colonel Holliday," said the Russian stiffly. "And as I have already informed you, my deception was completely necessary."

"You'll have to explain that," said Holliday. He dropped down in one of the stuffed chairs. Genrikhovich sat down in the recliner. Eddie stood for a moment longer, scanning the baseboards carefully and muttering in Spanish. He finally seated himself again.

"I know who you are, Colonel Holliday, and more important, I know what you are."

"So who and what am I?"

"In effect, you are the keeper of the king's keys; do you know what that is?"

"I'm a historian, Genrikhovich; of course I know what it is. It's what they sometimes call the chief yeoman warder of the Tower of London. For seven hundred years the chief yeoman has locked up the Tower every night at exactly nine fifty-three; he goes through a pass-and-be-recognized ceremony with the sentry." He recited the ancient exchange:

> *Who comes there?*
> *The keys.*
> *Whose keys?*
> *The king's keys.*
> *Pass, king's keys. All's well.*

Holliday frowned. "But I'm not sure what any of that has to do with me."

Genrikhovich smiled. "In this case the king in question happens to be Czar Nicholas the Second, emperor and autocrat of all the Russias, and now formally recognized by the Russian Orthodox Church as Saint Nicholas the Passion-bearer."

"I still don't see the connection," replied Holliday, his voice stubborn.

"You perform the same function within your order. With the exception of Brother Dimitrov at the monastery outside Ahtopol, you are the last of the White Tem plars, the keeper of their keys, their secrets, their wealth and their power."

"Fairy tales, Genrikhovich. There are no Templars, and the original Templars were anything but 'white.' They were bankers, builders, spies and speculators. Somewhere on the Pilgrim Road they lost their way. I'm not convinced they ever found it again."

"A cynical point of view, Colonel."

"I've fought in half a dozen wars, some legitimate, some not. Scratch any soldier my age and you'll find a cynic; believe me. I've seen too many boys with their guts all over the ground calling for their mothers to be anything but cynical, especially when it comes to the activities of medieval mercenaries hiding behind a cross."

"You imply they do no good at all."

"I don't know one way or the other."

Genrikhovich smiled calmly. "Yet here you are, Colonel, and no one forced you to fight for your country or for the downtrodden of other lands. You did it by choice. Free choice, Colonel. Your choice."

Holliday thought about what the Russian had said and suddenly realized that he had no pat answer to the question. In fact, the question had touched a nerve somehow. Why *was* he here? Why had he taken the notebook from Rodrigues in the first place? He'd taken on an enormous responsibility and he wasn't really sure whether he knew why. Was it some quest for a faith or a purpose that had eluded him all his life, or was it simply a knee-jerk call to duty he'd been trained for all these years? Don't think, do. The question nagged. He changed the subject.

"Let's get back to the matter at hand, Dr. Genrikhovich. Let's connect the dots, shall we?"

"By all means."

"You lied to me about speaking English. Why?"

"Because I didn't want there to be any hesitation or suspicion on your part when I spoke Russian to the people we will surely need to talk to on our journey. Your friend *Gospodin* Cabrera will provide you with the reassurance that what I say to these people is what I say to you."

"What exactly is this journey we're supposedly going on?"

"We know of three of the Templar swords. We must find the fourth."

"Why is it so important?"

"It will lead us to the Apophasis Megale, the Great Declaration of Simon Magus, just as Brother Dimitrov explained."

"And the key to the location of the sword is somehow held within the Kremlin Easter egg?"

"Yes, also as Brother Dimitrov told you."

"And how do you come to know this?"

"It is a long story, Colonel."

"I'm not doing anything else at the moment except

being chased by your New Age KGB friends. I've got plenty of time."

"They are not *my* KGB friends, Colonel. If you will recall they were shooting at me on that road as well as you."

"The story," Holliday prompted.

"Have you ever seen a photograph of Czar Nicholas the Second and George the Fifth standing together?"

Another crazy question that didn't seem to have anything to do with anything. "Not that I can recall," answered Holliday, irritated and exasperated by Genrikhovich's pedantically convoluted speeches. The man could have been a professor droning along in a lecture hall filled with bored students. The thought brought him up short; he'd done just that for more than ten years at West Point.

Genrikhovich cleared his throat and began speaking again. "Many people commented that they looked like brothers. Wearing the same clothes they looked like twins, although there were three years between them.

"The truth is that, while certainly not twins, the two men were half brothers, both sired by Edward the Seventh but birthed by different mothers. In the czar's case the woman was Empress Consort Maria Feodorovna, the wife of Edward's cousin, the czar Alexander the Third, while George's mother was Alexandra of Denmark, Edward's wife at age seventeen."

Holliday sighed. "Does all this information lead somewhere?"

It was Genrikhovich's turn to sigh. "Of course it's leading somewhere, Colonel. If I wanted to give lectures just to hear myself think I could do so at St. Petersburg State University, *nyet*?"

"Sorry," apologized Holliday, not quite meaning it. "Go on."

"The point I am endeavoring to make is that the two royal families were closer than even history tells us. The generally accepted reason for George the Fifth's not rescuing his cousin the czar and the czar's family during the 1917 revolution is that he feared just such a revolution in his own country. The facts offer a much simpler reason for King George's inaction—he was afraid that with his half brother in England there would be a dispute over the line of succession for the throne of the British Empire. There were already grassroots rumors of the two men's common father, and being the elder son, Nicholas would have had a legitimate claim. Had the czar shown any indication after his arrival in the British Isles of wanting the throne, there would have been chaos. The war was already bankrupting England; scandal over the monarchy would've been a disaster."

"And this relates to the four swords how?" Holliday asked.

"Both the czar and King George were members of the Templar order, and both were well aware of the dangers presented should anyone discover the secret held by the upper echelons of the Order of the Phoenix. Unfortunately, the czarina, Alexandra, became smitten with the monk Rasputin. In exchange for the key to the Phoenix secret, he promised to cure young Alexi, her young hemophiliac son.

"When King George learned of this he ordered his director of military intelligence, Sir Matthew Smith-Cummings, to—and I am quoting His Royal Highness here—'deal with the problem of the Russian monk.' Smith-Cummings then contacted the British ambassador in St. Petersburg, Sir George Buchanan, who dispatched three agents, Oswald Rayner, Captain Stephen Alley and Captain John Scale, to do the deed.

"All three men had close ties with Prince Felix Felixovich Yusupov, who organized the plot to rid the czar of Rasputin. Rayner and Scale had known Yusupov at Oxford. Stephen Alley had been *born* at the Yusupov Palace, where his father was one of the prince's tutors. He was a boyhood friend. Although most witness reports mention Rayner as being present, all three agents were present.

"It was Rayner who fired the fatal shot, however; of that there is little doubt. Rasputin took the key to the Phoenix secret to his watery grave in the Moika Canal, and for a hundred years it has been assumed that the secret was safe. It is only recently that a number of facts have come to light that would seem to indicate otherwise."

"Quite the story," said Holliday. "The king of En-gland, the czar of Russia, Rasputin the Mad Monk, Vladimir Putin's grandfather, Joseph Stalin, George Bush's great-grandfather . . . who's next, the president of the United States?"

"No, Colonel Holliday, your president at the time, Woodrow Wilson, was only peripherally concerned," Genrikhovich said blandly. "However, William Mc-Adoo, secretary of the treasury and the first chairman of the board of governors, was deeply involved. His ac-tions in 1916 and 1917 are still having repercussions today."

Holliday gave a dull laugh. "You make this sound like one of those new world order conspiracies the Internet prattles on about."

Genrikhovich shook his head. "There is nothing at all conspiratorial about it, Colonel. No one is trying to take over the world. Vladimir Putin simply intends to buy it, piece by piece; what he cannot buy he will sub-vert through power, fear or threat. He has begun the process already by co-opting the Orthodox Church in Russia to consolidate his power within the Federation. His next step is to find the key that was lost—the key that was known to Rasputin, the key that was the reason behind the creation of the four swords of Pelerin.

"Prime Minister Putin was once in the KGB, and much of his internal power stems from his control of the present-day FSB. I'm sure he is aware that you are the owner or at least caretaker of Hesperios, Sword of the West. I have no doubt that this is the reason for the pursuit following our meeting with Brother Dimitrov. He knows you are in Russia and he is hunting you; this is certain. One way or another you have very little choice. Either you help me find the location of the Great Declaration and destroy it before Putin gets it, or you will almost surely be killed."

"People keep on telling me that."

"It is a very simple truth, I'm afraid, Colonel."

"All right." Holliday sighed. "Where do we start?"

"At the Hermitage," said Genrikhovich, pride in his voice. "The largest single museum in the entire world."

10

Genrikhovich and Holliday walked west along the wide sidewalk of the Nevsky Prospekt with Eddie a full minute behind, watching for any close surveillance. It would be a hard call; even in October, St. Petersburg was full of strolling locals, tourists and other pedestrians window-shopping, stepping in and out of stores, appearing and disappearing in and out of metro stops, even walking dogs.

The broad avenue itself was crowded with cars and trolleybuses, their connectors crackling and flashing overhead as they passed. Nevsky Prospekt had been designed in the seventeenth century by Pyotr Alexeyevich Romanov, otherwise known as Peter the Great. Planned as the beginning of the road from St. Petersburg to Moscow, the avenue had always served as the city's main street, but its grandeur had become tarnished over the centuries by war, Soviet rule, overhead wires, thousands of streetlamps and the near-Vegas glitz of countless neon signs on storefronts from Gucci and Tiffany to Pizza Hut and McDonald's.

"Your friend is wasting his time," said Genrikhovich, happily sipping a Starbucks Frappuccino.

Holliday himself held a plain black coffee. "You don't think you might be under surveillance?"

"It is very doubtful. Not yet, at least. The discovery I made almost a month ago was accidental; the material was not classified."

"You came across the border with us."

"You give the Bulgarians far too much credit, Colonel Holliday. As far as bureaucracies are concerned things have changed little since the old days. If anything it is worse. In Bulgaria as in Russia we are still ruled by mediocrity, I can assure you."

"Those men who came after us didn't come out of nowhere," said Holliday. He could feel an itch between his shoulder blades as hypothetical crosshairs targeted him.

"They were watching Brother Dimitrov."

"And if they interrogate him?"

"He will tell them nothing, Colonel."

"Everybody talks eventually," answered Holliday.

"He is a *man,* like his grandfather. He would die first and take at least one of his interrogators with him."

"You seem very sure."

"I am a very small cog in the vast wheel of Mr. Putin's Russia. He cannot see me turning, at least not yet."

"What exactly are you the curator *of* at the Hermitage?" Holliday inquired. It was a simple enough question, but this was the first time he'd thought to ask it.

Genrikhovich smiled. "I am senior curator of the Hermitage archives." He took a slurp from his straw. "You might say I am a bureaucrat's bureaucrat, Colonel Holliday. The Hermitage archives contain a collection of letters, notes, purchase orders, provenance material and any other document or paper pertaining to the work of the Hermitage itself, going back to its origins with Catherine the Great in the mid–seventeen hundreds, as well as her purchase of several collections. I sometimes call myself the Keeper of the Filing Cabinets, the Troll of the Hermitage Basements, but it is a job not without interest."

"I can imagine," said Holliday. Genrikhovich was the museum's chief file clerk. On the other hand, as a historian Holliday was well aware of the value of old bits of paper and forgotten documents. The Rosetta stone was nothing more than a decree about the revoking of several tax laws for priests by King Ptolemy, and the attendant festivals and temples to be organized. The famous stone had been written in Demotic Egyptian, hieroglyphs and Greek as a way of ensuring that all officials, priests and the ordinary people could read it, but the trilingual document effectively provided a translation for a language that had confounded historians for the previous eight hundred years.

They reached the Moika Canal, and Genrikhovich paused, looking to the south. "Down there is the Yusupov Palace," he said, pointing down the winding narrow canal. There were barges and floating homes moored along the stone banks, but the buildings on either side were immense, huge mansions long since turned into government buildings and apartments. "It was from there that Rasputin came," said Genrikhovich, his voice somber. "He ran along the ice, with Yusupov and his British companions following the trail of blood and vomit he was leaving. Most assume he was heading for the stairs at the Fonarny Bridge, but I don't think he knew where he was going. I have seen the police photographs taken after he was pulled from the water. One eye was closed and there was a deep gash over the other. I think he must have been almost blind when Rayner caught up with him. According to Rayner's letter he said nothing before he died, but I'm not sure I believe that. What it did say was that their mission had been accomplished."

"Rayner wrote about the assassination?"

"Yes, in his report to the ambassador, which eventually was given to both King George and Czar Nicholas. He also sent a private letter to Stephen Alley, Prince Yusupov's 'special friend' at the palace."

Holliday glanced over his shoulder. Eddie was staring blankly into a store window a few hundred feet away. Holliday caught his eye and Eddie shook his head slightly. The Russian had been right about surveillance; they weren't being followed. Genrikhovich began walking again, and Holliday caught up with him, continuing their conversation.

"What do you mean, 'special friend'?" Holliday asked.

"He was . . . *pedik?*"

"Gay?" Holliday offered.

"Yes, gay, homosexual. They were lovers." He shrugged. "It made it easier for Alley."

"Made what easier?"

"Alley was a double agent. He worked for MI6 and also for the Okhrana, the czar's secret police."

"A tangled web." Holliday grunted. "You got this all from the Hermitage archives?"

"One thing leads to another. Assemble enough pieces and the picture suddenly becomes clear."

The two men walked on silently for a few moments, threading their way through the moving throng on the sidewalk. "Why would he say that they had accomplished their mission in his letter?" Holliday asked finally. "According to you this Stephen Alley and Prince Yusupov were there; they saw him fire the fatal shot."

"Ah, you are very quick, Colonel. It took me a little time to see the importance of that simple statement."

"What exactly is the importance?" Holliday asked.

Before he answered Genrikhovich drained the last of his coffee and tossed the empty cup into a waste bin. An old man dressed in Soviet camouflage fatigues instantly darted forward and retrieved the cup. He tilted it up to his mouth, trying to get a last few drops.

"If you read the autopsy report on Rasputin it is easy to see that he would have died of the wounds he received at the palace. He could not have survived for more than a few minutes on the ice. They didn't follow him to see that he died—they followed him to retrieve the key."

"The key to the location of this document? Simon Magus's declaration?"

The Russian paused, then spoke again, his voice ponderous and theatrical. "In a way, Colonel, but the key that Rasputin had stolen was very real. It was solid gold and exactly two and a half inches long. Rasputin had the key in his coat pocket. Rayner shot him in the forehead and retrieved the key before the madman slipped into the waters of the canal, his life gone."

"What did the lock open?" Holliday asked, playing his part in Genrikhovich's little drama.

"No lock at all," the old man responded. "It was the key to the music box in the base of the Kremlin Egg given to Czarina Alexandra Feodorovna Romanova by her husband, Czar Nicholas the Second."

11

The Russian State Hermitage Museum is a half-mile-long complex of German neoclassical buildings that stands on the eastern embankment of the Neva River in St. Petersburg, known as Leningrad during the Soviet era and still stubbornly called that by some older survivors of those bleak and sometimes desperate years.

The buildings, including the Old Hermitage, the New Hermitage, the Small Hermitage, and the immense Winter Palace, once home to the czars, were formally established in 1851 and held in excess of three million items from prehistoric and medieval times up to the present day.

During World War II, with Leningrad under siege, each and every item in the collections was cataloged, packed and moved on a series of freight trains to Sverdlovsk, deep in the heart of Russia on the east side of the Ural Mountains and a thousand miles from the fighting.

During this period the remaining Hermitage staff lived in the basements of the enormous museum, which, according to Genrikhovich, was where he was born during one of the artillery bombardments of the city in December of 1943.

By then some of Leningrad's citizens had been reduced to eating the dead frozen flesh of their companions, but in the end the Russian winter defeated Hitler just as it had defeated Napoleon long before him. Spring came, the city survived, and so did the Hermitage.

Oddly, the man who would eventually order the deaths of millions of his countrymen was first educated as a priest. Yet despite his training in the spiritual realm, Stalin, the peasant son of a Georgian cobbler in the village of Gori, had no real interest in art at all. He was no friend to the Hermitage, having sold off a huge part of their collection in the early 1930s to raise foreign currency. His appreciation of fine art ran to paintings of muscular men and busty women breaking the chains of their capitalist oppressors, fuming factory chimneys in the background. The women invariably wore kerchiefs around their heads and the men always seemed to have wrenches in their hands. His taste in music ran to old Georgian folk songs, his enjoyment of theater was distinctly lowbrow, and he ignored anything of a legitimate cultural or intellectual nature.

Genrikhovich, nine years old at the time, could still distinctly remember the party that was held in the basement of the Hermitage on March 5, 1953—the day Stalin died.

Holliday and Genrikhovich finally reached the vast expanse of Palace Square, with the breathtaking, red granite spear of the Alexander Column stretching one hundred and fifty-six feet upward into the icy, cloudless blue of the autumn sky. To the left, far across the rhomboid-shaped plaza, was the long curving arc of the Admiralty. To the right was the white-and-azure Winter Palace, once home of the czars, the place where the 1917 revolution began that changed Russia and the rest of the world, and which was now the largest building of the Hermitage complex.

The two men waited at the base of the Alexander Column and Holliday watched as the Cuban approached. The six-foot-six bald-headed black man was drawing stares from the pale tourists. As Holliday watched, four boys in their late teens converged on Eddie. Three of the four had shaved heads, the other a Mohawk. All four looked scrawny in cheap black leather jackets, skintight jeans and whatever passed for Doc Marten shit-kickers in Russia these days.

Eddie stopped and let the four teenagers come closer. One of them pulled something out of his back pocket and waved it in the Cuban's face. A switchblade, most likely. Holliday watched as Eddie bent his head forward as though he were listening to something the kid with the knife was saying. Eddie's legs told a different story

He'd eased one in front of the other and stiffened the rear leg, putting most of his weight on it. Holliday smiled thinly.

"Shouldn't we help him?" Genrikhovich whispered. "They are dangerous. *Shkoora-galava*. Bad people."

"He doesn't need any help," answered Holliday, watching the little drama unfold.

Eddie said something and the boy with the knife jabbed it toward the Cuban's belly. Eddie grabbed the boy's wrist and bent it back, the sound of the wrist bone snapping audible from a hundred feet away. The boy with the knife let loose a pitiful, high-pitched, screeching shriek.

The teenager on the Cuban's left stepped forward, arms flailing. Eddie bent the knife wielder's wrist even farther back and half turned, his forward leg snapping outward, catching the second skinhead in the crotch. The kicked boy dropped to the ground, screaming, hands between his legs.

Eddie cocked his left arm and gave the boy with the knife a hard fist to the throat. The boy turned blue, gagged and fell to the hard pavement, landing on his face and nose, gurgling, then passing out from the pain. The other two skinheads, eyes wide, stepped back. One of them turned his head and vomited.

Eddie dropped to one knee, took the switchblade from the now unconscious teenager's hand and snapped the blade off between two of the interlocking paving stones. He patted the cheek of the boy he'd kicked in the crotch, stood and stepped over the unconscious teenager and continued his interrupted stroll to the Alexander Column.

The boy who'd been kicked struggled to his feet and, still bent over, began screaming for the police at the top of his lungs. Not far from where Holliday was standing two *gorodovye*—junior police officers in dark green military uniforms complete with absurdly large peaked caps—were smoking cigarettes and studiously ignoring the screaming teenager. As Eddie passed the two cops the one closest to him grinned and gave him a discreet thumbs-up.

"Horoshuyu rabotu," the cop called out. *Good work.*

"Blagodaryu tebya, moi' droog." Eddie nodded. *Thank you, my friend.* The cop's smile grew even wider at the sound of the Cuban's fluent Russian.

"So what was that all about?" Holliday asked as Eddie joined them.

"The one with the knife wanted all my money and called me a *'negr huesos,'* which is a very unpleasant thing to say in Russian, believe me. I told him his mother was a Georgian goat and that he had been born through her . . . *ojete?* In Russian the word is *zhopa*."

Genrikhovich snickered.

"I think I get it." Holliday smiled.

Eddie shrugged. "He became very angry and he try to stab me with his knife, so I broke his wrist and kicked the other one in his *huevos minúsculos*."

"We must not draw attention to ourselves," chided Genrikhovich, clearing his throat. "It could be very dangerous."

"Should I have allowed the boy to stab me with his knife?" Eddie asked. "It looked as though he had not cleaned it in a very long time. The boy looked as though *he* had not been cleaned in a long time as well. I could have been given an infection."

Genrikhovich grumbled something under his breath and turned away, heading for the Palace Bridge and the small patch of green between it and the Winter Palace.

"Anybody on our tail?" Holliday asked Eddie as they followed the Russian across the plaza. To the south the immense golden dome of St. Isaac's Cathedral gleamed in the clear, crisp air.

"No one," said Eddie, shaking his head. "Nobody I could see, *mi amigo*." He shrugged. "But these days, who knows? Maybe there was a satellite looking down on us, or one of your drones."

They caught up with Genrikhovich as he reached the far side of the square and stepped into the park beside the Winter Palace. "You have a lot of skinheads in St. Petersburg?" Holliday asked as they walked beneath the trees.

"*Shkoora-galava*? Yes, they are a problem all over Russia, especially in the cities. They hate anyone who is not Russian and white. The worst kind of fascists. They could easily be my country's future, I'm afraid." The

older man shook his head. "They call themselves patri-
ots."

"'Guard against the impostures of pretended patrio-
tism,'" said Eddie, the English flawless. It was clearly a
quotation.

"Who said that?" Holliday asked. "Fidel?"

"George Washington," said Eddie. "We learned this
in school."

Holliday laughed. "You don't have skinheads in
Cuba?"

"In Cuba? No, it would not be allowed by El Comandante," said Eddie, smiling broadly, rubbing the
top of his smoothly shaved head. "And also the young
men in my country are much too *vanidoso* . . . con-
ceited about their hair. We only have *la cartelera de co-
caína* and purse snatchers, and, of course, like everyone
else in Cuba they are university educated."

Genrikhovich took them across the park to a narrow
set of stone steps that led down to a heavy wooden door
below ground level. A bored-looking soldier in camouflage fatigues was sitting on a stool beside the door,
smoking a cigarette and reading a copy of *Tvoi Den,
Your Day*, the Russian equivalent of the *New York Post*.

"Apaznaneya," the guard said, looking up from the
tabloid, his expression bored.

Genrikhovich dug around under his ancient cloth
overcoat and found a pale blue plastic identification
case. He snapped it open for the guard, who examined

it, dull eyed. The guard nodded, then gestured toward the door. *"Prayakets, professora."*

Genrikhovich bowed slightly, then motioned for Holliday and Eddie to follow him. The Russian dragged open the door and the three men went through into a short, dimly lit vestibule inside. The walls were green and white and the floor was cracked battleship linoleum. At the far end of the gloomy little room there was a metal circular staircase.

There was a desk to the left of the door with another guard seated behind it. This one had his nose buried in a copy of the Russian edition of *Maxim*. He was much older than the man outside, his nose bulbous and brick red. He smelled distinctly of alcohol.

The man looked up at Genrikhovich with the same bored expression as the first guard, and once again Genrikhovich showed his ID folder. This time the guard reached into a wooden box on the desk and handed Genrikhovich two plastic-coated pin-on cards that said, *Носетитель,* which presumably meant "visitor." The Hermitage curator pinned the cards onto Holliday and Eddie, then headed for the stairs.

12

The metal steps seemed to go on forever, their feet clanging noisily as they headed downward. The stairwell itself was lit bleakly every ten steps or so by short flickering fluorescents protected behind wire cages. Holliday felt as though he were descending to a castle dungeon. He wondered whether every step downward was taking him closer and closer to some unseen disaster.

Genrikhovich led the way, chattering on as they descended. "The basements beneath the Winter Palace were extensively renovated between the wars. The Armenian was no fool—he knew there would be another war and he prepared for it, even though Stalin fought him at every turn."

"The Armenian?"

"Joseph Orbeli, the director of the Hermitage from 1934 to 1951. He knew Hitler would come, so he turned the basements into concrete bunkers for the collections. The Winter Palace was bombarded dozens of times, but not a single artifact or object was ever damaged. A few people froze to death on the rooftop fire watches, but nothing was ever damaged and no one was hurt in the basement shelters."

They finally reached the bottom of the stairs and found themselves in the cavernous rabbit warren of chambers and rooms beneath the Hermitage. There was no plan to any of it; the refitting of the basement area had clearly been done ad hoc as funds or time or material demanded. Everything was done in rough concrete, some gray and solid-looking, the wooden grain of the forms still visible on the stony surface, while other areas were old and crumbling, too much sand or too little lime in the mixture. Stalactites of dripping mineral exudates dripped from parts of the ceilings, and there were white salt stains on the walls.

Genrikhovich led them down a succession of zigzagging unmarked green-and-white corridors and through huge arch-ceilinged chambers fitted with wood and metal racks filled with sturdy crates of all sizes and shapes. There was little signage anywhere except for small wooden plaques here and there with stenciled letter-number combinations. Cats wandered everywhere. They were every size and type, but they all looked extremely well fed.

"The Hermitage cats." Genrikhovich smiled. "A tradition here. Very useful too. Rats."

The Russian finally stopped in front of a plain, numbered door, took out a ring of keys and flipped through them, looking for the one he wanted. He found it eventually, turned the key in the lock and opened the door, ushering Holliday and Eddie into his private inner sanctum. The room was large, twenty feet on a side and low ceilinged, and covered in sagging acoustic tile, lit by banks of fluorescent tubes hanging down on chains. Two walls were filled floor to ceiling with old-fashioned wooden plan drawers of the kind architects used for storing drawings. The third wall was fitted with a long worktable with its own high-intensity lighting and a section that acted as a light table. There were two armless drafting chairs on casters, as though Genrikhovich had once had assistants. Above the table were rows of metal racks and shelves stuffed with thick numbered and lettered binders, all in gray slipcases. The area to the right of the desk contained an institutional-looking metal desk and a wooden rolling office chair. There was an old PC on the desk sitting on a boxy hard drive.

"So, here we are," said Genrikhovich, closing and locking the door behind him. He sat down in the chair in front of the desk. There was also a modem and a touch-tone multiline phone. The room was completely functional except for a small framed photograph on the desk. It showed a woman and a boy. The woman was wearing a drab, poorly fitted dress. She was holding the hand of a young boy of about ten. He was wearing a young pioneer's uniform.

"You and your mother?" Holliday asked, nodding toward the picture.

"My wife and my son, Yuri. They were visiting my wife's parents in Arzamas in the Gorky oblast. Her father was a retired machinist there. It was his eightieth birthday and he wanted to see his grandson. June fourth, 1988. A train carrying one hundred and eighteen tons of hexogen—you know hexogen?"

"RDX." Holliday nodded. It was one of the best-known military explosives ever made.

"Yes, RDX. The tanks exploded. My wife's family lived in a small block of flats next to the railway line. They were all killed, vaporized. There was no funeral. There was nothing to bury."

"I'm very sorry," said Holliday.

Genrikhovich shrugged and sighed. "It was a very long time ago. More than twenty years." Even so the Russian's eyes were welling up with barely contained tears.

Holliday nodded. He knew what that was like and knew that the sadness and the pain never really left you. He still dreamed of Fay sometimes, usually a Fay who was young and vibrant and healthy, but just as often he dreamed of her gaunt and dying, her eyes rimmed with the dark shadows that predicted her inevitable death. He often wondered now whether that kind of pain grew more painful as you became older and came closer to death yourself.

"So," said Genrikhovich, regaining his composure. "We come to the beginning of it all."

Genrikhovich took out his keys, found one and fitted it into the drawer of the desk. He took out a plain green file folder and took a single sheet from it, placing it delicately on the light table. He flicked a toggle switch and the milky sheet of glass making up the surface of the table glowed. Holliday swiveled in his drafting chair and stared.

"What is it?" Holliday asked, wondering what it was he'd come so far to see. In the end it was nothing more than a small rectangle of paper, obviously old, pressed between two sheets of celluloid, themselves yellowed with age. The document had a pale mimeographed bust of Stalin in three-quarter profile at the top, surrounded by flags. The lines and squares on the paper were filled with figures. There was a signature at the bottom, faded to a yellowed sepia and unquestionably done with a straight pen. The name was Boris Vasilyevich Legran. The date was June 7, 1933. There was a pale blue stamp-pad scrawl beneath Legran's name.

"Who was Legran?"

"Briefly he was the director of the State Hermitage. More so he was a crony of Stalin's."

"What does it say?"

"It's a purchase order made out to Torolf Prytz for the construction of a gold key two and one half inches long," Genrikhovich said. He took another celluloid-enclosed document out of the file and laid it beside the first. The second document showed a diagram of an old-fashioned skeleton key with dimensions marked. "These are the specifications for the key."

"This would seem to be true." Eddie nodded, reading over Holliday's shoulder.

"Who was Torolf Prytz?" Holliday asked. "It doesn't sound like a Russian name to me."

"There were few goldsmiths left in the new Soviet Russia after 1917, as I am sure you can understand," answered Genrikhovich, his tone dry. "And none capable of the master craftsmanship to re-create the key. Torolf Prytz was a Norwegian master goldsmith. Legran commissioned the key from him, with Stalin's countersignature below." He pointed to the scrawl beneath Legran's signature. "He always used a signature stamp except on documents he signed in public."

"What is this supposed to prove?" Holliday asked.

"Nothing on its own," said Genrikhovich. "It is merely the first piece in the puzzle."

"And the next?"

Genrikhovich took something that looked like an old-fashioned photostat of a letter, written on CCCP or Soviet stationery with the words, Народный комиссариат внутренних дел. Below was the wreathed red sigil of the Soviet Union. It was dated March 1934. The letter was countersigned in a scrawl much like the signature stamp on the purchase order for the Norwegian goldsmith.

Holliday pointed to the Cyrillic words on the letterhead. "Eddie?"

"*Narodnyy komissariat vnutrennikh del*, NKVD," translated the Cuban.

Genrikhovich nodded. "It is a letter from Beria, the head of the NKVD, to Legran, the director, berating him because the key does not work and serves only to operate the music box within the 1906 Kremlin Egg. He asks for Legran's resignation. The letter is countersigned in ink by Stalin and asks for the money spent on the gold key to be returned." The Russian shrugged. "Of course, the operation of the music box was all the key was ever designed for in the first place."

"Did Legran resign?"

"The following day." Genrikhovich nodded.

"Where did the letter come from?"

"Legran put it into his personal correspondence file. Eventually all the official correspondence comes to the archives. I was adding the material to Legran's general documentation file when I saw the letter, so I removed it."

"I'm still not sure where all this is going," said Holliday.

Genrikhovich picked up the phone on his desk and spoke in Russian for a moment. Holliday stiffened.

"He is asking for a file," murmured Eddie, translating. "Nothing more than that."

A few minutes later a young man appeared carrying a pale pink cardboard file case. He gave it to Genrikhovich, who signed a small chit in return, and then the boy left after a pleasant *spasiba* and that was that.

"Look," said the Hermitage document curator. He took an item from the pink file case. This was an eight-by-eight transparency of the base of what appeared to be an octagonal piece of onyx covered by a green felt cover. Genrikhovich took out a second transparency, which he laid beside the first, and then a third. Both the second and third transparencies showed the same eight-sided onyx base with the green felt removed. The second transparency was black-and-white, while a third was in color. The second transparency had the date 1906 drawn on it in white ink. The date on the color transparency was digitally stamped August 12, 2012. The base of the second transparency had the appropriate Fabergé hallmark stamped on it:

Фаберже

БА

And so did the second, but with one small change:

Фаберже

JVA

"I don't get it," said Holliday.

"By the 1880s Fabergé was the imperial court jeweler. It was one of the functions for the Hermitage to document and photograph each of the Fabergé eggs given to the empress by the czar. The first black-and-white transparency shows the base of the Kremlin Egg, also known as the Uspenski Cathedral Egg, made by Fabergé in 1903, although it wasn't given to Alexandra until 1906, for a variety of reasons. The bottom was covered with felt so it wouldn't scratch delicate surfaces. The master goldsmith in charge of the Kremlin Egg was Johan Victor Aarne, a Finn who worked in the Fabergé shop in St. Petersburg from 1891 to 1904, when he returned to Finland. The Cyrillic hallmark 'БА' is his signature, the punch for making it his alone to use." Genrikhovich paused. "Three months ago some of the Kremlin treasures were taken out of the collection for repairs and for cleaning. Included among them was the Kremlin Egg; the clockwork mechanisms had become clogged with dust and dirt over the decades, and several of the larger jewels had become loose in their settings.

"Since the Hermitage has the largest and best conservation unit in the Federation, the items were sent here. As chief archivist I was responsible for the documentation of the treasures as they came into the Hermitage, and our photographers took a series of comprehensive detailed exposures of each and every item. The second transparency of the Kremlin Egg was taken at that time."

"Different marks on the base," said Holliday.

"Precisely. The JVA mark from the second transparency is also that of Johan Victor Aarne, but it was not used by him until his return to Vyborg, Finland, in 1904. He used the mark between that date and his death in 1934."

"So sometime in that thirty-year period he made a perfect copy of the egg."

"Yes," said Genrikhovich. "The one on display in the Kremlin Armoury is a fake."

13

The big black ZiL 114 limousine and its front and rear guard of Mercedes G55 four-by-fours sped across the granite cobblestones of Red Square, scattering the small crowds of tourists as it raced towards Spasskaya Gate, the official entrance to the Kremlin.

The thin, partially bald man brooding in the deep leather seat of the passenger compartment looked more like an accountant than the director of the FSB, the feared secret police agency that held sway over the Russian people, but Alexander Vasilyevich Bortnikov liked his unassuming look. Especially the glasses Vladimir had suggested. Bortnikov had nearly perfect vision, but he liked the studious, professorial aspect his oversize spectacles gave him.

The limousine slipped through the broad opening beneath the tower, breaching the ancient fortress with amazing ease. Ivan the Terrible would have spun in his grave. Bortnikov smiled thinly. What was it poet Mikhail

Lermontov had said about this place—"the legendary phoenix raised out of the ashes"? If only he knew how appropriate those words were.

As the wall in Berlin had crumbled, so had great Russia's hopes for the future. Now, with his old friend Vladimir putting the iron back into the Rodina's soul, there was hope once again . . . and it was the Phoenix that would give Russia that chance at restoring her greatness.

The limousine slowed somewhat as it came through the opening in the massive wall and rolled ponderously past the old Supreme Soviet Building. It threaded its way through the maze of buildings until it finally reached the courtyard of the old State Kremlin Palace, once the home of the czars when they were in Moscow.

Vladimir kept his official prime minister's office in the Russian White House, the modern, Stalinist-era building that was home to Parliament. But he was never one to cut himself off from the real seat of power and maintained his real and private office in a suite of rooms that had once been the apartment of one of the Romanov princes.

The limousine stopped at an entrance at the rear of the building, and Bortnikov waited while Tolya, his chauffeur and sometime bodyguard, opened the door for him. He climbed out of the leather seat and stood briefly in the cool late-afternoon sunshine. He nodded to Tolya, told him to go and get himself a cup of coffee somewhere, and entered the building.

He climbed two flights of narrow stone stairs and

continued down a long, ornate hallway, the ceiling arched and covered in gilded cherubim and angels. The walls of the corridor were bright blue watered moiré silk, and every few feet there were marble busts depicting an assortment of green gods and goddesses. He reached an arched white door at the end of the hallway, opened it and stepped inside.

Beyond the door was a large vestibule with an ornate gilded desk on the left and a guard seated behind it in full, red-breasted Kremlin guard uniform, complete with the huge Pinochet-style peaked cap and shiny cavalry boots. As Bortnikov stepped into the room the young man snapped to attention, heels clicking, white-gloved hand snapping to the peak of his idiotic cap, his eyes unblinking. The FSB director smiled pleasantly.

The boy was smooth cheeked and very handsome, just his type. There was sweat forming on the young fellow's forehead. Power was a wonderful thing. Bortnikov gave him a little nod, then crossed the vestibule to a set of double doors. He opened the one on the right and stepped into the sitting room of Vladimir Putin's private office.

There was no desk, only chairs and tables and glittering blue stone "Imperial Porphyry" columns. The tall windows were covered in bloodred velvet fringed with gold. The chairs were gilt and red upholstery in the Louis Quinze style, the carpets covered with rich "tree of life" patterns from Azerbaijan. The tables by each chair were chased silver and crystal, and the central coffee table the chairs surrounded was a circular slab of inlaid marble held up on curved gold legs with lion's-paw feet. On the coffee table was a solid-gold platter holding three sweating bottles of red-labeled Istok vodka, a dozen green-and-gold bottles of Baltika 9 beer and the appropriate glassware.

Three of the four chairs around the table were already occupied. To Bortnikov's left was the balding, narrow-faced Vladimir Vladimirovich Putin, prime minister of all the Russias. Directly in front of the FSB director was Dmitry Anatolyevich Medvedev, the diminutive, boyish-looking Russian president and Putin's successor in the job. The gray-bearded older man on the right, wearing a very expensive pin-striped suit from Bond Street instead of his ornate robes, was Vladimir Mikhailovich Gundyaev, known during his days in the old KGB by his code name "Mikhailov" and otherwise known as Kirill I, patriarch of Moscow and all Rus, primate of the Russian Orthodox Church—effectively its pope and, by the numbers, the most powerful of all the Orthodox patriarchs.

Gundyaev was the oldest of the four by a few years, but all of the men were in their late middle age. Friends since boyhood, all four had been in the Leningrad Oblast KGB during the same period.

Bortnikov turned and closed the door firmly behind him. He turned back to his companions, a hand raised in greeting, then sat down in the fourth chair. Putin stood, went to the coffee table and poured out four generous shots of vodka into the crystal old-fashioned glasses. The other three men stood and Putin passed the drinks around. *"Podnaseets Kloob Leningradski!"* toasted the prime minister. *To the Leningrad Club.*

"Kloob Leningradski!" the other three responded.

"Daneezoo!" Bottoms up, Putin ordered. All four downed their drinks in a single swallow. Putin, the host, refilled them, and the four old friends sat down again.

"Perhaps we should sing patriotic songs," said the gray-bearded Gundyaev. He began to sing the moody, solemn chorus of *"Gosudarstvenniy Gimn SSSR,"* the anthem of the Soviet Union, in his strong, baritone voice:

*Slav'sya, Otechestvo nashe
svobodnoye, Druzhby narodov nadyozhny oplot!
Partiya Lenina—sila narodnaya
Nas k torzhestvu kommunizma vedyot!*

*Glory to the Fatherland, united and free!
The stronghold of the friendship of the people!
The party of Lenin, power of the people,
It leads us to the triumph of Communism!*

"I really don't think that will be necessary, Vladimir Mikhailovich." Putin laughed. "Singing such a song outside this office might get you into terrible trouble with the proletariat."

"But it is such a nice song," complained the primate. He'd obviously been drinking before Bortnikov got there. "It has gravity, strength, power. Not like that rude stuff you hear in the streets now." The head of the Russian Orthodox Church launched into a reasonably good imitation of a beat-box song called "Black Boomer" by Seryoga.

"You seem to know the words quite well, Your Holiness," said Putin.

"I hear it when I go to the radio station for my Sunday sermon to the people. It distresses me."

"What on earth is a 'black boomer,' I wonder?" Medvedev asked, sipping from his glass.

Putin shrugged. "According to my daughter Yekaterina, black boomer refers to the pistol the man is carrying—a black boomer. On the other hand, my daughter Maria says the 'black boomer' in question is the young man's vehicle, a black BMW. I tend to agree with Maria."

"Perhaps we should get down to business," said Bortnikov, putting his half-filled glass down on the side table beside his chair.

"Ah, yes." Putin nodded. "What have you to tell us, my dear Alexander Vasilyevich?"

"The American we were told about and his Cuban companion crossed the Turkish border and went with an unidentified third man to the monastery of Saint Simeon the Plowman at Ahtopol in Bulgaria."

"The place Beria went to in 1945." His Holiness nodded. "And where he retrieved the secret sword."

"Which told us nothing," said Putin. "Only gave us more riddles to solve."

"At any rate they went there and were observed by several CSS thugs."

"They were followed?"

"Of course."

"By the Bulgarian State Security people?" Putin asked.

"No, by our men."

"And?"

"They were killed."

"The American and his friends?" Medvedev asked nervously. "They killed an American?"

"No," said Bortnikov, blood coming into his face, not from embarrassment but from rage. He reminded himself about his doctor's warnings concerning his blood pressure and lit a cigarette to calm himself down. "Our people," he said after a moment, drawing on the cigarette. He took a swallow of vodka. "All of them."

"This American has . . . how do you say it in English . . . skills?" Putin said. He'd been working hard to improve his English for the past two or three years and was now reasonably fluent. His daughters were always teaching him little colloquialisms.

"I would say he has excellent skills," said His Holiness, raising an eyebrow.

"Where are they now?"

"We lost track of them for a while and then they showed up in Odessa. He visited a document thief and was provided with everything he needed."

"You know the names they are traveling under now?"

"Not yet, but there are not many Americans in Russia at this time of year. Somewhere along the line he will have been required to show his identification. We know he did not enter Russia through any known airport or train station, so in the end it will simply be a process of elimination."

"How long?" Putin asked.

"A matter of days. Maybe less."

"We don't want them harmed," cautioned His Holiness, pouring himself a foaming glass of the potent Russian beer. "You have a tendency to be overzealous in your actions." He paused. "And perhaps your people are not as good as you have boasted on more than one occasion. You are not a street policeman anymore, Alexander Vasilyevich." The primate's tone was chiding, and the FSB director bristled.

"No, Your Holiness, and neither are you a parish priest taking the confessions of your people and then passing them on to Vladimir Vladimirovich anymore," replied Bortnikov, glancing at Putin. He turned back to the primate. "I leave the running of the Church to you, *Preeyatyel Papa*. You leave the running of the Sluzhba Vneshney Razvedki and the FSB to me."

"We should stop arguing like children in the school-yard," said Putin. "This is about neither the Church nor the Foreign Intelligence Service, nor the FSB. It is about the four of us in this room and our great duty, and it is about the Order of the Phoenix. Most important, it is about Russia, our motherland, the Rodina and her future. Remember that."

Bortnikov's cell phone chirped loudly. He slipped it out of his breast pocket, thumbed it on and held it to his ear. His face brightened as he listened. Finally he ended the call and put the phone back in his pocket.

"They have discovered who the third man accompanying Holliday and the Cuban is. His name is Victor Nikolaevich Genrikhovich, and he is a curator of documents at the Hermitage."

"Dear God," whispered Medvedev, the president. "We could be ruined."

"Don't worry," said Bortnikov. "He is being arrested as we speak."

14

The telephone trilled. Genrikhovich stared at it as though the plastic device were a scorpion. It rang a second time. He picked it up and listened. The blood drained from his face and Holliday thought he was going to faint. Genrikhovich hung up the telephone and dropped into his old wooden chair.

"We have been betrayed," said the curator, his face the color of ash.

"Who?" Holliday said quickly, getting up from the drafting chair.

"One of the secretarial people staffing the basement level. She is an informer for the FSB. The file boy must have told her I was here."

"Who warned you?"

"A friend. It is not important."

"How long do we have?"

"According to my friend, not long. They are sending a squad of OMON."

"Shit," breathed Holliday. OMON Black Beret squads could be armed with anything—AK-47s, PK machine guns, Bizon folding-stock submachine guns, AN97 assault rifles with under-barrel grenade launchers. Their motto was, "We know no mercy and do not ask for any." Their unit insignia was the roaring head of a white Siberian tiger. Not exactly comforting news. "How many exits?"

"Dozens, scores," answered Genrikhovich. "I have never counted."

"How will they come?"

"Probably the same way we did. Either that or through the courtyard entrance to the basement level."

"What's the quickest way out?"

"Those two exits. The others lead onto the square or onto the Neva Embankment."

"Do they have a boat unit?"

"In St. Petersburg, yes. They will be waiting."

"That's out then," said Holliday. Something was niggling at him in the outer suburbs of his brain, but he couldn't quite see it through the clutter of a billion other pieces of useless historical information. Who really cared if the thing they used to pull back the spring on a French crossbow was called a goat's-foot lever? And why was he thinking about key lime pie? Or Orson Welles, the theme music for *The Third Man* echoing furiously in his head like a burrowing earwig?

"We are running out of time, *compadre*," urged Eddie calmly.

Key lime, Harry Lime, the character played by Orson Welles in *The Third Man*. The cats. The Hermitage cats. Where did the rats come from?

"Are there any old tunnels down here, maybe left over from World War Two?" he asked suddenly.

"My father never told me of any. . . ." Genrikhovich paused for a moment, then nodded. "St. Petersburg has always had terrible problems with sewage. Hundreds of years ago houses would connect their wastewater pipes to the small storm sewers. Everything became terribly polluted. Nothing was done until 1924 or 1925. They began building outfall tunnels on the embankments. The war stopped the system, and when the war was over they began an entirely new system."

"Is there one of those embankment outfall tunnels near here?"

"One was dug directly beneath Palace Square to connect the Neva with the outflow from the Moika Canal. It was built between the Hermitage Theatre and the Old Hermitage."

"Can we get to it from here?"

"I expect so." Genrikhovich nodded.

"Then let's get the hell out of here," said Holliday, grabbing Genrikhovich by the arm and pushing him toward the door.

"The file!" Genrikhovich wailed.

"Bring it, *amigo*," Holliday said to Eddie as he thrust Genrikhovich forward.

"Sí, compañero," answered the Cuban, stuffing the transparencies into the pink accordion folder, along with any other documents on Genrikhovich's desk. He followed Holliday's back as he went through the door.

"Left?" Holliday asked, still gripping Genrikhovich's arm.

The older man nodded mutely, his breath coming in short, unpleasant-sounding pants.

Turning left, they headed down a narrow, linoleum-floored corridor. It was green to the wainscoting and yellowing dirty white above, like everything else Holliday had seen of the Hermitage. On the floors above him were the treasures of centuries, and all he could see was green-and-white walls and tangles of pipes and conduits overhead. They reached a stone wall about a hundred yards along, probably some sort of supporting buttress. A gouged hole had been hacked through the stonework and a tall metal door fitted, the masonry roughly patched around it. Holliday hauled it open and they stepped through into another blank, empty length of corridor. As they set foot in the passage, red lights in the ceiling every twenty-five feet or so began to blink furiously, and Holliday could hear the distant sound of a wailing siren.

"They are locking the place down! We are trapped!" Genrikhovich moaned.

"They haven't caught us yet," said Holliday. He grimaced, imagining what would happen if and when they did. In the old days it would have been a quick trip to the cellar of the Lubyanka at 19 Dzerzhinsky Square in Moscow and a single tap to the back of the head with a nine-millimeter Makarov. Now he wasn't sure what the procedure would be. Certainly nothing pleasant.

They reached a massive industrial boiler room, machinery already clanging and booming as the ancient furnaces began the long, ponderous chore of heating a building the length of a football field with a thousand drafts and leaks from a time when peasants, coal and entire forests of firewood were cheap and accessible.

A dozen men in blue coveralls and wearing goggles and hard hats swarmed over a maze of interconnected up-and-down catwalks, tending the machinery like something out of *Metropolis* or *1984,* worker ants tending a series of fat, ancient and rusty brown queens. Steam rose everywhere, and the hot, wet air echoed with the sounds of men calling to one another above the clatter of the pipes. Nobody noticed Holliday, Eddie and Genrikhovich, or if they were noticed they were ignored.

"There," said Genrikhovich, pointing. Holliday looked. At first glance it appeared to be the remains of what once might have been a coal bin, but then he saw. Behind a bulbous electrical generator there was a man-high vent covered by a heavy mesh grille. Holliday herded Genrikhovich toward the opening with Eddie following, the Cuban's sharp eyes watching the workers carefully.

Holliday reached the grille, Genrikhovich crowding

in behind him. "We must hurry, please," he said, his voice whining, one hand clutching Holliday's wrist. Holliday shook it off. He could feel warm air pushing on the back of his neck and knew, intentionally or not, that the big vent was exhausting the hot air out of the boiler room. Somewhere there'd be a big white plume of condensation riding the cool air outside.

The vent was about eight feet in diameter, hinged on one side and locked on the other with a padlock through a tongue and hasp. The metal was iron and it was flaked heavily with layers of rust and grime. If Genrikhovich was right, this had been intended as one of those 1925 outfalls and never used. The padlock was a long laminated brass shackle style with the name VARLUX along the bottom, and clearly a copy of an American Master brand lock. The padlock looked fairly new. He checked the bottom of the lock. There was a faint MADE IN CHINA stamp. Everything was made in China these days. It wasn't a good sign.

Holliday looked around. A long, adjustable spring-handled monkey wrench lay on top of the generator casing. He picked up the wrench, put the short, flat-sided grip into the shackle of the lock and pulled hard. There was a dry snapping sound as the tongue of the hasp snapped off the vent grille. Eddie darted forward and caught the lock before it hit the floor.

"Gracias," said Holliday.

"No es nada, mi amigo," replied the Cuban softly.

"Your Spanish is becoming *muy fluido*." He handed the lock to Holliday, who slipped it into the pocket of his jacket.

He dug the short arm of the wrench through the grille and pulled. There was a ratcheting squeal and it opened six inches. He looked over his shoulder but no one seemed to have noticed. He pulled again. There was a second high-pitched grinding sound from the hinges and the screen opened two feet. "Go!" Holliday whispered to Genrikhovich, pushing him through the opening. He turned to Eddie, but the Cuban was already moving behind the big generator. "What the hell are you doing?" Holliday hissed at his friend.

"Momentito," whispered Eddie, disappearing behind the big piece of electrical equipment. Still, no one paid any attention to them. Holliday waited, his nerves winding up like a clockwork engine. He could feel the fear tickling the hairs at the back of his neck, and out of the corner of his eye he could see one of the blinking red lights, which no one else seemed to have noticed. His mouth was dry as sand. In a few seconds one of the workers would turn and see the light, even if the sound of the siren was buried under the hum and drone of all the machinery in the boiler room.

Finally the Cuban returned. He was holding a giant six-volt dry-cell searchlight.

"I saw this. I thought perhaps it would be good to see where we are going, no?"

"Yes." Holliday grunted. The Cuban was right. "Go and find Genrikhovich," he ordered, "He won't have gone far. I'll stay here and close things up."

Eddie nodded. Still holding the monkey wrench, he slipped through the opening and disappeared into the darkness. Holliday followed, then turned and eased the grille until it was open only three or four inches. He fished the lock out of his pocket, hung the shackle over the remains of the hasp and eased the door shut. If anyone gave it a casual look the vent would have appeared to be locked. He turned and stumbled into the darkness.

15

Wearing white gloves, as required, Cardinal Antonio Niccolo Spada, Vatican secretary of state, prefect of the Congregation for the Doctrine of the Faith, better known as the Holy Inquisition, sat in the private manuscript reading room of the Vatican Library, carefully turning the pages of the original manuscript on vellum of *The Rare and Excellent History of Saladin* or *al-Nawadir al-Sultaniyya wa'l-Mahasin al-Yusufiyya* by Baha' al-Din Ibn Shaddad.

Seated across from the hawk-faced cardinal, smelling like an ashtray as usual, was Father Thomas Brennan, head of Vatican foreign intelligence, once known as Sodalitium Pianum, its name now changed to that of a much more bureaucratic and thus anonymous group, the Committee for Doctrinal Research and Investigation.

"North, south, east and west," murmured Cardinal Spada. "Four holy swords, Polaris, Octanis, Aos and

Hesperios. Hesperios, the Sword of the West, was given to Adolf Hitler by Mussolini after it had been discovered on an archaeological dig near Naples, and eventually found its way into Colonel John Holliday's hands seventy-odd years after it was dug up. Aos, Sword of the East, was held by the monk Helder Rodriques, in the Azores. Polaris was hidden in a Bulgarian monastery; in 1944 it was given to Lavrenti Beria, head of the NKVD, who in turn gave it to Stalin. They have learned nothing from these three swords, and what is worse, *we* have learned nothing."

"So the secret must lie with the fourth, Octanis, Sword of the South," said Brennan. "Sounds like something out of *Harry Potter* or *Lord of the* bloody *Rings*—four swords to rule them all and in the darkness bind them." The Irish priest snorted. "What a load of bleeding bollocks, boyo," he said. He scratched at the gray-white stubble on his cheeks with three stubby fingers yellowed with nicotine. "It's fantasy, Your Eminence. Fecking silly fairy tales from a thousand years ago. *A Thousand and One Arabian* fecking *Nights*, yeah?"

Spada frowned, staring across the old scarred table at Brennan, wondering what on earth could have called such a man to God and holy orders, and, even more dumbfounding, what seminary could have educated him, and what bishop could have possibly seen fit to ordain such an uncouth, foulmouthed lout from the wilds of County Offaly

Brennan caught the look and smiled, showing off his small and nicotine-stained teeth. "I know what I am, and who I am, and where I came from, and where I am now, Your Eminence, believe you me. I know all that and I know what you think of me. But that doesn't matter, really; does it, Your Eminence? Because when you get right down to it, you and me are the very same. I know all your dirty secrets and you know mine."

"That wouldn't be a threat, would it, Father Brennan?" Spada said mildly.

"Certainly not, Your Eminence!" Brennan said in mock horror. "God's blood, Cardinal! It's just my way of saying I know who the shark is and who the feckin' remora is in this relationship, and I'll happily clean the bits of flesh from between the shark's teeth, and I'll be your Gollum searching for your precious Sword of the South for as long as you want me to, because that's my fecking job, yeah?"

"That may not be necessary, in point of fact," said Spada. He nodded toward the old vellum manuscript on the table in front of him. "This particular book of *Arabian Nights,* which is a biography of Saladin by one of his closest advisers, mentions not only the Four Swords of Pelerin; it also mentions a gift of Saladin to the eighth grand master of the Templars, Odo de St. Amand. It was a fifth sword, *Al Husam Min Warda*, the Sword of the Rose. When Odo and King Baldwin the Leper, king of Jerusalem, were trapped after a battle, Odo gifted it to Reginald of Sidon, the man who rescued them. The Sword of the Rose was never heard of again."

"More fairy tales," said Brennan.

The cardinal could see that Brennan desperately wanted a cigarette, so he kept on talking, just to draw things out a little longer. Brennan could do with a dose of history anyway. Spada smiled. "Sidon was a territory in the Holy Land during the Crusades. But what you may not know, Father Brennan, is that it is also the origin for the so-called Protocols of the Elders of Zion, the fictitious Prieuré de Sion, the Priory of Sion, and half a dozen other misuses, large and small. The misinterpreting of a single word can sometimes be very important." He gestured at the book on the table in front of him. "For instance, Saladin's biographer was very careful to use the word *'husam'* for sword, rather than *'saif.' Husam* is the word used for an ordinary soldier's weapon, a real sword, while *saif* could be misinterpreted as a metaphorical sword—*Saif al-Haqq*, the Sword of Truth. *Saif al-Islam*, the Sword of Islam. The Christian Sword of the Lord. He was telling us that the fifth sword, the Sword of the Rose, is very real."

"We're in Dan Brown territory now—seeing things that aren't there, weaving conspiracies out of thin air," scoffed Brennan.

"He's a storyteller; that's his business," answered Spada. "And he's obviously doing something right, no matter what you think of his abilities." The cardinal paused. "That's hardly the point, though, Father Brennan."

"Well, what the hell *is* the point?" said the Irish priest and spymaster. He waved a hand at the stacks of ancient manuscripts and bound volumes all around them in the large, rectangular room. "This dry stuff is the past—our problems are in the present and in the future."

"This dry *stuff,* as you call it, Father Brennan, is history. Within the walls of the Vatican is every secret ever whispered from lips to ears or written down for the last two thousand years and even farther into the distant past. Almost everyone has heard the aphorism from George Santayana, who said that those who do not learn from history are doomed to repeat it, but very few heed his cautionary warning." The cardinal paused for a moment, his eyes scanning the stacks. Finally he spoke again.

"Alexander the Great could not conquer Afghanistan, but more than two thousand years later the Russians *and* the Americans tried and both failed. Napoleon invaded Russia, only to be defeated by winter, but Hitler thought he could do better, for some reason. Mussolini called himself caesar, and instead of being stabbed to death on the Ides of March he was hung upside down on an Esso station sign at the end of April." Spada shook his head wearily.

"Christ said: 'He who heard and did nothing is like a man who built a house on the earth without a foundation, against which the stream beat vehemently; and immediately it fell. And the ruin of that house was great.' But that didn't stop people from building Pompeii under a volcano, or New Orleans on a swamp, where hurricanes were a yearly event." The aging cardinal sighed. "History is not just who we *were*, Father Brennan; history is who we *are*."

"That's all well and good, Your Eminence, but how does history help us with our problem with Kirill the First and all his nefarious pally-wallies in the bloody Kremlin?"

Spada shrugged and closed the book in front of him, then slipped off the white gloves. A young priest came shimmering out of nowhere and gathered up the book on a special neutral-pH plastic tray and scurried off. When he had vanished again the cardinal spoke, his voice angry.

"We barely have a foothold in Russia—less than three-quarters of a million people, only a few thousand more than the Jews. Putin has made the Orthodox metropolitans into political oligarchs, while our churches are stoned and shot at. He's using the Church as a tool for expansion into foreign territories—*our* territories. The world has been fooled into thinking that the Russian bear is sleeping peacefully and that today's problem is the Middle East or China, but it's not. It was Russia before the Cold War, and it is *still* Russia. Russia and her schismatic, unholy, image-worshiping Mafia of a religion is still the problem. They have a stranglehold on Europe's gas and oil, they bring more gold out of the ground than Canada and Africa combined and they still have twenty-two thousand tanks that are designed for the autobahns of Germany and the autoroutes of France and the rest of Europe. The Russian bear has one eye open even when it's dozing."

"So what are we going to do about it?" Brennan asked.

"You've had a watch on Holliday since Washington; am I right?"

"Yes, not closely, but we're aware of his movements."

"And?"

"He was with his niece and her husband in Ethiopia and then vanished into the interior for several weeks. He reappeared in Khartoum nine days ago and flew to Istanbul. He had two others with him, one a Russian named Genrikhovich, a curator of documents at the Hermitage in St. Petersburg, the other a black man. We don't know who he is."

"An African? American?"

"Not unless Africans speak fluent Russian, as this one does."

"Cuban, perhaps?"

"Could be. Anyway, after they crossed into Bulgaria we seem to have lost track of him."

"Find Holliday," said Spada. "We know he is a formidable adversary and he may well be on the trail of *Al Husam Min Warda*. Find him and we may well find the Sword of the Rose and its secrets."

"But what secrets are we talking about?"

"The rose is a potent symbol in many religions. To us it is representative of the early Christian martyrs and the Holy Mother. In other religions it is the symbol of silence. In Rome, a rose laid by the doorstep once indicated that there was a secret meeting in progress. There is the symbolism for the five petals—the five wounds of Christ and the five panes in the rose window of a cathedral." The cardinal paused.

"The fifth sword of the sorrow piercing the Holy Mother's heart is mentioned in Matthew as the great darkness that fell upon the Earth as Christ was raised upon the cross." Spada lifted his shoulders wearily. "It could mean a hundred different things or a hundred different places."

"The book in Arabic gave you no answers?" Brennan asked.

"One," said the cardinal, his voice thoughtful. "In the Koran there is a verse—'If you wish to see the glory of God, contemplate a red rose.'" Spada pushed back his chair and stood. "There are also those who say that the rose is the symbol of the prophet's blood."

Brennan nodded as though he understood, which Spada knew he did not. The Irishman patted the pockets of his frayed black priest's jacket, no doubt assuring himself that cigarettes and a lighter were there and ready the moment he stepped outside the library's ancient doors. He turned away, but the cardinal's dark, forbidding words stopped him, and Brennan turned to listen.

"Remember this, Thomas Brennan: that while you serve me, remora to the shark, so I in turn serve others much more powerful. More powerful than the Holy Father, more powerful than any president or king.

"Memento puteus, sacerdotis," Spada said in Latin. "Remember this well, priest."

More fatuous philosophy, Brennan thought. "I'll remember, Eminence, if you tell me just what exactly it is that you want me to do."

"I want you to call the Peseks, for one thing. He's a Czech who was brought up in the Communist era; he almost certainly speaks Russian. I don't know about his psychopathic wife and her ghastly hatpin. Whatever the case, Holliday must be dealt with once and for all, and you must bring the Sword of the Rose out of Kirill's grasp."

"And Kirill himself?"

"If we are to survive this, Brennan, the Orthodox Church must be shattered to its core, its hegemony over the Russian people destroyed. To kill a serpent you do not cut off the tail, Father Brennan; you lop off the head."

" 'Will no one rid me of this troublesome priest?' " the Irish priest quoted with a smile.

"Why, Thomas," said the cardinal. "You know your history after all."

16

After ten minutes in the outfall vent, Holliday and the others reached a side passage. From the smell of it the narrower, brick-lined tunnel led to the sewers. Holliday stopped, turned and listened. So far there were no sounds of pursuit, but he knew it wouldn't last. It was more than likely that the OMON squad would have at least one or two Spetsnaz special forces types on board, and those guys were relentless. They'd eventually spot the broken hasp on the vent in the boiler room and they'd come after them like baying hounds after a fox.

There was a rusted grille over the tunnel just like the one at the outfall opening, but Holliday used the monkey wrench and levered it off, tearing the old hasp off completely. It didn't matter; if the OMON squad got this far, trying to fake them out was a waste of time.

"This way," said Holliday.

"It smells of . . . excrement," said Genrikhovich,

balking and wrinkling his nose. Holliday was suddenly very tired of the Russian. He sighed.

"The outfall almost certainly empties into the river, and they'll be waiting for you. Personally I couldn't care less whether you come with us or not. It's up to you: knee-deep in shit or a bullet in the brain."

Eddie handed Holliday the battery-powered lamp and the two men climbed up into the sewer tunnel. For a few seconds there was silence from behind them, but alone in the dark, reality set in, and Genrikhovich came after them. The deeper they went into the tunnel, the worse the smell became until it was almost overwhelming.

"*¡Querido Dios!*" said Eddie, gagging. "*¡Mierda Ruso huele mucho peor que la Cubana, creo que!*"

Holliday didn't need a translation. "No kidding," he said with a grunt. They pressed on, the walls and arched cciling of the tunnel growing damp and mildewed as they continued deeper down the passageway. The bricks of the floor were crumbling with dampness, and every now and again there was a flash of dark shadow that skittered away, chittering sounds of irritation fleeing from the bright beam of light cast by the searching beam of the lamp.

"*Ratas,*" grumbled Eddie. "*Odio las ratas de mierda.*"

"We know," said Holliday. Ten minutes after entering the side tunnel they reached what appeared to be a main channel. There was a raised concrete step on either side of a broad, sluggishly flowing stream of brown muck, the thick stew of effluent scattered with floating islands of things more solid that defied description.

The concrete construction was old and crumbling, patched here and there with varying grades of cement. The raised sides of the trough were about three feet above the lavalike flow of the waste, which was flowing right to left. The sides were about two and a half feet wide, covered in sludge and treacherous-looking, the danger made worse by the fact that the walls curved upward, forcing anyone foolish enough to be here in the first place to walk in a half crouch.

Genrikhovich stared, horrified. *"Reka diaryei,"* he said.

"Reki Rossii diaryei," corrected Eddie. *A river of Russian diarrhea.*

Holliday grimaced at the revolting image and swallowed hard. "I'm lost," he said. "Which way do we go, left or right?"

Eddie spoke up immediately. "The flow of the *mierda* is from west to east, if that is any help. Perhaps *un poco más al nordeste* as well."

"You're sure?" Holliday asked.

"Yes." Eddie nodded firmly. "I have a thing . . . *una brújula*, in my head," explained the Cuban. Holliday frowned. Eddie turned to Genrikhovich. *"Kompas?"* he asked in Russian.

"A compass?" Holliday said.

"*Sí, compañero*, a compass. It never fails me."

"If this is true we should go east," Genrikhovich suggested. "West is the Neva. East is the center of the city. Perhaps we could find a way to the metro."

"All right." Holliday nodded. "Stay close and watch your step." He ducked down and headed upstream along the slime-covered bank of the swirling river of sludge.

Within minutes of entering the sewer tunnel all three men were filthy as they were forced to reach out and steady themselves against the walls, their clothing scraping the slime-covered bricks and their shoes caking with ancient excrement. As they continued down the passage, each at various times would slip and tumble into the stream of sewage. Finally, covered in filth, they gave up all attempts to keep themselves even partially free of the stinking, oozing effluent and walked along knee-deep in the stream, the footing more solid under them and with far more clearance for their heads. More than once Holliday had felt some strange sort of abnormal movement within the flow they pushed against, and he could have sworn something unthinkable had brushed against his sodden pants legs. Something swimming.

After what seemed to be an eternity they reached some sort of two-story hub with sewers on the upper levels sending putrid waterfalls of effluent slopping down into a large pool, the pool itself having several even larger outlets.

Holliday shook his head in amazement and disgust. Catwalks encrusted with filth and mold stretched over the pool—obviously people were actually meant to come to this horrible cathedral, complete with a cathedral organ of accreted matter that ran down the curved brick wall in pipelike stalactites.

On the far side of the pool, reached by one of the catwalks, they found a small concrete chamber that was probably used as a rest stop by sewer workers. Eddie found it excruciatingly funny that the room came with its own toilet cubicle, and for a time he couldn't stop laughing and muttering under his breath in Spanish. There was also a set of lockers in the room, which held complete sets of protective clothing, along with hard hats, oxygen tanks and masks.

"We change," said Holliday. "We can't go back to the real world covered in crap. At least these will make us look official."

"We are above the metro station at Pushkinskaya," said Genrikhovich.

"How do you know that?" Holliday asked.

Genrikhovich pointed to a metal sign half-obscured with old sludge:

Пушкинская M

"We're *above* the station?"

"St. Petersburg metro lines had to be dug very deep

to reach bedrock. The whole city is built on the Neva and the Fontanka estuaries."

"And if we go up?"

"It is the Vitebsky railway station."

"Where do trains go from there?"

"Mostly to Western Europe. Also to Kaliningrad and Smolensk, if I remember correctly."

Eddie shook his head. "They will have eyes at the train stations, even if they are only electronic."

"How far are we from the Hermitage?"

"A mile. Perhaps a little more than that."

Eddie frowned. "It is not far enough, *mis compadres*. They will have a security cordon at least that far out by now."

Genrikhovich spoke up. "My sister Marina and I have a dacha in Novoye Devyatkino. It is the last stop on the number one metro line."

"I very much doubt your sister would appreciate a couple of fugitives as houseguests," said Holliday.

"Marina is rarely there. She works at the United Nations in New York. I am there more than she is."

"We need to get as far as we can, *mi coronel*." Eddie shrugged. "I would like to have a wash of my body, too, I think."

"All right." Holliday nodded. "The end of the line it is."

17

Marina and Victor Genrikhovich's dacha, or summer place, in Novoye Devyatkino looked like Hansel and Gretel's gingerbread house in the middle of Chicago's infamous Cabrini-Green public housing development. Once upon a time, Novoye Devyatkino had been pleasant countryside with scattered farms and the summer homes of the wealthy, set on the banks of streams and rivers, or the shores of the several lakes dotting the area.

Large woodlots of ash and alder, birch and pine covered the landscape, interspersed with rolling hills and meadows bright with wildflowers. In the fifties, following Stalin's brutal purges, Leningrad had seen something of a ghastly architectural renaissance, and a new kind of forest had grown in Novoye Devyatkino, a forest of blank-faced concrete apartment buildings that looked more like gray high-rise gulags than places for families to live.

The quality of workmanship had been uniformly terrible, the landscaping and services nonexistent, and the day-to-day existence of people forced to live there simply to justify the terminus of the metro main line had been bleak. By the seventies the whole area was a semi-slum; by the fall of the Soviet Union it had become dangerous.

With the disappearance of Communism, Novoye Devyatkino went through yet another transformation. The old high-rises were knocked down—at least most of them—and new apartment buildings were erected, these with elevators that actually worked, enough square footage to be livable, and enough schools, shopping, restaurants and recreational services to make the revived suburb an attractive, modern alternative to St. Petersburg's enormous nineteenth-century apartment blocks, with their clanking plumbing, leaking faucets and drafty windows, not to mention their exorbitant rents.

Through it all a few of the original family cottages had remained. The Genrikhovich dacha was a two-bedroom two-story with a board-and-batten second floor with brick facing and fieldstone below. The little house had a steeply sloping roof covered in split cedar shingles and trimmed in rustic gingerbread. There was a makeshift carport tacked onto one side with an old UAZ Buhanka parked beneath it. The Buhanka, or "loaf" in Russian, was a knockoff of the old VW bus. This one was covered in patches of primer paint and looked almost as old as Genrikhovich.

The big living room had a large stone fireplace with a dining room and country kitchen in the rear. There was a floor-to-ceiling brick-and-board bookcase in the living room crammed with what turned out to be English-language crime novels going back to the nineteenth century.

Marina had squeezed in a powder room where there had once been a pantry, and large windows in the dining room had been replaced with French doors leading out to a small deck. There were two bedrooms and a full bathroom separating them on the second floor.

The furniture was old and mostly Victorian, with braided rag rugs and a few willow-twig armchairs that looked extremely uncomfortable and had probably come with the house.

"It was part of my great-grandmother's dowry when she married my great-grandfather," said Genrikhovich. "She was the daughter of an admiral and he was a professor at the old Naval Guards Academy. He taught celestial navigation and mathematics. They kept him on after the revolution because, as he put it, 'Even Stalin could not alter the course of the stars.' He was good at his job, so they let him keep the dacha; it has remained in our family ever since."

It had taken them almost an hour to descend through a series of tunnels and manholes to the Push-kinskaya metro station. They'd come up on the track bed in their rubberized protective suits, suddenly finding themselves in the ornate, arched, pale marble station. Genrikhovich led them onto a Number One line train, and by the time they reached the end of the line at Novoye Devyatkino they had the entire car to themselves, the stench emanating from the suits having driven everyone else away.

Marina Genrikhovich's dacha was on a narrow lane well away from the nearest apartment block and was completely private. While Genrikhovich ran himself a bath, Holliday and Eddie took a bar of soap down to the fast-running creek at the end of the property, stripped off the suits and took the plunge. The water was freezing but neither man cared. They were more than willing to endure the cold just to get the smell of the sewers off.

"Your sister must be a large woman, *amigo*," said Eddie, slipping into a red dragon-motif silk bathrobe that came only to his knees. Genrikhovich had built a blazing fire, and Eddie sat on a velvet footstool, warming up.

"Yes. Even as children I was the one who ate no fat and Marina at no lean. She has a freezer in the kitchen with enough food to last through the next ice age."

"Good," said Eddie. "I could, how you say it, eat a horse."

"I think she has some *sudzhuk* sausage, if you'd like some."

"What is this *sudzhuk*?" Eddie asked

"Horse meat. It is a delicacy in the Ukraine." Genrikhovich shrugged. "You said you could eat one."

"Jesucristo, los rusos están locos," said the Cuban in his dragon robe. *"No, muchas gracias, mi amigo. Tal vez la próxima vez.* Maybe next time."

Holliday had fared a little better in the clothing department and had managed to squeeze himself into a spare pair of Genrikhovich's trousers and an old sweater that fit him like a sausage skin.

"The first order of business is getting some clothes. Eddie doesn't have anything fit to wear, and I wouldn't want to go too far dressed like this."

"No problem," said Genrikhovich. "I will drive Uncle Joe to the *univermag* and get what you need, and then I will make us something to eat. You have money?"

"Sure, I've got money," said Holliday. "But what's a *univermag* and who is Uncle Joe?"

"A *univermag* is a . . ." Genrikhovich turned to Eddie.

"A *univermag* is a . . . *¿cómo usted lo dice, almacenes grandes?*" The Cuban snapped his fingers. "A *departamento* store, a mall."

"And Uncle Joe?"

"Dyadya Dzho, Kreml' Highlander," Genrikhovich tried to explain.

"Stalin," Eddie translated dryly.

"The minibus outside—it is the name Marina and I gave to it."

"That thing actually runs?" Holliday asked, astounded.

"Certainly," said Genrikhovich. "It is a classic."

True to his word, the Russian drove off in the rumbling, popping Uncle Joe and reappeared after what seemed to be a very long time, beaming and carrying a number of shopping bags. He'd purchased three complete sets of clothing, including a blue-and-white satin Dynamo Moscow bomber jacket for Eddie and a military-style *ushanka* fur hat with an old hammer-and-sickle emblem on the front for Holliday.

As dusk fell and the evening air cooled, Holliday and Eddie dressed themselves in their new outfits and sat down to a remarkably tasty meal prepared by Genrikhovich—broiled steak with onions, mushrooms and fresh tomato slices from the little vegetable garden beside the cottage. With dinner finished and coffee in hand, they gathered around the fire in the living room once more. Genrikhovich had even managed to get Eddie a box of Partagás Habaneros cigars at the *univermag*, one of which the Cuban was happily enjoying.

"Much better," said Holliday. "You have skills as a cook, Dr. Genrikhovich."

"Please," said the Russian, "you must call me Victor."

"All right, Victor," said Holliday. "The meal was great, but we still have a real problem."

"Which is?"

"If the FSB knows who you are they'll eventually find this place. We can't stay long, and the phony IDs we picked up in Odessa are useless now."

"The dacha is still under my great-grandmother's family name—Kornilov—but you are right; they will find it eventually. As to the matter of our papers, I have been giving this a great deal of thought and I believe I have discovered an answer."

"Do tell," said Holliday.

"It is in these books." Genrikhovich smiled, waving a hand toward the rickety brick-and-board bookcase.

"Which books?" Holliday asked.

"A number of them," answered Genrikhovich. "From Baroness Orczy's *The Scarlet Pimpernel* and Mark Twain's *The Prince and the Pauper* to Wilkie Collins's *Armadale* and even Ian Fleming's *Moonraker*."

"I'm not seeing it," said Holliday, shaking his head and wondering what the old man was so excited about.

"*The Talented Mr. Ripley? The False Inspector Dew?*"

"Nope," said Holliday. Eddie puffed on his cigar, the titles going right over his head.

"*The Day of the Jackal?*" Genrikhovich said, exasperated.

Finally Holliday got it. Each of the books the Russian had mentioned involved someone taking on somebody else's name.

"Identity theft," he said.

"Yes." Genrikhovich nodded. "In particular, a technique called 'ghosting,' taking the identities of the newly dead."

The Russian reached into the inside pocket of his frayed suit jacket and brought out a slip of paper. He handed it to Holliday. It appeared to be a list of addresses.

"What's this?" asked Holliday.

"When I went to the *univermag* I was thinking about this problem, so I stopped at FloraQueen, a florist store, yes? They send flowers."

"We've got the same thing in the States." Holliday smiled.

"Yes, well, it seems that tomorrow there are to be six funerals of people from Novoye Devyatkino, three Orthodox, two nondenominational and one Jewish. The Jewish cemetery is in Obukhovo in the far southern part of the city. The Orthodox cemeteries are at the Alexander Nevsky Monastery in Ligovka-Yamskaya in the east, and the two nondenominational funerals are being held at the Novodevichy Cemetery near the Moscow Triumphal Gate.

"All of the cemeteries are at least an hour away by metro from Novoye Devyatkino. Three of the interments are scheduled to take place at eleven in the morning, two will take place at one in the afternoon, and one will take place at two. During those periods the apartments of the deceased will presumably be vacant." The Russian grinned ghoulishly. "I have known very few corpses who took their passports, identification and wallets with them to the grave." There was a long silence.

"¡Es brillante!" Eddie whispered finally, eyes wide.

Genrikhovich beamed. He looked at Holliday. "What do you think?"

"Victor," said Holliday, "I think we may have seriously underestimated your potential. You have a truly criminal mind."

18

The apartment occupied by the late Ostap Obelovich Cheburashka and his wife, Tatanya, was located in one of the older high-rises in Novoye Devyatkino. The simple lock had been easily slipped with a credit card. The apartment was a three-room affair with a living room/ dining room, a kitchen and a bedroom. Presumably there were toilet and bathing facilities elsewhere on the floor. A mezuzah was stuck to the doorframe, and a menorah sat on an old, scarred sideboard, the nine candles no more than inch-long stubs. Ostap Obelovich had died just in time. Beside the menorah were pale, overexposed photographs of a young man and his wife, the man the picture-perfect proletarian worker, the young woman virginal and expectant. Khrushchev's Russia and the new Five-year Plan, a plan that had gone on forever and finally come to nothing. The apartment smelled of borscht and cigarettes and lemon vodka and failed dreams. Somewhere along the way Ostap Obelovich had lost the young wife, because there was no sign of her in the apartment. The bed was single, the clothes were all his and there was dust everywhere.

In the bedroom someone had laid out a lace doily on Ostap Obelovich's dresser, atop which lay a ring, a watch, a worn plastic wallet and a bar of medals. The watch was an old Pobeda "Victory" from before World War II, probably given to Ostap by his father, Holliday guessed. Among the medals, he recognized the Afghan medal of valor. There was also a photograph in another silver frame, this one showing an older, bearded Ostap, half in and half out of the turret of an Ob'yekt 166K T-62K main battle tank. Holliday recognized the terrain—Afghanistan, not too far from Kabul. 'Seventy-nine to 'eighty-nine, a decade of loss, frustration and in the end humiliation and the first real sign that the Russian bear was a little sickly and not the threat that it once had been. If the CIA had been keeping a more careful watch, they would have seen the first critical chink in the armor that led to the collapse of Karl Marx's perfect state a few years later.

The final truth of the man named Ostap Obelovich Cheburashka stood half-hidden in the shadows beside the dresser. A thing of worn leather straps and rivets and pink-enameled aluminum that had served as Ostap Obelovich's right leg, almost certainly taken in Afghanistan, where Holliday had lost his eye. Different war, different time, same place, which was how it always was, going back to the days of Alexander. People killing and dying for the same pieces of land for millennia. A leg lost for what? Some posturing general in the Kremlin? It was all a waste, no matter which side you were on.

"Bad thoughts?" Eddie asked quietly.

"Sad ones," said Holliday. And then he did what a good soldier always did—put the thoughts away and got down to business. Twenty minutes later, with the dead man's passport, transit papers, veteran's identification and wallet, they left the apartment and headed to the next address on their list. Holliday had left the watch, the ring and the medals behind. By midafternoon they had three new identities and headed back to the dacha in Novoye Devyatkino.

They spread their haul out on the plain maple table in the kitchen. They'd had enough time to get into all six of the apartments on the list with little or no difficulty, but they'd abandoned two, one because of the advanced age of the deceased—there was no way any of the three men would pass as Pyotr Fomitch Kalganov, a ninety-three-year-old retired schoolteacher, or İsmail Gasprinsky, a Crimean Tatar with a bit of Cossack thrown in.

"Okay," said Holliday, "I'm Dimitri Valentin, Victor is Ostap Cheburashka and Eddie is Vladislav Nikolayevich Listyev, and his story is that he is the bastard child of a professor and his young African student at Patrice

Lumumba University. He's lived his whole life in Russia, which is why he speaks the language so well." Holliday picked up one of the transit passes allowing the bearer to travel outside his own city. "And just thank God these are probably the only documents we'll need to show, because trying to doctor the passports just won't work, and from the looks of it the late Dimitri Valentin spent his whole life working at the Leningrad Steelworks before he got laid off in 1990. If we get seriously looked at by anyone, my advice is to run like hell, because these things won't stand up to any kind of scrutiny."

"Ahora bien," said Eddie. *"¿Qué hacemos?"*

"What now?" Holliday said. Eddie nodded. Holliday turned to Genrikhovich. "Good question," he said. "What now?"

There was a long silence. Genrikhovich pursed his lips and pushed his spectacles higher up his long, thin nose. He nodded finally and began to speak.

"I have thought on this," said the Russian. "And again we are linked to history. The Kremlin Egg, the one that actually sits in its display cabinet in the Kremlin Armoury with all the other great treasures of the Romanovs, is a fake—brilliantly made, certainly, but a fake nevertheless. We know this fake was made sometime between 1904 and 1934 for some purpose—most likely to keep whatever secret it holds safe and away from people like Stalin or more likely Lavrenti Beria, who we discovered was involved at least as far back as 1944, when he received the third sword."

"Polaris, Sword of the North," said Holliday.

"Precisely," said Genrikhovich. "He may well have deciphered whatever the message was on the sword, or perhaps not. If the message led him to the Kremlin Egg, as I think it did, then he would have been frustrated by the copy."

"That doesn't do much for us," said Holliday. "The egg could have been switched at any time—the mark on the base indicates when it was made; it gives us no clue as to when the egg was exchanged."

"Not anytime, Colonel Holliday—it could only have been exchanged on one occasion."

"When?"

"Stalin had used the Romanov eggs and other czarist treasures as a way of getting foreign currency. He even ordered five hundred paintings and sculptures in the Hermitage to be auctioned. This is how your Armand Hammer, the baking soda tycoon, came into possession of so many of the eggs."

"Is there a point to this?" Holliday asked, a little irritated. Genrikhovich had an annoying habit of going the long way to get where he was going.

"Context, Colonel Holliday. As you know perfectly well, history is context."

"Jesucristo." Eddie groaned softly.

"Go on," Holliday said.

"On the twenty-second of June 1941, the Third Reich declared war on the Soviet Union. The following day preparations for the evacuation of the Hermitage began. By the first of July, less than two weeks later, two heavily armed and guarded trains took over one-point-five million objects from the Hermitage to safety. By the twentieth of July almost everything had been removed. Stalin, ever the pragmatist, decided that the Kremlin treasures should be crated up and removed as well, the Kremlin Egg among them. They remained hidden away until October of 1945, when the treasures were returned to the Hermitage and to the Kremlin Armoury. That is the time I think the real Uspenski Cathedral Egg was switched with the forgery—while they were in hiding."

"Where were they hidden?" Holliday asked.

"The town of Sverdlovsk, which is ironic, really."

"How so?"

"You may know of Sverdlovsk under its original name," said the Russian. "And the name it is known by today—Yekaterinburg."

"Where the Romanovs were murdered," said Holliday. He'd read a spy novel about it once. The book had an odd title. Then he remembered. *The House of Special Purpose.* He nodded.

"Quite so," said Genrikhovich. "Comrade Lenin's euphemism for the Ipatiev House. The czar and his entire family were shot in the basement there in the early-morning hours of July 17, 1918. Which is doubly ironic."

"Why?" Holliday asked.

"There were three places in Sverdlovsk where the Hermitage and Kremlin treasures were stored—an art gallery, a Catholic church and the Ipatiev House, which by then had been made into an antireligion museum."

"The Kremlin Egg had been stored there?"

"I checked the inventory ledgers—the crate with the egg was listed as being warehoused there for the duration."

"What are the odds of there being anyone there who'd know anything?"

"Quite good, actually." The Russian smiled. "The House of Special Purpose was demolished in 1977 by order of Boris Yeltsin, but in late 1999 an Orthodox church was built on the site, the Church on Blood in Honour of All Saints Resplendent in the Russian Land. There is a museum to the Romanovs there—its director is the son of the staff member from the Hermitage who was in charge of the Ipatiev House inventory during the war."

"So we go to Yekaterinburg?"

"That would be my suggestion." Genrikhovich nodded.

"How do we get there? The FSB will be watching the train stations and the airport."

"We drive to Tosno; it is about fifty kilometers from

here. They will not be watching the train station there. It is the first stop on the St. Petersburg–Moscow line."

"I thought the highway police had roadblocks every few miles."

"That was in the old days. They're lucky to have the manpower for a roadblock every hundred kilometers now, if that. And I know how to deal with the highway police. By necessity they are little more than uniformed thieves. A handful of rubles will be our passports as long as we keep your Cuban friend hidden in the back of the van. He is too much of a curiosity, I am afraid."

"When can we leave?"

"Early tomorrow morning. The Red Arrow leaves St. Petersburg every day at one in the afternoon. It stops in Tosno twenty-five minutes later. We must be there to meet it."

"Red Arrow?" Eddie asked.

"A very famous train," said Genrikhovich, smiling. "Its nickname is *Letayushchii Bordel*."

The Cuban laughed. "The Flying Brothel?"

19

Brinsley Whitman Havers, at thirty-eight, was the youngest assistant to the assistant national security adviser in the history of the White House. It was an accomplishment of which he was immensely proud, especially since he had been born Paramahansa Kumar Aggarwal in May Pen, Clarendon Parish, Jamaica, bastard stepson to Rambhan Kundgolkar Aggarwal, a wholesale dealer of Trout Hall oranges.

His mother, Aishwarya Vrinda Aggarwal, had been only seventeen when she married the much older Rambhan Kundgolkar, who, in the final analysis, was unable to consummate the marriage, let alone impregnate his young bride. It was hardly surprising then that Aishwarya Vrinda separated from her family in Mangalore by ten thousand miles and, consequently lonely, would look elsewhere for love. Even less surprising that she would find it in the figure of a well-known "randy man" about town named Nedrick Samuels, whose friendship was mistrusted by most husbands and resisted by few wives.

Paramahansa Kumar was the result of the illicit liaison, a responsibility unacknowledged by young Nedrick, who discreetly removed himself to St. Ann Parish as soon as Aishwarya Vrinda began to show evidence of her infidelity. In the old days back in Mangalore, Aishwarya Vrinda would almost certainly been whipped, either by her husband or by her own father, but considering his own inabilities, Rambhan Kundgolkar decided to accept the child as his own, despite the fact that the boy was several shades darker than anyone in the Aggarwal family had ever been.

On the death of her husband when Aishwarya Vrinda was twenty-eight, she liquidated all of the older Aggarwal's assets and moved to East 28th Street in New York City, where she opened an Indian grocery called Aggarwal's. Five years later both she and her son were bona fide American citizens. Their red-and-gold Jamaican passports were ceremoniously burned in the trash barrel behind that first store. Soon, Aggarwal's resided all over the state.

At the age of eighteen, before enrolling in Harvard Law School and with his mother's permission, Paramahansa Kumar Aggarwal legally changed his name to Brinsley Whitman Havers and left his past, and what was left of his Jamaican accent, behind. He casually let his fellow students know that he was actually Brinsley Whitman Havers III, cultivated the nickname "Whit" and never looked back.

And here he was, summa cum laude from Harvard, a thirty-eight-year-old boy wonder in the White House coming down from the second floor of the West Wing for a meeting with his boss and the national security adviser himself.

Whit Havers reached the bottom of the stairs, turned to his left and knocked on the door of the national security adviser's office.

"Enter," came the gravelly voice of General George Armstrong Temple, the NSA himself. Whit did as he was told and stepped into the office. There were tall windows on two sides, to the north looking down the main drive from the Pennsylvania Avenue entrance, and to the west overlooking West Executive Avenue, now closed to public traffic. Like most of the windows in the White House, the panes in the national security adviser's office were bulletproof.

The general had no desk. Instead, he worked at a long conference table set with twelve armchairs. The general was in his shirtsleeves, which were rolled up to his elbows. His trousers were held up with braided leather suspenders. Bright red half-lens reading glasses sat on the end of his blown-out drinker's nose.

He was at least a hundred pounds overweight, smoked cigars constantly and wheezed when he talked. There was a pool on the second floor based on how many months into the term he'd last before keeling over. Whit hadn't entered the pool; the general was like Dick Cheney—his heart was made of concrete and his liver was made of cheese, but he'd probably outlive all of them. People as mean and hard as that never died; death was too scared to come within a mile of them.

The only other person in the room was J. Hunter Kokum, Whit's boss, the assistant NSA. Kokum was in his sixties, pale as a ghost and thin as a scarecrow. In his spare time he raised Thoroughbreds in Kentucky. His last job had been as assistant director of plans at the CIA. Before that he was deputy director of the FBI.

Always a deputy, or an assistant, never the thing itself, which was just the way J. Hunter Kokum liked it. He was an éminence grise and the power behind the throne. He'd discovered that in political life it was safer that way. His family were oil billionaires.

"Sit," said General Temple.

Whit sat at the chair closest to him, which happened to be the farthest away from the general.

"Tell the general about Pierre Ducos," instructed Kokum.

"Well," began Whit. He didn't make it any further than that.

"Wait a second." The general grunted. He lit a fresh cigar. "No iPad, no Zoom, no Android, no BlackBerry? Not even a goddamn file folder?"

"Whit likes to keep things in his head," murmured

Kokum, his voice mild, a faint smile on his thin lips. "He feels it's safer that way."

"Is that right?" Temple said, impressed. Kokum liked to show Whit off like a pet monkey, which the young man hated, but went along with because he knew that one of these days he'd have Kokum's job. Not this president, maybe, or the next, but eventually.

"Ducos," repeated Kokum.

"Pierre Armand Ducos, French. Parents Marie Yvette Ducos, deceased, and André Ducos de Saint Clair, one of the hereditary dukes of Burgundy, also deceased, making Pierre Ducos, their only child, heir to the dukedom and the title."

"A duke." The general wheezed, puffing on his cigar. "Goddamn royalty, what do you know?"

"Ducos is an *avocat*, supposedly a simple lawyer living in the village of Domme in the Aquitaine region of France. The village has less than a thousand inhabitants. Seven hundred years ago the town was a Templar stronghold. There was even a rumor that the Holy Grail had once been hidden there."

"You said 'supposedly a simple lawyer'? What does that mean?"

"Ducos handles the estates of three men, trustees of a company called Pelerin and Cie. Pelerin is a front, a shell company controlled entirely by Ducos. It has majority holdings in three Swiss banks, two banks in the Caymans, major holdings in Bank of America, JPMorgan Chase & Co., MetLife and smaller holdings in several others. It has large holdings in the Standard Oil Investment Group, Halliburton, Exxon Mobil, LUK-OIL. . . ."

"The big Russian oil combine?" General Temple said, staring.

"Yes."

"Go on, son."

I'm not your son, Whit thought. I'm not anybody's son except my mother's. He smiled. "The list is almost endless, sir. Pelerin has effective assets of more than a trillion dollars in virtually every country in the world, including China."

"All controlled by some lawyer in west bum-bugger France? It makes no sense."

"No, sir, it does not."

"There is an explanation?"

"There are rumors, sir."

"What rumors?"

"Rumors of an organization for which Ducos is as much a front as Pelerin and Cie."

"The Rosicrucians, the Masons, Opus Dei, the Illuminati, the Dan Brown Fan Club, the goddamn Shriners?"

"No, sir."

"The Bilderberg Group, the New World Order, the Republican National Committee? Spit it out, man; I don't have all goddamned day."

"Yes, sir. I am aware of that, sir. The problem is, General, for a secret society to be secret, nobody outside the society can know about it."

"You said there were rumors. What rumors?"

"There seems to be a connection with the Cambridge Five—Philby, Blunt, Burgess, Maclean, Cairncross and Leo Long."

"That's six," said Temple.

"Yes, sir, there're some who say there were even more. At any rate, they were in a club called the Apostles, and in the end, of course, they were all working for the KGB. It's also interesting to note that Colonel John Holliday's uncle, Mr. Henry Granger, knew Philby, Blunt and Burgess through his dealings with MI6 during the Second World War."

"I'm starting to get a bit of a brain freeze, lad. Remind me again who this Colonel Holliday is and his connection to Ducos."

Whit sighed. He'd written a dozen position papers and briefs about this for Kokum, but it seemed that the general hadn't read any of them. "On some level Ducos is no more than a trustee for Pelerin and Cie. Holliday is the one who has all the accounts, codes, passwords and what have you to actually access the funds involved."

"And how did this colonel come by all these codes and passwords?"

"He was given a notebook with all the information in it."

"Who gave it to him?"

"A monk in the Azores named Helder Rodrigues."

"Why?"

"We have no real idea, and Rodrigues is dead. Murdered by a German white supremacist named Kellerman whose father was a Nazi."

"A secret society so secret no one knows about it, a monk in the Azores with a trillion-dollar notebook, Nazis and a Frenchman. Pull the other one, boy."

Whit bristled slightly at the use of the term "boy," but he let it pass. Temple was old-school, and he was also his boss's boss. "There is documentation for all of it, sir. I can bring it to you if you'd like."

"Jesus, no," said the general. It was Temple's turn to sigh. "Look—Mr. Kokum tells me that all our best intelligence says Putin and some of his pals are in a snit. We want to know why. No fifty-page essays, just put it in a nutshell and toss it down the table if you would. Pretend it's a rebuttal at the Debate Society finals, Harvard Lion Kings against Tufts Half Vote. You've got thirty seconds. Go."

Whit was stunned. The rebuttal at the Lion Kings–Half Vote debate had been his moment of absolute triumph. How did Temple know about that? There was more to the general than met the eye. Which was why he was the national security adviser, of course.

"Ten seconds gone, Mr. Havers."

Whit closed his eyes. He could do this. "Somehow Ranger Lieutenant Colonel John Holliday, formerly of the West Point Military Academy, has stumbled onto a secret the Russians have kept quiet since before the Russian Revolution. Putin is about to make a move to consolidate his power and turn Russia into a superpower again. Holliday could ruin everything for him."

Temple turned to Kokum. "Do we want that?"

"Definitely not, General. In five years or less Russia will be the largest source of foreign oil available to us. The Middle East and North Africa have gone to hell ever since people started getting smart and realized their leaders had rocks in their heads. We need Putin. We need to keep him happy."

"Do we have anyone in the area?" Temple asked blandly. He rolled his cigar around in the ashtray in front of him.

"Do we?" Kokum asked, turning to Whit.

"Yes, sir."

"Who?"

"A man named John Bone."

"Any connection to us?"

"No, sir, he's a freelancer."

"American?"

"Irish by birth. He lives in London. Right now he's in Amsterdam on another assignment for us. That new WikiLeaks thing you wanted handled."

"A bit of preventive medicine, as I recall," Kokum said.

"Yes, sir." Whit nodded.

"What's his record?" Temple asked.

"Thirty-two professional fights, thirty-one wins, all KOs, one draw."

"What was the draw all about?"

"The subject was hit by a car an hour and a half before the fight."

"All right," said the general, sticking the cigar back into the corner of his mouth. "Blue message to this fellow." He nodded down the table toward Whit. "Your man here pulls the strings. Let's see if he's as good as he thinks he is."

Kokum smiled thinly. "I don't think Mr. Havers has the sort of experience required for this kind—"

"He's the case officer, Kokum. Over and out."

Jeezampeas! Whit thought to himself, reverting to his mother tongue. He loved the arcane beauty of West Wing language. A "blue message" didn't mean anything at all—it could have been red, white or pink. "Message" was the operative word. "Message" with a color as a prefix was a euphemism as clear as the old-fashioned "terminate with extreme prejudice." It was a kill order. Lieutenant Colonel John Holliday was as good as dead.

20

The public's ideal of a professional assassin runs to one part Sean Connery in a toupee, two parts Daniel Craig and perhaps a dash of Matt Damon—handsome, muscular, unemotional, a magnet for women and a lover of all the finer things in life. Most important, one way or another, no matter which side he is on, the professional assassin is a patriot.

John Bone was none of these things. He was fifty-six years old, tended to a middle-aged man's potbelly, had thinning carroty hair, wore spectacles and liked nothing better than a nice cup of tea and a plate of eggs, chips and beans for brekkie. He loved cats, cried over certain rock-and-roll songs from the sixties, and ran a small, marginally profitable business designing and printing menus for restaurants, which he ran out of a tiny office above a sex shop on Dean Street in London's Soho district. Academically, he had excelled only in languages, for which he had a great facility, and now spoke six quite fluently.

He had been married for seventeen years to a simple, pleasant woman named Alice, had twin teenage girls, Hailey and Hannah, 3.2 million euros in a bank of the island of Guernsey and another 5.8 million euros in a bank in Liechtenstein.

He regularly took his family to Torremolinos on the Costa del Sol, where he liked to sail Flying Junior–class dinghies. He generally sailed alone, since Alice was afraid of water and the girls had never really been interested. His favorite color was Lincoln green, his favorite song was "She's Not There" by the Zombies, his favorite actor was George Clooney and his weapon of choice for close work was a pearl-handled straight razor he kept in his shaving kit when he traveled. Distance work—sniping, rockets and the like—he left to other experts. His wife, Alice, never asked about his frequent overseas trips, and Bone never offered any explanation.

John Bone had no military service or training that anyone knew of, and no one knew very much about his background. He first came to the attention of intelligence in 1980 following the assassination of Walter Rodney, a Marxist candidate in the Guyana elections of that same year. Rodney was blown up in his car with a homemade bomb that he was about to plant at a local police station. According to witnesses Rodney was given the bomb by a sergeant in the Guyana Defence Force named Gregory Smith. The Guyana Defence Force later insisted that they had never had a man named Gregory Smith in the GDF at any rank.

The Central Intelligence Agency, which had Walter Rodney under surveillance at the time, could well believe it; there were very few Guyanese citizens with flaming red hair, pale, sunburned skin and freckles who spoke with a pronounced Dublin lilt in their voice. John Bone was twenty-four years old at the time. It was later discovered that Bone had been in the employ of the incumbent president, Forbes Burnham, and the military leaders of the People's National Congress. It was unclear whether this was Bone's first assignment, but the CIA and a number of other agencies followed his career with great interest, using him on a number of occasions.

On this particular October evening he was in Amsterdam standing at the Chipsy King on the Damstraat enjoying a large paper cone of garlic fries smothered in mayonnaise. Years ago, when he'd first come here, the thought of chips with mayo was quite revolting, but now he'd rather acquired a taste for it—at least while he was in Amsterdam. Putting mayo on his chips back home would give Alice a heart attack. He smiled, thinking of Alice. Everything a man could want, she was— kept a good house, handled the money, kept his books at the office and raised the twins, who'd been a handful from day one. On top of that she was still a cracker in bed, even after seventeen years. A treasure.

He ate a few more chips, picking up the saltshaker on

the outside counter and giving the cone another shake. Stupid, really, considering his age and his blood pressure. Eating more chips, he kept his eyes on the entrance to the Doria hotel across the narrow street. Like a lot of Amsterdam hotels, the lobby was on the first floor, not the ground, the entrance squeezed in between a pizzeria and a Mexican grill named Gaucho's.

He'd been given the assignment by his usual contact in the Netherlands—Guido Derlagen, a shaved-headed "security consultant" with hands like hammers and a face like an ax. Bone liked him, but he didn't trust him. When you got right down to it, Bone didn't trust anyone when it came to business, but so far the Dutchman's word had been good. Bone wasn't entirely sure where Guido had sprung from, but he was willing to give odds on its being the AIVD—the General Intelligence and Security Service, like marbles in your mouth if you tried to pronounce it in Dutch.

This time he was fairly sure he wasn't working for the Netherlands, though. The target was a top executive in the WikiSpout organization, one of six who knew where the main servers were located and how to access them. She was the pro tem leader, named Caroline Halle Muller, a Dane. According to Derlagen she lived on the fourth floor of the Doria hotel, directly across from him.

She finally appeared, looking just like the photograph Derlagen had shown him: a few years on the wrong side of thirty, hair pulled harshly back off her unsmiling face and done in cornrows that were far too young for her, a skirt too short for heavy thighs. She wore Birkenstocks, of course, and held a giant old-fashioned briefcase clutched in her hand. Oversize glasses on a chain bounced on a pendulous chest covered by a blouse, a tweedy cardigan. No romance in this woman's life and never likely to be any. She had a Cause with a capital *C*, and that was better than acting like rabbits any day of the week.

She turned in under the small red awning over the narrow doorway and headed for the fourth floor. Bone continued to plow through the cone of chips until he reached the last little crispy bits in the bottom. He crumpled the cone and looked around for a trash bin. There wasn't one, so he put the greasy bit of paper into his Windbreaker pocket. It was past due for the laundry anyway, and he didn't like to litter, especially when his DNA was involved. Funny thing, that: he came out of a time when fingerprints were the only real worry, and since his weren't on any official record, that was that; but now they could track you down from a bit of belly button lint or a fleck of dandruff. It was sad, really. Science and accountancy seemed to have taken over the world—it was all bits and bytes and double helixes. He sighed and headed across the street, hanging back to let a flock of bicyclists go by.

He went up the stairs. There was a cramped little registration desk on the first floor, but there was no one on duty, which was a blessing. He continued all the way up to the fourth floor, stopping at the top to catch his breath. He could feel his heart pounding away in his chest, and he calmed himself by thinking about the fact that'd he never been a smoker, so that was one thing in his favor, at least. He reached into the right-hand pocket of his Windbreaker and took out a single latex glove. He slipped the glove onto his right hand, then reached back into the pocket for his razor, which he opened and locked.

Breathing back to normal, he walked down the narrow, dimly lit corridor to the door of her room: 422. He knocked quietly. There was no response, so he knocked again.

"Who is it?" Her voice was muffled but he could hear the irritation in it.

He put on his best Dublin drawl. "John Drennan, Ms. Muller. The *Irish Independent?*" Bone was using the name of one of the paper's political writers. "Your office said I could find you here."

The door opened and there she was. "They shouldn't have done . . ."

He moved the blade in his right hand in a firm, continuous motion that slid easily through skin, flesh, arteries, veins, layers of cartilage, ligaments, muscles and mucous membranes that made up the trachea, all the way through to the muscles and glands at the back of the neck, finally scraping the C4 vertebra of the spine. The Muller woman's instinct was to bring her hand up to the wound, but she only succeeded in pushing her fingers into the bloody ruin of her neck, tipping her almost severed head back at an absurd angle so that her last conscious vision was probably the nubby plaster of her hotel room ceiling. Bone pushed her back into the room with his gloved hand. She sank to the floor and toppled backward. He stepped into the room, careful to avoid the spreading lake of blood around the dead woman's head. The room was small and utilitarian. A bed, a stand-alone wardrobe, an upholstered chair, a wooden chair and a plain desk under the window. The briefcase was on the desk. Bone opened it and saw that the Dell laptop was still inside. He closed the briefcase, picked it up and walked out of the room. Three minutes later he was back on the Damstraat; fifteen minutes later he was back at his own hotel. He phoned Derlagen.

"It's done; I have it."

"Good," said the Dutchman. "I'll meet you in the usual place." The usual place was the waiting room of the Centraal Station. "I have another job if you want it."

"I was hoping to get home for the weekend. The girls have a choir concert on Sunday."

"Up to you. Priority fee if you want it."

"Where?"

"How's your Russian?"

"Ochen' horosho," answered Bone in a Moscow accent. Pretty good. "Any competition?"

"The locals. The Catholics and those mad Czechs they use from time to time."

"The Peseks? That crazy bitch and her knitting needle?"

"The same."

"Bloody hell," muttered Bone. He thought for a moment. "Triple fee and I'll do it."

"I'll see what I can arrange," answered the Dutchman.

Pierre Ducos, advocate in the little hilltop town of Domme, sat at his table in his favorite restaurant, the Cabanoix et Châtaignes on Rue Geoffroy de Vivans, and enjoyed the hearty lamb stew that was the restaurant's specialty, and for good reason. He would follow it with a sorbet and a coffee and then return to the office. Madame Beauregard the widow would be seeing him that afternoon on a matter that she deemed to be of extreme urgency, but probably had something to do with her fears that her grandson, a student in Paris, was actually a homosexual, and was there anything within the law that Advocat Ducos could do to stop it?

He finished the last of the stew and sat back in his chair, waiting for Jeanette, the only server in the old, low-ceilinged place. She was also the owner's daughter and was having an affair with the young chef. Ducos knew this because Jeanette, the young chef and the owner were all his clients. He smiled; sometimes it was difficult to remain objective in a small town like this.

Jeanette appeared. "I'll bring out your sorbet in a moment, *m'sieu l'avocat*."

"No hurry," answered Ducos. "I think I'll step outside for a cigarette. I must make a call anyway."

"À votre service, m'sieu l'avocat."

Ducos smiled, stood up and made his way across the dimly lit and crowded room. Cabanoix et Châtaignes was everything he liked about Domme—it was strong, with its dark oak rafters, thick plaster walls and slate floors as old as time. It was always crowded with people he knew, and more than anything else it was predictably excellent. The menu changed with the seasons and the whims of the chef, but whatever he chose from the menu he knew without doubt that it would be marvelous. If there was one thing Pierre Louis René Marie Joseph Ducos appreciated—nay, demanded—it was consistency. There was nothing he liked less than a thing out of place, time out of joint or an event unforeseen, and that was what he was faced with now.

He lit a cigarette and took out his cell phone. He tapped out a long series of numbers and waited. It answered after a number of rings.

"Sir James? *C'est Ducos.* . . . Quite well, thank you. We have a situation that must be resolved. It has to do with number five. . . . Yes, Sir James, the Rose . . . Yes, Holliday . . . Russia, I'm afraid . . . I assume they are aware of this. . . . All right. I'll inform Barsukov tomorrow. His people will deal with it, I assure you. . . . Of course I'm aware Barsukov is in prison. What does that have to do with anything? The prisons in Russia are *run* by the Mafia, Sir James. . . . Of course. Every step of the way, Sir James. There is far too much at stake to let it go on any longer. . . . And a good afternoon to you, Sir James."

Ducos closed the phone, pocketed it and stood there for a few moments enjoying the last of his cigarette, thinking about the Greek tragedian Aeschylus and his favorite quotation from the man: "God is not averse to deceit in a holy cause." Smiling, Pierre Ducos stubbed out the remains of his cigarette on the cobbles and went back into the restaurant for his well-deserved sorbet and coffee.

21

The Red Arrow Express turned out to be the train once used by the local St. Petersburg party bigwigs and other members of the local apparat, complete with private and semiprivate compartments, ornate dining car, red velvet upholstery, fringes on the window blinds and the showers, all on a train that took only eight hours to reach its destination. Following Genrikhovich's instructions they drove the rattletrap old Volga to Tosno and boarded the train without incident. They had purchased a four-bunk compartment even though there were only three of them. They wolfed down the contents of the little food boxes that were waiting for them on each of the bunks and then went to bed. Holliday stayed awake in the darkness, looking out into the night at the dark pastoral scene of birch trees and small farms as they sped past, and then he, too, fell asleep. He woke with the others just before the train pulled into Leningradsky station, exactly on time.

They left the train with the other passengers and made their way into the terminal building, a tall, rectangular hall lined with small shops and restaurants. If there had ever been benches for waiting or lockers for luggage they were long gone.

"We can't stay here all day," said Holliday. According to Genrikhovich, there were two daily trains to Yekaterinburg each day—the Ural Express, which left Moscow Kazanskaya station at four fifty in the afternoon, and the Rossiya, or Trans-Siberian Express, which left Moscow Yaroslavskaya station at nine oh five in the evening. Both trains took twenty-six hours to complete the journey.

In the end they decided on the Trans-Siberian. It was larger, more anonymous and not as destination-specific as the Ural Express. They crossed the expanse of Komsomol Square, bought their tickets in the booming, eighteenth-century station, then had breakfast at a nearby McDonald's, Holliday fascinated by Genrikhovich's almost magical ability to eat endless amounts of junk food.

They spent the rest of the day playing tourists and buying supplies for their trip, including backpacks, changes of clothing and a small digital camera to give their touristy playacting a bit of verisimilitude. They rode the magnificent subway, took pictures of one another in Red Square, rode a glass-topped tourist boat along the Moskva River and spent half an hour standing behind barricades on the Arbat watching Arnold Schwarzenegger and Brian Statham shooting a scene from *Red Heat II.*

Every once in a while during the strangely pleasant day in Moscow, Eddie or Holliday would drop back to see whether they were under any sort of surveillance. Neither man could detect anything out of the ordinary. They had lunch at a Kentucky Fried Chicken on the Arbat, a Pizza Hut dinner off Red Square, and made it back to the station in time to load up on snacks and bottled water for the trip and then climbed on the train. They made their way to their four-berth compartment somewhere close to the front of the long blue-and-red train. It was barely six feet wide, the lower berth upholstered benches during daylight hours, the upper berths permanently made up as beds. The narrow window was covered by a plush fringed curtain that seemed to belong to another age. A narrow hinged table pulled up on a folding single leg between the lower berths. They were each handed a packaged meal of burger, nibbed wheat, sweet corn and peas in a plastic container by their *provodnitsa*, a female, uniformed carriage attendant. The *provodnitsa* told them that there was a samovar at the end of the carriage with hot water available at all times of the day as well as powdered coffee. The attendant told them that if they required more or different food it could be obtained in one of the two dining cars on the Rossiya. She then gave them a brief official smile, cast a single nervous glance in Eddie's direction and withdrew. At nine twenty-five on the dot the Trans-Siberian Express gave a single long blast on its horn and eased smoothly out of the station. They were on their way.

One of Genrikhovich's purchases had been a cheap two-liter bottle of KiN horseradish vodka, which he brought out and began to drink as soon as the train began moving. Holliday and Eddie each had one shot of the foul stuff, agreed that it tasted like someone burning truck tires and switched to the powdered coffee. Between shots Genrikhovich ate bites of his packaged meal—one shot for each bite. By the time he'd finished the meal the Russian was drunk and almost unconscious. Together Holliday and Eddie managed to lift him onto one of the top bunks. Fortunately the bunk had a built-in guardrail.

With Genrikhovich snoring above them the two men sat on either side of the table drinking glasses of black instant coffee and staring out into the darkness. They had long ago left Moscow behind them as the long winding train clattered and rumbled its way east toward the distant Ural Mountains.

Eddie turned the switch on the little ventilator fan and lit one of the cigars he'd purchased in the lobby of the infamous Ukraine Hotel. "Tell me, Doc, why are we doing these things? I like excitement, yes, but I think this is getting a little crazy." The Cuban shrugged. "You have told me the story of this monk, Helder Rodrigues, and the promise you made him when he was dying, but even promises come to their end, *compañero*; am I right?"

"Well, in the first place our snoring, farting friend in the top bunk is right—we've gone too far to back out now. It's simply a matter of survival, of getting out of this whole thing alive. We've got the FSB after us and God only knows who else."

"That is not what I meant, *compañero*, and you know it." The Cuban shrugged his powerful shoulders. "This thing, whatever it is, has a. . . . *sujeción*, a grip on you." Eddie smiled broadly in the darkness. "You are my friend and I go where you go, do what you do, but I would like to understand better the reason for all of this. I am old-fashioned, Doc; if I die I would like it either to be as a very old man with a pretty girl in the bed with me or for some great cause."

Holliday stared out the window, the darkness broken every few minutes by the distant, dim light from farmhouses—lives lived that he would never know, dramas unfolding that he would never witness, nothing more than a passing wraith in the night. Finally he turned back to Eddie.

"At first, when I discovered the sword in my uncle Henry's house I thought I was part of something important, something ancient and good. Uncle Henry was the only real family I ever had, and I thought there couldn't be anything better than following in his footsteps. That's why I got my degree and my doctorate in history, to be like him. After getting out of the army I taught at West Point, a teacher like my uncle Henry. He was magic to me. He showed me that history was everywhere, from the blood-rich soil of Antietam to the seventeenth-century graffiti on the walls of the palace at Versailles. He showed me that there was sometimes more history in the writings of Charles Dickens and Mark Twain than there was in a hundred history textbooks.

"When I learned of his connection to the Templar tradition and eventually of his role in protecting that great treasure in the caves of the Corvo volcano in the Azores, I loved him even more. He was truly a knight in shining armor to me."

"You are sounding like he is no longer the shining knight for you," said Eddie.

"I learned that he was only a man. A spy for his country and a man who killed more than once to get what he wanted. A man who crossed boundaries that perhaps should have been left uncrossed. And that was only my uncle. The more I investigated his fellow 'knights,' these new Templars, these holy men and their holy cause, the more I saw them for what they truly were— some of them, anyway—what they had always been: avaricious, greedy men piling up wealth and power for their own sake. It's one secret society at war with another. This Order of the Phoenix, or whatever Putin and his oligarchs call it, and whoever or whatever the Templars are now—it is enormous power versus enormous power, and there can be only one left in the end. That's what this fifth sword is all about. North, south, east and west, with the fifth sword in the middle, the Rose Sword and whatever secret it holds. The Rose Sword, the last sword, is everything to them."

"And the secret of this sword's location is somehow in the egg of the Fabergé given by the czar?" Eddie asked.

"That would seem to be the accepted idea. Find out the secret of the Kremlin Egg and you find the sword. Find the sword and you find the real secret the Templars have been hiding from the world for the last seven hundred years."

The two friends sat in the dark together talking, sharing their pasts, their glories and their tragedies. Eddie spoke of being black in Cuba, and even after Castro's revolution how white and separate the country remained, without one black minister in the government or black general in the military.

He joked about his early days as a criminal, stealing mangoes off the trees that lined the main boulevard of Miramar, the police hot on his trail, of being beaten and bullied for his strange name in his early school days, and fabricating makeshift weights from cans full of cement and iron bars. On the other hand he spoke well of his education—a university engineering degree—and of his early military career, learning to fly anything from little single-prop Zlin Z 26 trainers to massive MiG-29 Fulcrum fighter jets.

Finally he spoke of his days in Africa, his final disillusionment with a revolution that supported other, poorer countries with multimillion-dollar aircraft and pilots while simultaneously being so corrupt at home that the government was unable to feed its people a daily meal of beans and rice, and where nurses and secretaries and even doctors became prostitutes in the evening to make ends meet. A country where everything was blamed on the "embargo" and where tomatoes rotted in the fields for want of the machinery to pick them, while in Havana the black market thrived and people with the right connections watched Miami satellite TV on wide plasma screens.

For his part Holliday spoke of growing up poor, of his early escape into books given to him by Uncle Henry and of his drunk and often abusive father. He spoke about the army as another kind of an escape, the training making a man out of a boy and how the wars he'd fought had seemed to steal small parts of his soul. He spoke about his love for his wife, Fay, and her sudden passing, and of his love for teaching history. He talked about his niece, Peggy, and Rafi Wanounou, the good man she'd married, an Israeli archaeologist. He talked about his regret at not having had children, and together the two men talked of their mutual love of base-ball.

Both men fell asleep around one thirty in the morning just after leaving Vladimir, Eddie's namesake and the first station stop and locomotive change for the Trans-Siberian. The rocking motion put an already tired Holliday into a deep and dreamless sleep that was suddenly and forcefully interrupted by Eddie seemingly only a few seconds later. Holliday craned his neck and saw a weak line of light coming through the break between the curtains covering the window. He remembered Eddie pulling them closed just before oblivion reached up and grabbed him. He looked at the glowing dial of his old Hamilton wristwatch. Five o'clock in the morning Moscow time, dawn wherever they were right now.

Eddie was shaking him by the shoulder. "Wake up, *mi coronel*; we have a problem."

"What problem?"

"It is Genrikhovich, the Russian."

"What about him?"

"He is gone."

22

"What do you mean, gone?"

"I woke up to use the *excusado* . . . the toilet. When I came back I heard no snoring from above me, so I looked and he was not there. I thought perhaps he'd needed the toilet himself and went to the one in the next car along, but he was not there either."

"What about the *provodnitsa*, or whatever the hell they call her?"

"Asleep, presumably. She was not at her post by the samovar at the end of the car."

"It's a train, for God's sake. He's got to be somewhere."

"I have looked from one end of the train to the other, *mi compañero*. He is vanished. *Desaparecido*."

"Where the hell are we?" Holliday asked, sitting up groggily.

"Somewhere between Nizhniy Novgorod and Yosh-kar-Ola."

"Where the hell is that?"

"Nowhere," said Eddie.

"Have there been any stops since we went to bed?"

"Nizhniy Novgorod."

"Could he have gotten off the train there?"

"It is very doubtful, *mi coronel*. He would almost surely have awakened me."

"You're sure?"

"Positive. When I got up for the toilet he was snoring. When I returned he was not. I was gone perhaps three minutes at the most."

"If that's true he wasn't as drunk as we thought."

"This is my thinking as well, Doc. He tricked us."

"Why?"

"There is only one way we will know."

"Find him."

"*Sí.*"

The train was made up of fifteen cars: three first-class, like the car Holliday and Eddie were in, each with ten compartments with four bunks each. Beyond that was the dining car, a bar lounge car for snacks and overpriced booze, four second-class cars that were like old-fashioned American Pullmans, two seats down, one bunk up, and then six third-class coaches with eight bunks crammed into each compartment. At the end were the baggage car, the generator car and the locomotive. They searched the train again from end to end, but there was no sign of Genrikhovich. They checked all the toilets and asked all the *provodnitsas,* but no one had seen anybody fitting Genrikhovich's description. Both of the conductors agreed that the train was completely full and all their passengers were accounted for. Unless Genrikhovich had somehow managed to crawl under somebody's bunk, he simply wasn't on the train.

On their way back to their compartment they stopped in the plainly decorated dining car and ate an early and expensive breakfast of meat-filled *pelmeni* in piping-hot broth, a slice of heavy bread, some sort of smoked fish with the head still on and a gigantic chrome thermos of black, very strong coffee.

"Did somebody take him or did he run on his own?" Holliday wondered.

"There couldn't have been much of a struggle—I would have heard, or the *provodnitsa* would have. No, *compadre,* we must accept that leaving us was his idea."

"But why come all this way, lead us along, bring us into the middle of nowhere? I don't get it, Eddie."

"Nor do I, *mi coronel,*" responded the Cuban. He stared out the window. Holliday could see flickering bright images of a wide river through the trees. Most probably the Volga. He was riding through Russian history. Finally Eddie spoke again. "Have you ever played chess, *compañero?*"

"When I was a kid." Holliday nodded. He sipped some of the scalding coffee. "My uncle Henry taught me. He said it formed the basis of most military strategy."

"It was compulsory in my group of Young Pioneers. Our leader wanted to become the Cuban Boris Spassky."

"What's your point?"

"We are playing a game of chess and we have no idea what pieces we are—pawns, rooks or knights."

"My vote would be pawns. Genrikhovich had a good story and we fell for it. I think the real analogy is that we don't even know which side of the board we're playing on, black or white."

"Maybe red and white would be more *apropiado*, considering where we are."

"Lets get back to the compartment; we've got some decisions to make."

"*Sí, mi coronel*, such as deciding whether we should stay on the board or absent ourselves, yes?"

"You bet your ass, Eddie."

By the time they made their way back through the creaking, swaying cars the sun was fully up. Holliday wanted to ask their *provodnitsa* whether she was sure she hadn't seen Genrikhovich earlier that morning, but she wasn't in her usual place at the samovar or in her little cabin at the end of the car. Even *provodnitsas* took pee breaks, he supposed. He turned around and went back to their compartment. He slid the door open. Eddie was seated on the right-hand bunk. The *provodnitsa* was seated across from him. Instead of a little silver tray with glass cups of amber-colored tea, she was holding a nasty-looking Serdyukov SPS automatic in her hand, the nine-millimeter cannon of choice for the FSB.

"Zakryt dver," said the woman, twitching the automatic in Holliday's direction.

"She wants you to close the door," translated Eddie.

"I figured that," said Holliday, sliding the door closed behind him.

"Sadit'sya," the woman ordered, pointing to the bunk beside Eddie. Holliday sat down.

"Bylo radio soobshchenie, Ya, chtoby derzhat' vas zdes', poka politsiya prihodyat."

"It seems there was a radio message. She is to hold us here until the police come," Eddie translated.

"When's that?"

"Kirov Pass. Nine forty-five."

"Ninety minutes."

"Long time."

"Heavy gun."

"A kilo, at least."

"Zavali yebalo!" the *provodnitsa* hissed.

"Shut up?" Holliday asked.

Eddie smiled. "Something like that." The Cuban paused. He glanced toward Holliday. *"¿Entiende usted? Hay que matar a ella."*

"Matar?" Holliday asked.

"Asesinato, hacerla una muerta."

"Zavali yebalo!" the *provodnitsa* repeated.

"Gotcha," murmured Holliday. The question was, how? If she somehow managed to fire the gun it would be a disaster, even if she missed. The noise would be deafening. The bullets for the SPS were designed to go through thirty layers of Kevlar, a requirement in these times, when the bad guys wore better body armor than the cops. The shock of a bullet like that hitting either one of them at such close range, even in an arm or leg, would be enough to shatter bone and induce instant shock. A hit to the body would probably be fatal.

The *provodnitsa*'s grip on the weapon wasn't very practiced; her right hand was wrapped around the grip, her index finger on the trigger. Her left hand was on her knee, rubbing back and forth nervously. The safety on the pistol was in the down position, meaning that it was off. The hammer was at full cock.

"On three," said Holliday softly. "I go low, you go high."

"Sí, entiendo." Eddie nodded.

"One, two."

"Zavali yebalo!" the *provodnitsa* yelled.

"Three."

"Svyatoe der' mo, smotrite na chto!" Eddie yelled, looking out the window.

It was just enough. The woman's eyes flickered and the gun moved a fraction of an inch. Holliday's right arm snapped across the space between him and the woman, his hand folding over the slide of the pistol, his thumb jamming between the hammer and the firing pin. For his part Eddie lurched forward, his left hand in a rigid four-fingered blade smashing into her larynx, crushing it.

Holliday tore the gun out of her hand, wincing with pain as the hammer slammed down on his thumb. He moved to one side, giving the Cuban room to maneuver. Eddie put one knee into the woman's diaphragm, took his left hand from her larynx and grabbed her hair with his right, pulling her head back as far as he could. He slammed his left hand under her chin and there was a distinct snap as her vertebrae parted company with one another. She flopped down onto the bunk. The smell of urine filled the compartment as her bladder voided.

"Now what?" Eddie asked.

"Stuff her in one of the upper bunks and then get the hell off this train."

23

The two men jumped off the Trans-Siberian Express just as it slowed to begin the sharp curve past the small village of Chandrovo. They swung down on the long steel handrails on either side of the doorway, dropping down in a roll on the cindered track bed, then scrambled into the ditch. They hunched low as the train rumbled past in the early-dawn light. Apparently no one had seen their escape.

"Not so bad." Eddie grunted, getting to his feet.

"Sure," said Holliday. "We just jumped off the Trans-Siberian Express in the middle of nowhere after breaking a young lady's neck."

"*Compañero,* it was I who broke the young lady's neck, and she was holding a pistol in our faces."

"True enough," said Holliday. They watched as the train disappeared into the distance. "I wonder how long we've got."

"They will look for the *provodnitsa* and perhaps find

her. The police were to be waiting at Kirov. According to the schedule they will not arrive there until ten o'clock. At best we have three hours, but I would not bet on it."

"So what's our best bet for getting to Yekaterinburg?"

Eddie pointed to the west across a series of rolling fields. In the distance, perhaps a mile away, Holliday could see the bright gleam of water. "The Volga," said the Cuban. "It flows to Kazan. Perhaps we can catch a local train there."

"What are we supposed to do, swim?" Holliday asked.

"You didn't study Russian geography in school the way we Habaneros did." Eddie grinned. "It is the Volga. We will find a boat there; I guarantee it."

"Lead the way," said Holliday. They climbed out of the ditch, ducked under the farmer's fence and headed for the distant river.

Whit Havers knocked on Assistant Deputy Director of National Security J. Hunter Kokum's office door—located directly across from General Temple's own office on the main floor of the West Wing—then stepped inside. Kokum, thin and gray, sat behind his desk, flipping through red-tabbed security reports, his trademark scowl on his face.

"What?" Kokum asked without looking up.

"Report on Black Tusk," said Whit, using the appropriate code name pulled from the classified security computer file for the present operation in Russia.

"Any word?"

"Yes, sir, the asset was contacted in Amsterdam and agreed to take on the contract. Assuming that the targets would not be using regular air transport to reach their destination, he waited in the appropriate Moscow train station for the targets to appear."

"And did they?"

"Yes, sir, at approximately seventeen hundred hours local time yesterday. They purchased a second-class compartment and boarded the train a few moments before it was to depart."

"The asset is traveling with them?"

"No, sir. He saw them onto the train and then flew on ahead. He's already in Yekaterinburg."

"And if the targets leave the train before then?"

"Yekaterinburg is their destination one way or the other. It doesn't really matter how they get there."

"You seem pretty sure of yourself, Havers."

"It's logical, sir."

"When you've done this for as long as I have you'll come to understand that logic has very little to do with intelligence matters."

"Yes, sir," said Whit.

"What about Ducos?" Kokum asked. "You have the Frenchman under surveillance?"

"Yes, sir."

"What's he up to?"

"He appears to have gone on vacation, sir."

"Where?"

"A town at the edge of the Pyrenees. A little village with an old castle on a hill. Montségur, I think it's called."

"Find out about it."

"Yes, sir."

"Enjoying your first assignment as a case officer, Mr. Havers?"

"Yes, sir," Whit answered—what the hell else was he supposed to say?

"Know why we have case officers for projects like this, Mr. Havers?"

"To oversee the operation," answered Whit.

"That's part of it, certainly, but it's not the most important part, Havers."

"No, sir?"

"No, Havers. The real reason is to have someone to flush down the shithole when the whole thing comes apart."

Yevgeni Ivanovich Barsukov, imprisoned head of the notorious Tambov Gang of St. Petersburg, lounged in his cell at Vladimir Central Prison, smoking a British Senior

Service cigarette and reading an American edition of *TIME* magazine.

On the table beside his comfortable upholstered chair was a large goblet of freshly squeezed orange juice and a lightly toasted English muffin slathered with butter and Dutriez Bar-le-Duc red currant jam.

At fifty-eight, Barsukov looked at least fifteen years younger. His graying hair was dyed the same brown it had been all his life, his neatly trimmed mustache and Vandyke beard colored to match.

He wore contact lenses rather than submit to spectacles, and although he had thickened slightly through the middle during his time in jail, he worked out several times a week and lifted weights on occasion. It was hot in the cell, and Barsukov was stripped to the waist, the five stars tattooed on each shoulder and the large crucifix across his chest clearly visible. Even if an inmate had never met Barsukov, the tattoos would tell the man that Barsukov was "prince of thieves," a man of great power and position.

The cell was large, twenty feet by thirty or so, with four tall windows facing east. Most cells at Vladimir contained six inmates, but Barsukov shared with only one other, Sergei Magnitsky, his bodyguard and private chef. At the moment Magnitsky was preparing Barsukov's breakfast of oladyi pancakes and sausages with a pair of George Foreman grills kept on one of the broad concrete windowsills.

Barsukov was serving a fourteen-year sentence for fraud and money laundering. Magnitsky had been convicted of no crime but had simply joined his boss in prison out of choice. In fact, both Barsukov and Magnitsky had committed murder many times over during the course of the last twenty-five years, but neither man had ever been convicted.

By Western standards, Barsukov's lifestyle seemed wildly at odds with being incarcerated in what was without a doubt the most dangerous and violent prison in the Russian Federation, but Barsukov was more than the leader of a major gang outside the prison—he held the unofficial rank of *smotryashchiye* within the prison. If a prisoner needed an argument settled or was experiencing other problems, he would come to Barsukov, who served as the "watcher" or mediator, often the only thing between total chaos and a prison that ran on an even keel.

As Magnitsky waited for the sausages to cook he brought his boss a fresh cup of his preferred dark arabica coffee. Barsukov took an approving sip, then placed the cup on the side table beside his goblet of orange juice. He butted his cigarette, picked a fleck of tobacco from his lower lip, then took up his cell phone. From memory he dialed a number; he was old-guard, rarely writing anything down, and never committing a name or a number to the memory of an electronic device. The line rang twice before it was answered.

"I am looking for Father Deacon Ivan Yevseyevich Veniamino; is he there? No? Then perhaps you can give him a message for me; my name is Vladimir from St. Petersburg. That's right. Please tell Father Deacon Veniamino that the bells should be rung in turns tonight. Yes; the bells should be rung in turns."

He flipped off the phone and dropped it onto the table. Magnitsky would take it apart and dispose of it later.

"Come on, Sergei, those sausages must be done by now."

"Coming right up, boss."

It took them the better part of an hour to reach the shallow banks of the wide, slow-moving river, and another twenty minutes to find a short, waterlogged pier jutting drunkenly out into the water, built on rusted, half-submerged fifty-gallon drums. A long, high prowed rowboat was tied up loosely to the pier. Several inches of water in the bottom of the boat smelled of old fish and dead worms, but it seemed solid enough. There was a wooden box of fishing tackle—very heavy line, big three-barbed hooks and below-the-surface floaters. There were also two pairs of heavy work gloves in the box and a ball-peen hammer, probably for killing whatever fish they caught.

"Sturgeon poachers," said Eddie. "We read about

them in school. They fish for the big female sturgeon, then dye the eggs black to make look like beluga caviar from the Caspian Sea. Fish can be an easy hundred pounds, even more."

Eddie sat down at the oars, and Holliday unlooped the rope from the pier, then settled down by the transom. Both men pushed off, and in a few moments they were well out into the swirling currents of the dark river, Eddie doing little more than guiding their passage. The river was quiet as they moved through the early-morning mist, the silence interrupted only by the sounds of waterbirds by the shore taking to the air. After the constant clatter of the train it was a peaceful change. Holliday vaguely remembered a scene from *The Great Escape,* one of his favorite movies from the early sixties. Charles Bronson and John Leyton casually pick up a rowboat on the shores of the Danube and calmly row to safety. If it were only that easy.

They switched positions every hour or so and, taking the current into consideration, by noon Holliday figured they'd moved about fifteen miles or so downriver.

"How far to Kazan?" Holliday asked, getting behind the oars once again. Eddie settled by the transom, looking downriver.

"Perhaps fifty kilometers. I'm not really sure."

Holliday rowed, his tired muscles already complaining. The mists were gone and a chilly breeze was blowing across the river, setting up little storms of ripples that he had to fight against to stay in position. After fifteen minutes or so Eddie suddenly told him to pull for shore.

"Why?" Holliday asked.

"I saw something," said Eddie.

Holliday looked back over his shoulder, but all he could see was a stubbled field that had long since been harvested and a large, well-worn barn with an equally worn sign in large, flaking white letters on the side. The rowboat nudged the muddy bank.

"We may be in luck, I think," said Eddie. A straight dirt road led directly to the barn's big double doors. The Cuban pointed to the sign on the barn at the edge of the farmer's field.

"I don't get it." Holliday shrugged, staring at the incomprehensible assortment of Cyrillic letters.

Юрия культур пыли службы

"Yuriya kul'tur pyli sluzhby," said Eddie, grinning from ear to ear.

"You got me. I still don't know what the hell you're talking about."

"The sign says, 'Yuri's Crop-dusting Service,'" Eddie replied. He grabbed the hammer from the box of fishing tackle and stepped out of the boat. He climbed up the riverbank, heading for the barn. Holliday was right behind him.

Reaching the barn, Holliday saw that what he thought had been a dirt road was actually a short runway, less than two hundred yards long. Eddie stood at the barn doors. They were locked securely with a large brass padlock. The hasp, however, was screwed on the outside of the door, and it took only a few whacks with the hammer before the hasp had splintered away from the door. Holliday looked around. There was a cluster of farm buildings in the distance but they were a good mile or so away.

Eddie hauled open the barn doors and stared. *"¡Absolutamente perfecto!"*

To Holliday it looked like a biplane left over from the First World War. The rust-colored primer and mottled brown paint on the aluminum hull were worn down to the metal in some places, and the fat rubber tricycle tires were totally bald. Spray nozzles lined the trailing edge of the lower wings, and there was an even larger nozzle directly behind the single, four-bladed rotary engine.

"What is it?" Holliday asked.

Eddie stepped up to the aircraft, running his big hand over the engine nacelle like a man examining a racehorse. "She is a *Kukuruznik*, a Maize Worker. Her real designation is an Antonov An-2. They used to use them a lot in Cuba but now there are only a few. There is even one of them in the Air Force Museum in Habana."

"I'll bet," said Holliday. "Can you fly it?"

"Pero por supuesto, mi amigo—of course I can fly it."

24

Holliday followed Eddie around the biplane's sturdy, stumpy wings to the midsection of the fuselage. The more of the plane he saw, the more he realized that the mottled paint job was probably done that way on purpose. It was camouflage. There was a large, upward-hinged cargo door with a smaller passenger door inserted within it. Eddie pulled the simple twist handle on the passenger door and boosted himself up into the plane. Holliday followed.

"*¡Hijo de puta!*" Eddie breathed. "*¡Es un mal olor!*"

The Cuban was right: the inside of the aircraft smelled, and it wasn't crop-dusting chemicals. Holliday recognized the rubbery, earthy stink immediately: baled, processed Afghani opium. Yuri was no farmer's friend; he was a drug smuggler, and apparently on a fairly large scale. Instead of insecticide tanks there were a pair of large fuel tanks just behind the wings. Holliday tried to visualize a map of Asia. It was probably about fifteen hundred miles from here to one of the northern towns of Afghanistan, Herat, maybe. With the two extra fuel tanks, an old plane flying low, under the radar and following the mountain passes, would have an easy time of it.

They made their way forward to the cramped cockpit. The glass in the windows was flat, and the cockpit was so heavily tilted Holliday couldn't see the ground.

Eddie settled into the left-hand pilot's seat and let his fingers wander over the controls. He reached into the side pocket of his seat and pulled out a folder full of charts and began going through them.

"These will take us to Yekaterinburg." He nodded.

"You're the pilot," said Holliday. "Tell me what you want me to do."

"Go to the back of the plane. See how much fuel is in those tanks. When you have done that go outside and take away the *calzos,* the . . . how do you call it, chocks. Then come back and sit yourself beside me, okay?"

"Okay." Holliday nodded. He went back to the tanks and tapped them; they appeared to be about half-full. That done, he jumped down from the doorway, pulled out the wooden chocks that stood against the wheels and then climbed back into the plane. He closed the passenger door, twisting the handle firmly, and went back to the cockpit. He sat down across from Eddie, staring at a hundred dials and switches in front of him. It was impossibly complicated.

"You can really fly this thing?"

"Yes. She is *una vaca,* a cow, but she will do as I tell her, I think."

Eddie reached down and fiddled with some kind of push-pull button low on the dashboard, the fingers of his right hand easing forward a small throttlelike handle on the console between the seats. A sharp coughing noise followed and the four-bladed propeller spun through a few rotations. Eddie pushed the lever a little farther forward and the propellers began to whirl, gouts of black smoke blasting out into the inside of the barn. Eddie pushed the throttles forward a little more, the sound of the engine roaring almost painfully.

Holliday caught motion from the corner of his good eye and he turned, peering out through the windshield. In the distance off to their right he could see a rooster tail of dust or smoke.

"We'd better get moving," said Holliday. "I think Yuri's onto us."

"I cannot," said Eddie, pushing the throttles even farther forward. He hauled back on the half-wheel yoke directly in front of him. "I must run the engine up to clear the oil from the pistons. If I do not do this the cow will die, yes?"

"Do what you have to do, but hurry it up," said Holliday. The plume of dust had resolved itself into an old GAZ-67, the Russian knockoff of a jeep crossed with a tractor. Holliday could make out at least four people in the vehicle. One of them was standing up and gripping the handles of what looked like a mounted fifty-caliber machine gun. "How long?" Holliday asked, raising his voice over the phlegm-rattling noise of the engine.

"A few seconds more!" Eddie called out. A few seconds more and the fifty-cal was going to be within killing range. The five-inch-long shells would go through the skin of the old plane like a rat through cheese. Holliday watched as the truck bounced closer on the invisible track through the fields. Another thirty yards and it was going to be too late.

"Go! Now!" Holliday yelled. The first ranging burst from the truck was chewing up the dirt runway a few yards ahead. Eddie released the yoke and pulled the throttle all the way back. The Antonov jumped forward like an overweight greyhound chasing a rabbit. Holliday and Eddie were thrown back into their seats as the first burst of machine-gun bullets struck the plane, clipping the undercarriage and the belly of the fuselage only seconds before the Antonov took to the air. A second burst hammered through the lower starboard-side wing, but by then it was too late—the Antonov was climbing at an insane rate of speed, all with Eddie's hands clear of the yoke. He worked the pedals and the plane banked away from the airstrip and the murderous fire of the machine gun. Only then did Eddie grab the yoke and gently ease the old airplane into level flight. The Volga was five hundred feet below them and the machine-gunning Gaz was a memory.

"You always fly with no hands?" Holliday asked.

"You do not lead *una vaca* by her horns, *amigo*; you let her find her own way. It is the same with this aircraft." He stroked the yoke in front of his hands. "When you taxi the Antonov the yoke is the brake. Pull the yoke to raise the nose and you will stand the aircraft on its head."

"Glad I wasn't trying to fly it." Holliday laughed.

"*Yo también, compadre*—me, too." Eddie grinned. He reached into the side pocket on his left and pulled out the bulging chart book. Flying the plane with his knees, he leafed through the charts until he found the one he wanted. He studied it for a moment, then stuffed the chart book back into the side pocket. He adjusted the Antonov's course slightly and they slowly lost altitude until they were only three hundred feet or so above the ground.

"How far to Yekaterinburg?" Holliday asked.

"Two hours, maybe, two and a half, no more than that."

"Where do we land?"

"A good question, *mi amigo*," answered Eddie. "A very good question."

The International Cathar Historical Society met in the village of Montségur each year. Montségur was a favorite of groups interested in Cathar history, of which there were a surprising number, and the ICHS didn't stand out among them in any special way. Each year they organized tours of the massive Cathar stronghold on the steep hill that loomed above the town, as well as seminars and readings about the twelfth- and thirteenth-century sect that split from the Catholic Church, believing it to be irretrievably corrupt.

The Cathars also believed that each man had the individual spark of God within his soul and needed no organized religion to keep that spark alive. To them Christ was a prophet and philosopher and no more divine than any other ordinary man.

Most interesting, at least to the International Cathar Historical Society, was the fact that the Cathars believed that they were the true inheritors of the Apostolic Creed, not the Roman Catholic Church. It was this connection with the Apostles that attracted the ICHS, since they were in fact known to one another as the Apostles, a group of twelve men organized secretly in the early thirteen hundreds to protect, preserve and enlarge the assets of the Poor Fellow-Soldiers of Christ and of the Temple of Solomon, more commonly referred to as the Templars.

The Apostles had never been knights of the order, but they had been and continued to be its bankers, its accountants and its bookkeepers. With their ink-stained fingers the monks and laymen of the order had survived long past the vaunted holy men, the knights and the grand masters, most of whom were tortured or burned at the stake, or both. The scribes, the note takers, the money changers and the moneylenders had gone on undisturbed and tranquil in the immutability of numbers, of money owed and money lent.

The motto of the Templar Knights had been, *In hoc signo vinces—By this sign we shall conquer.* The motto of the Apostles was, *Aqua profunda est quieta—Still waters run deep.* Better to survive shyly for your purpose than to die any number of glorious and useless deaths.

The twelve Apostles—and there were always twelve who came to Montségur each year—were from every inhabitable continent, and in their way represented every major power on the planet. None of the twelve ever answered to their real names when they met, although some knew of one another and did business together. When they met they were Peter, Andrew, James, John, Philip, Bartholomew, Matthew, Thomas, James, son of Alphaeus, Thaddeus, Simon and Judas Iscariot. In this way, as Apostles died and were replaced, continuity, which was their watchword, never changed— always twelve, always the same.

As always when the Apostles assembled together they spoke in Berrichon, the obscure and now vanished vulgate Latin tongue that the Templars had sometimes used in coded communications with one another.

Pierre Ducos was Peter, not the first Apostle but, as the Greek version of his name suggested, the Apostles' "rock." Usually it was Ducos who offered the official greeting and prayer as the twelve men gathered in the private dining room of the Hotel Costes. The sumptuous meal had been laid before them, the wine poured, and the waitstaff had withdrawn. It was a prayer little known and even more rarely heard.

"May the grace of the Holy Spirit be present with us. May Mary, Star of the Sea, lead us to the harbor of salvation. Amen.

"Holy Father, eternal God, omnipotent, omniscient creator, bestower, kind ruler and most tender lover, pious and humble redeemer; gentle, merciful savior, Lord! I humbly beseech Thee and implore Thee that Thou may enlighten me, free me and preserve the brothers of the Temple and all Thy Christian people, troubled as they are.

"Thou, O God, who knowest that we are innocent, set us free that we may keep our vows and Your commandments in humility, and serve Thee and act according to Thy will. Dispel all those unjust reproaches, far from the truth, heaped upon us by the means of tough adversities, great tribulations and temptations, which we have endured, but can endure no longer. Amen."

There was a chorus of mumbled amens and then the clatter of cutlery. Sir James Sinclair, otherwise known as Simon to the group, was the first to speak. "In our discussions over the last few weeks most of us have voiced concerns regarding the man Holliday. Rodrigues had no right to give the list to him."

"Rodrigues was dying, as I recall," answered Ducos. He took a sip of his wine, a very fine Margaux. "And in point of fact, Holliday's uncle was one of us many years ago. He has some right to the notebook."

"He was never pledged to the order," said Judas, a plump banker from Switzerland. "He has no idea of the laws and ordinances. He is not one of us; therefore he has no rights at all."

"From what we've seen he wouldn't have abided by the laws and ordinances anyway," snapped Sir James Sinclair. "He is a rogue and he cannot be tolerated."

"Enjoy your ratatouille before it gets cold, my dear Simon; there is nothing worse than soggy vegetables," said Ducos. "The situation is in hand. The Russian has promised me that when Holliday reaches the church in Yekaterinburg, he will be dealt with."

"And if he doesn't go to the church?" Sir James asked, taking of a forkful of the aromatic vegetable stew.

"If he does not go to the church, my dear Simon, then we have nothing to worry about, *n'est-ce pas?*" The lawyer smiled, watching as the Scotsman's protests were silenced by the marvelously cooked meal. "We have been one step ahead of the unfortunate colonel and his golliwog friend from the very beginning."

25

Landing near Yekaterinburg presented no real problems, to Holliday's surprise. With the main airport out of the question when flying a stolen plane, Eddie artfully set the old Antonov down in a farmer's fallow field. Safely back on the ground, the two men found an old set of abandoned railway tracks leading into the town of Sredneuralsk less than a mile from their landing spot. Both men carried the backpacks they'd taken from the train, and Holliday still carried the Serdyukov SPS automatic he'd taken from the *provodnitsa*. According to the charts, Sredneuralsk was about twenty-five miles from Yekaterinburg.

Reaching the town, they passed a gigantic factory that emitted the reeking odor of processing chickens. In the center of Sredneuralsk they found a large yellow building that looked as though it might have originally been some wealthy landowner's mansion but which turned out to be a hotel.

They stopped there for a meal in the sparsely decorated café and Eddie asked their waiter how they could get to Yekaterinburg. The waiter, a grizzled, rheumy-eyed man in his sixties with a long stained apron tied to his front, was surprised at being addressed by a black man in fluent Russian, but then he beamed, showing off a gleaming set of Stalin-era steel teeth. "Tourist, yes?" he asked in English. "I am Ivan Chaplitzky, owner of Tsentral'nyi 'otel, of course." He poured coffee into their thick pottery cups from a sterling-silver pot that appeared to be at least a hundred years old. Something buried in a backyard before the revolution and dug up after the revolution failed seventy-four years later, thought Holliday. "You are, of course, tourists, I am sure."

"Yes," answered Holliday. "I'm American and my friend is Cuban."

"Viva Fidel, okay?" Ivan chuckled. "Your friend has very good Russian."

"Spasiba," said Eddie.

"Priglashaem Vas," said Ivan the waiter. "You say that you wish to get to Yekaterinburg, of course?"

"Yes." Holliday nodded.

"I take you," said Ivan. "I have taxi, of course. One thousand rubles. Pay U.S. I take you for fifty dollars."

"All right," said Holliday.

"Each way," said Ivan.

"We're only going one way," said Holliday.

"But I must come back, of course." Ivan shrugged.

"Of course," said Holliday.

Ivan's taxi turned out to be a mid-fifties ZiL 111 hearse that looked a lot like a 1955 Chevy Bel Air, which he'd borrowed from his undertaker brother Dimitri. Ivan stuck a magnetized plastic sign on the door and another one with suction cups on the roof, switched the license plates and they were off. Forty-five minutes later he dropped them in front of the glass-and-steel arch of the Hyatt Yekaterinburg in the middle of a bustling city of a million and a half people. The sleepy little town on the edge of the Urals had come a long way since the czar and his family had been assassinated there in 1917. So had the czar, for that matter. After lying in the bottom of a coal mine in a swamp for the better part of a hundred years, Nicholas had been elevated to sainthood in the Greek Orthodox Church, with a cathedral built on the site of the very spot where he'd been gunned down.

Holliday and Eddie booked a suite using their phony passports, praying that news of their exploits hadn't reached this far, this soon. Once in the suite they cracked open the minibar and settled down in the front room with a couple of tall bottles of Stary Melnik Gold.

The two men, both·exhausted by their day, sat silently for what seemed to be a very long time. When the silence was broken it was Eddie who spoke. *"Ahora el tango, el bolero siguiente."*

"Translation?" asked Holliday sleepily, stretched out on the couch.

"Something my grandmother said when I told her I was tired." The Cuban smiled. "Now the tango, then the bolero."

"In other words, we're not finished yet. You mean Genrikhovich?" said Holliday.

"*Sí.*"

"Was he snatched or did he leave the train on his own?"

"It is the question, *mi coronel.*"

"The only reason we're here is because of his suggestion. I'm not sure whether I believe him now."

"I do not trust him, either," said Eddie, taking a long swallow of beer.

"So what would your grandmother say?"

"*La discreción es la mejor parte del valor,*" answered the Cuban.

"Good advice."

"It worked for her, *mi compadre*; she lived to be a hundred and ten years old."

"So what would Granny do in this situation?"

"I think Genrikhovich mentioned a name, no?"

"Anton Zukov." Holliday nodded.

"If Genrikhovich has set us up for some kind of trap, it will be in the museum at the church, where *Gospodin* Zukov works."

"Ergo, we don't go to the church; we find out where Mr. Zukov lives and pay him a visit at home."

Eddie shrugged. "It is what my grandmother would have done." The Cuban smiled. "But first she would have had a siesta, I think."

"Truly, Eddie, your grandmother was very wise. I'll take the couch; you can have the bed."

By the time they woke up night had fallen. They ordered room service dinners and then they got down to work. There were seven A. Zukovs listed in the book, and Eddie began phoning them all. He told them he was a reporter for *Moskovsky Komsomolets,* the national newspaper, doing a story on the Hermitage during the Great Patriotic War, and understood *Gospodin* Zukov's father had come to Yekaterinburg with the treasures. Four of the people who answered said he had a wrong number and hung up. The fifth didn't. Eddie and the man talked for a few moments before the Cuban set down the telephone.

"He thinks it is a little strange to do interviews so late in the evening, but he agreed. One hour."

Anton Zukov lived on Vokzal'naya Ulitsa, about three blocks from the railway station. The apartment building was a Constructionist-era monstrosity that looked like a tin can cut in half. It was reddish stucco over concrete, with a garden area between the curving, crumbling arms of the structure. Once upon a time the garden was probably supposed to be a communal effort tended to by the building's occupants, but by the state of the shrubbery it looked as though the plot had died along with the Soviet Union. The lobby had suffered in the same way. There was nobody at the reception desk, and two elevators, one of which had its door gaping open and cables dangling from the ceiling. It was obviously under repair, but it looked as though it had been that way for a very long time. Zukov lived on the ninth floor, and after a ten-minute wait the elevator arrived and took them ponderously upward with enough rattling and pausing that Eddie and Holliday agreed that it was the stairs on the way down.

Zukov answered the door. He had an egg-shaped head with thinning salt-and-pepper hair, developing jowls, a small mole to the left of his wide, downturned mouth, gold wire glasses and a tweed jacket. He looked like an English professor from a Midwestern university. He took one look at Eddie and smiled thinly.

"Vy ne iz gazety Vy?" You are not from the newspaper, are you?

"Nyet," said Eddie.

Holliday took the black Serdyukov automatic out of his pocket and held his arm loosely at his side. "We just want to ask you some questions."

"An American with a gun and a black man who speaks Russian. How intriguing." He stood aside. "Do come in. Make yourself comfortable."

"After you," answered Holliday.

211

"As you wish." Zukov nodded. He led them down a narrow hallway. On Holliday's left a pair of large urns flanked what appeared to be a dark, brooding self-portrait of the French artist Nicholas Poussin. The interior of the apartment was even more surprising—contemporary white leather furniture in a conversation square looking toward a wood-burning fireplace, more art on the whiter walls and good rugs covering a dark cherry hardwood floor.

They sat down across from one another on the white leather couches. Zukov pulled out a blue-and-yellow pack of cheap Belomorkanal cigarettes and lit one with a giant agate lighter on the glass coffee table in front of him.

"Tell us about the Kremlin Egg," said Holliday.

Zukov's braying laugh caught both Holliday and Eddie by surprise. The Russian man began choking on his cigarette smoke and coughing. Finally he sat back against the leather cushions, perched his glasses up on his forehead and wiped his eyes with a thumb and forefinger.

"What's so funny?" Holliday asked.

"You've been talking to Genrikhovich, haven't you?" Zukov asked, grinning broadly.

"You know this man?" Eddie asked.

"Of course I know him. I know him just like you know a scab on your knee you want to pick off."

"The egg," reminded Holliday, the automatic pistol in his lap.

"Genrikhovich believes the Kremlin Egg holds some kind of secret that Rasputin took with him to his grave and which the Leningrad Four discovered."

"The Leningrad Four?" Holliday asked.

"Vladimir Vladimirovich Putin; Dmitry Anatolyevich Medvedev, the president; Vladimir Mikhailovich Gundyaev, better known as Kirill I, patriarch of Moscow; and Alexander Vasilyevich Bortnikov, head of the FSB. They were boyhood friends in St. Petersburg, they were all in the KGB and they have all risen to great power. Genrikhovich thinks they're part of some ancient society called the Order of the Phoenix or something equally melodramatic."

"There is no Order of the Phoenix?"

"Not to my knowledge."

"The Kremlin Egg?"

"It was never here. It always remained in the Kremlin Armoury. It wasn't part of the evacuation, something I could never make Genrikhovich believe, I'm afraid. He said Golitsyn's son would back up everything he said."

Holliday only knew of one person named Golitsyn. "Anatoliy Golitsyn? The KGB defector who exposed Philby and the Cambridge Five spy ring back in the sixties?"

"The very one." Zukov laughed. "Except Anatoliy Golitsyn never had a son, only a daughter."

"What did Genrikhovich say to that?"

"He said the son was illegitimate, by a secretary

named Maria Ivanova, who worked for the KGB in Leningrad—pardon, St. Petersburg. According to Golitsyn there is even some connection to Putin or Stalin or something equally foolish. The boy took the mother's name—Anatoliy Ivanov. According to Genrikhovich this spectral bastard works in Moscow and has an apartment on Sivtsev Vrazhek Lane in the Arbat district."

"Did you check it out?" Holliday asked.

"Don't be ridiculous. I had neither the time nor the inclination. Genrikhovich loves to weave endless tales of dark conspiracies, secret societies, the KGB infiltrating the Church, the Romanovs, anything to get attention. Anatoliy Ivanov was nothing but a figment of the man's fevered imagination. He is, as you Americans say, a fruitcake."

"So we've been screwed," said Holliday.

"*¿Qué?*" Eddie said.

"*Vy byli rez'bovym,*" explained Zukov.

"*Hijo de puta,*" said the Cuban.

26

Alexander Bortnikov, director of the Russian FSB, stared out the window of his seventh-floor office and looked down at Lubyanka Square. The statue of Iron Felix Dzerzhinsky was gone, but people still avoided walking in front of the old All Russian Insurance Company building the statue had faced. The memories of the blood-soaked dungeons and torture chambers in the basement were too fresh for some Russians. It looked cold outside, and a harsh wind was blowing scraps of newspaper and dust from the gutters. Winter was coming.

Bortnikov turned away from the windows and walked back to his desk. The office had once belonged to Lavrenti Beria, head of the NKVD and later the KGB, a small, round-faced bald man with a pointy chin and a small mouth who looked far more like a bookkeeper than he did Stalin's favorite goblin, and the man responsible for the deaths of millions of Russian people at Stalin's command.

Everything was the same as it had been in Beria's time; the parquet floors had been maintained, as had the waist-high silver birch wainscoting that ran around the large, high-ceilinged room. The dark green paint on the walls above the paneling was unchanged, and even the small electric brass button beneath the desk was still there, used to summon the guards who would escort his new victims to the basement cells.

Bortnikov sat down at his desk and smiled grimly at the heavyset, gray-haired man across from him. "So, Tikhonov, what can you tell me about Holliday and his Cuban friend?" Alexander Tikhonov was director of the FSB's Special Purpose Center, a catchall subdirectorate useful for everything from disposing of bodies to manufacturing letter bombs and arranging traffic "accidents."

"We're assuming that they reached Yekaterinburg. Apparently they stole a crop-dusting plane, which we have since discovered was actually being used to smuggle drugs from Afghanistan."

"Has the owner been arrested, questioned?"

"It was attempted. The man resisted and was killed."

"Too bad. I thought that Holliday was an Army Ranger. How is it that he could fly an airplane?"

"It was the Cuban. His name is Edimburgo Vladimir Cabrera Alfonso. According to our friends in Yasenevo he flew MiGs, among other things." Yasenevo was a town just beyond the Moscow Ring Road and was home to the headquarters of the SVR, Russian Foreign Intelligence.

"Edimburgo?"

"Presumably his mother liked Scotland."

"He speaks Russian?"

"Fluently."

"How did Holliday meet him?"

"This past summer. The Cuban was a river pilot in South Sudan. It is a long story, I'm afraid."

"All right, enough about this peculiar Cuban. Yekaterinburg . . ."

"The stolen aircraft was found in a field a kilometer from the town of Sredneuralsk. There are several taxis there. Presumably they took one to Yekaterinburg."

"Are we sure of that?"

"They booked themselves into the Yekaterinburg Hyatt using the Michael Enright and Simon Toyne passports they bought in Odessa."

"And they weren't caught?"

"As Kafka said, 'Every revolution evaporates and leaves behind only the slime of a new bureaucracy.'" Tikhonov smiled. "The information was received too late. Twenty-four hours too late. They are gone."

"So we are slime now, Tikhonev?" Bortnikov laughed. "In Stalin's day you would have been taken to the basement here and given a single bullet to the back of your head."

"In Stalin's day I never would have said such a thing, tovarich Bortnikov," Tikhonev said, using the old Russian word for "comrade."

"I will have a conversation with Director Skorik about his failure to have identified the use of the passports." Vladimir Skorik was head of the FSB Information Security Center. One of the center's primary functions was to monitor foreign passport use within the Russian Federation. Holliday and the Cuban had apparently slipped through the cracks for a vital twenty-four hours.

"They never visited the church?"

"No. We had two men outside and two in. They never set foot in the church or the museum."

"You're sure?"

"Positive," replied Tikhonev.

Bortnikov leaned back in his chair. "What will they do now, I wonder?"

"If they didn't go to the church, perhaps they've given up," said Tikhonev. "Maybe they're looking for an exit strategy."

"I doubt it. From what I can gather about Holliday he is not a quitter." Bortnikov sighed. "Nevertheless, you may be right. I want their photographs at every border crossing out of the Federation and at every highway roadblock. Cover the airports, domestic and international, as well as the train stations. I want them caught, Tikhonev, and caught soon."

"I think it's crazy," said Holliday. "It would never work." They were standing in the green-tiled basement preparation room of Dimitri Chaplitzky's mortuary. Dimitri's brother, Ivan, their waiter at the Central Hotel in Sredneuralsk the day before, was also with them, along with his dark-suited, dour-faced brother. Dimitri Chaplitzky bore a remarkable resemblance to Ichabod Crane in Walt Disney's version of the Headless Horseman tale. As well as the two brothers, there were two of Dimitri's clients, both dead, both male, both extremely ugly and both turning the color of Stilton cheese.

"No, not crazy, please, misters. My brother, Dimitri, and me are doing it again and again."

"But how do you get past the roadblocks?"

"It is simple, misters. Between here and Moscow there are only three major towns: Perm, Kirov and Nizhniy Novgorod."

"Okay." Holliday nodded. "I get that."

"Yes, okay, okay, but listen to me. To the roadblocks between here and Perm we are a *katafalk*, how you say, hearse taking bodies back to Perm for insertion in the ground or *krematsiya* or whatever family wants. You understand?"

"Yes."

"Between Perm and Kirov we say the body is going to Kirov."

"And from Kirov to Nizhniy Novgorod . . ."

"Yes, yes. We have papers for all places."

"What if they look in the coffins?" Holliday asked.

"They will not."

"Why?"

"It is tradition in Russian Church not to embalm the bodies."

"But we're not dead—yet," Holliday said.

"When we are . . . moving other things we make sure they are not opening the *grob*, the coffin, another way," said Ivan.

"How?"

Ivan nodded to his brother, who went to a tall stainless-steel refrigerator. He opened the door and removed a large plastic bag. He brought the bag across to one of the empty preparation tables and set it down. Holliday and Eddie stared. The bag was full of a variety of human feet in various stages of putrefaction.

"Santa María, madre de Dios," whispered Eddie.

"Feet?" Holliday grimaced.

"Yes, feets," said Ivan, smiling. "Grieving families do not notice they are missing. We also have cousin with shoe store. *Vy ponimaete, gospoda?*"

"Da." Eddie nodded. "We understand."

Anton Pesek, sixty-something son of a high-ranking official in the Czech State Security Service, the *Státní bezpečnost,* and brought up during the Communist era, took the train from Prague to Moscow even though it involved the tedious business of buying a Belarus travel visa and then paying a bribe to the border guards. If it weren't so predictable it might have been funny when the visa ended up being out of order, but as it was the process was simply boring. There had been several terrorist attacks, including a suicide bombing at Domodedovo, Moscow's main airport, but so far no one had seen fit to plant bombs or seek martyrdom with a few pounds of Semtex strapped to their hairless holy chests at Belorussky railway station. Besides which, entering Moscow at the train station was much more discreet than at the airport, where video security abounded. As a professional assassin Pesek had to bear such things in mind.

Anton was a dapper man, slim, a little on the short side, with a well-trimmed Vandyke beard, hair graying at the temples. He had a predilection for slot machines, expensive shoes, American cigarettes, and Bacardi and Coke, the last two severely cut back lately after several queasy and somewhat frightening moments alone in hotel rooms and one emergency room visit while on vacation in Tuscany with his wife and fellow assassin of somewhat dubious sanity, the Canadian Daniella Kay.

Pesek sported a two-inch scar on his neck, usually covered by the collars of his expensive Turnbull & Asser shirts. The scar was the result of a fight he'd had in Venice some years before with Lieutenant Colonel John Holliday. The knife, Pesek's own, had come within half a centimeter of his right carotid artery, and had the blade come any closer or gone any deeper Pesek wouldn't be worrying about his intake of Marlboros or Bacardi and Coke; he'd be occupying his assigned space in the family plot at Cemetery Šárka in Prague. Pleasant enough when the leaves turned in the fall, but it wasn't on his list of preferred destinations.

Holliday was his reason for being in Moscow, but not for revenge. Being injured or killed was part of the pact you made with the Old Man of the Mountain when you took up the assassin's creed. Pesek bore the American no malice—he had in fact saved the man and his cousin Peggy from a fate worse than death in Prague's notorious Pankrác Prison the year before.

This time his assignment came from the chain-smoking priest Thomas Brennan, who ran the Vatican Secret Service for his odious master, His Eminence Cardinal Antonio Niccolo Spada, the Vatican secretary of state. The job had been simultaneously irritating and interesting.

"Holliday is on the trail of a holy relic that he must not be allowed to discover. All we know at the moment is that it involves the Kremlin Romanov Egg, also known as the Uspenski Cathedral Egg. He may well attempt to appropriate the egg."

"You mean steal," Pesek had replied.

"Yes."

"Where is it at present?"

"The Armoury at the Kremlin."

"Buona fortuna a lui." Pesek, who spoke Italian as

fluently as he did English or Russian, laughed. "There is no chance."

"Nevertheless, Mr. Pesek, we would appreciate your assessment of the situation."

"I am an assassin, not a thief, Father Brennan."

"We will pay you extra for your assessment."

"For whatever it is worth."

"For whatever it is worth. Regardless of your report it will be necessary to remove Colonel Holliday from the equation."

"You mean kill him."

"Yes, kill him."

Pesek left the train station by taxi and traveled to the Ritz-Carlton Moscow, where he rented a large corner suite on the top floor that looked down Tverskaya Street and not only gave him a perfect view of the Spassky Tower and the main public entrance to the Kremlin, but also offered a bird's-eye view of the Tverskaya metro entrance, Holliday and his new *černoch* friend.

Pesek settled down in the lavish living room of the suite with a bottle of ice-cold Coca-Cola and two small bottles of Bacardi. What was the old Japanese proverb? *If you sit by the river long enough, you will see the body of your enemy float by.* Eventually Holliday would come, and eventually he would die.

27

John Holliday strolled across the interlocking paving stones of Red Square and tried not to think of the decided queasiness in the pit of his stomach. The reaction didn't come from the faint odor of rotting human feet that he was sure clung to his skin even after three showers. He knew that instead it came from sitting in on too many intelligence briefings, squinting at grainy photographs and trying to identify the types of missiles mounted on carriers paraded through the square on May Day each year, or identifying which bigwigs had appeared on the podium and which ones had been discreetly airbrushed out.

The tall, thick walls of the Kremlin, the stone mass of the government-only GUM store, and the goose-stepping guards in their silly peaked caps marching back and forth like toy soldiers in front of Lenin's tomb were as familiar to him as a recurring nightmare, even though he'd never been here before. It was like a monstrous case of vertigo that was way out of his control.

The Chaplitzky brothers had taken Holliday and Eddie to the rural dacha village of Peredelkino, about twenty kilometers from Moscow. According to the Chaplitskys, the dacha, an outsize log cabin, had once belonged to an obscure Russian writer in the 1970s, but now it looked more like a warehouse, most of the rooms stacked with boxes of iPads, laptops, GPS units, Black-Berrys and other electronic devices.

On the trip to Moscow there had been only one scary moment. A roadblock guard outside of Perm had insisted on opening Eddie's coffin, a flimsy fiberboard creation with a fake satin lining and bronze-colored plastic handles. Lying in the coffin beside him, Holliday could only hold his breath and listen.

Dimitri had pried open the upper half of Eddie's coffin. The stink of the half dozen feet in the open baggie between Eddie's legs and the whispered word *"holera"* from Dimitri had been enough to send the guard away as fast as his legs could carry him. The rest of the trip, while disgusting, was uneventful.

And now here they were at the red beating heart of Ronald Reagan's Axis of Evil. Holliday had never seen the Russians in quite that light, but for an American boy brought up in the fifties and sixties they were certainly the main enemy, with an occasional serving of Chinese as a side dish.

When Holliday was growing up, everything Russian had necessarily been dark, brooding and corrupt, where everyone was named Boris or Igor or Natasha, and the men never shaved. Khrushchev pounded his shoe in the U.N. The Russkies never could have come up with the H-bomb on their own, and *Sputnik* was the greatest blow to the American ego since the British burned down the White House in 1814.

Time, events and a whole lot of reading of history had altered his perspective somewhat, but, as a soldier and sometime intelligence officer, his adult life had always centered on the Soviet Union as the bull's-eye on the target. By the same token, the same time and events had altered America as well, and these days Holliday could almost sympathize with Putin's feeling that the great motherland's grandeur had been tarnished.

Afghanistan had been a travesty; everyone drank far too much vodka, and the entire Russian Federation appeared to be a fiefdom of organized crime. The United States had gone through its own transformation, from the avenging angel that had won World War II and saved the world to the quagmires of Vietnam, reality television, childhood obesity and Wall Street recklessness. Meanwhile, both nations suffered the cultural degradation of McDonald's, Pizza Hut, KFC and IKEA.

As they passed under the high curved arch of the Spassky Tower, it occurred to Holliday that maybe the Internet crazies weren't so far off the mark with their global conspiracies; he found himself thinking of Rex Deus and Kate Sinclair and her sinister forces, of the priest Brennan and the Vatican Secret Service, and of this new group mentioned by the Bulgarian monk—the Order of the Phoenix.

Between them and the other half dozen or so shadowy alphabet organizations he knew about, maybe the world really was controlled by forces beyond the control of the ordinary person. He laughed aloud, his voice echoing from the ancient stone of the tunnel-like entrance to the Kremlin.

"What is so funny?" Eddie asked.

"I was just thinking of Glenn Beck and Sarah Palin fighting back-to-back, beating off the Communist hordes for truth, justice and the American way."

The Cuban snorted. "They should have come to Habana and stood with me for ten hours in the hot sun listening to El Comandante speaking in the Plaza de la Revolución; they would have died of boredom."

"You actually did that?" Holliday asked, surprised. Eddie had never struck him as a dedicated *comunista*.

"Naturalmente." Eddie grinned. "In the old days they gave you lunch in a box and beer to make crowds for the cameras. In later times the police rounded you up and took you there in buses—if you did not go, you didn't work for a week. *¡Viva Fidel!*"

The two men came out from under the arch. On their left were the gardens in front of the two so-called

Nameless Towers of the Kremlin Wall, and on their right was the neoclassical yellow-and-white Presidential Administration Building. For a crisp fall day there were a surprising number of tourists wandering around, some unsupervised, but most in regimented tours led by guides speaking English, Mandarin, Japanese and German. The Cuban approached one of the big-hatted, ornately uniformed guards posing for pictures in front of the main entrance.

"Kak my mozhem poluchit' v Oruzhyei'noi' palate?" Eddie asked. The guard stared at the Cuban, his jaw dropping like an old-fashioned steam shovel in a cartoon. He gave Eddie a stuttering reply, then watched, still openmouthed, as the tall black man rejoined Holliday. "We go past the big cannon and keep to the right until we come to the Armoury. It is a palace with a green roof," Eddie reported.

The czar's cannon turned out to be a gigantic thirty-four-ton bombard with a bronze barrel and one-ton cannonballs from the sixteenth century. It had never been fired. Right beside it was the Czar Bell, two hundred tons of bronze that broke in the casting pit, and was never hung or rung. It seemed a little odd to Holliday that the Russians, not to mention the old-guard Communists of the Soviet Union, would be so proud of such useless white elephants that had no purpose except to express some sort of weird cultural impotence. Who knew? Maybe it was the reason Russians drank so much vodka.

They followed the guard's directions and eventually found the Armoury, which really did have a green roof.

"A question, if you do not mind, *compadre,*" asked Eddie as they stared up at the rococo-style building.

"What is it?"

"What are we doing in this place?"

"We're casing the joint." Holliday smiled.

"*¿Qué?*" Eddie asked.

"Forget it," answered Holliday. "Let's go see this egg everyone's been talking about."

"Tell me, where we are on this Black Tusk thing?" J. Hunter Kokum, the assistant deputy national security adviser, asked. The pale, white-haired man in his two-thousand-dollar funereal Brioni suit leaned back in his antique button leather office chair and stared across Charles Dickens's darkly varnished, honey-topped mahogany writing desk, an object that had cost him almost a million dollars at a Christie's auction and almost caused an international incident. Seated across from him, Whit Havers cleared his throat nervously.

"After completing the Amsterdam assignment, Bone met with our contact there and then went to Yekaterinburg to wait for the targets."

"What happened?"

"According to Bone, they never went near the church at the Ipatiev location. They did meet with a man named

Anton Zukov, the curator of the Ipatiev House museum, which is contained in the basement of the church they built to memorialize the Romanovs."

"This is starting to sound like *Dr. Zhivago*." Kokum grunted.

"Who?" Havers asked.

"Forget it." Kokum sighed. "Before your time." He glanced at a black-tabbed file on his desk. Black tabs were like black American Express cards—not many people had access to them. Whit Havers certainly didn't. He wondered whether it had anything to do with Black Tusk. Kokum looked up from the file as though suddenly remembering that Whit was still in the room. "What happened when they talked to Zukov?"

"Zukov told them that Genrikhovich was a pathological liar, that the Kremlin Egg had never even been in the Hermitage, let alone evacuated from it. Apparently the egg has always been in the Kremlin, except when it was sent out for cleaning and repair. It is there to this day."

"How does Bone know they spoke to Zukov?"

"He followed them, sir."

"And how does he know what was said? Did he bug the place or something?"

"No, sir. Bone questioned Zukov about the matter after Holliday and the other man had left."

"Questioned him?"

Havers cleared his throat uncomfortably. " 'Interrogated' might be a better word, sir."

"Ah," murmured Kokum. "And if this Zukov fellow decides to talk about his interrogation by Mr. Bone, what is he likely to say?"

"Very little," answered Havers. "In fact, it is highly unlikely that he will say anything at all."

"And why is that, Mr. Havers?"

"Because Mr. Zukov now resides in a swamp in the Koptyaki forest about thirty kilometers outside Yekaterinburg, sir."

"Ah," said Kokum, tenting his fingers together. "Your idea?"

"Yes, sir," said Havers.

"You're better at this than I thought, young man."

"Thank you, sir."

"Don't screw it up." The narrow, cold face of the silver-haired man spoke volumes: Fuck up and it will be your head on the block, sonny boy; that's what you've been right from the start: a sacrificial lamb.

"No, sir." Havers felt a faint shiver, and the Harvard-educated, once-upon-a-time Jamaican unaccountably found himself wondering which half of his DNA he'd picked up from his real father, the inimitable Nedrick Samuels. He prayed it wasn't the strand controlling flight under pressure.

* * *

The treasures of the Kremlin Armoury are contained in nine chambers on two floors of the mid-nineteenth-century building. The ten Fabergé eggs are located in the second large room on the second floor of the building. Once again Holliday was struck by the almost masochistic fascination of the old Soviet regime in keeping the ancient, beautiful and incredibly valuable regalia of their oppressors on display, including Ivan the Terrible's throne.

The ten eggs in the Kremlin Armoury collection were all held in a single large display case, arranged on dull brown, felt-covered tiers shaped roughly like an ancient Mayan stepped pyramid. The Kremlin Egg, also known as the Uspenski Cathedral Egg, occupied the highest level—the place where the bloody human sacrifices were usually made—not a far-fetched metaphor when dealing with relics from the last of the czars and the beginnings of the Russian Revolution.

Although the eggs were housed in a two-hundred-year-old building, the lighting within the Armoury was definitely state-of-the-art. Holliday had no doubt that the display case with the egg collection was made of bulletproof glass, and a careful look at the base of the display revealed the wires and leads going to motion detectors or pressure alarms or both. With several thousand well-armed presidential guards and forty-foot-thick walls it would take more than George Clooney and his franchised entourage of crooks to spirit away the Kremlin Egg from this place.

"I have the same question, *compadre*: what are we doing in this place?" Eddie whispered.

Holliday purposefully walked away from the brightly lit egg display and wandered casually into the next room. Neither the guards nor the sprinkling of visitors were paying any attention to them. "Genrikhovich said the Cathedral Egg we just saw on display is a fake."

"And we know Genrikhovich is a liar." Eddie shrugged.

"I don't think he was lying about that," said Holliday.

"Why not?"

"Because he had no reason to. People usually lie for a reason."

"Not if they are *demente*, crazy," answered the Cuban.

"Just for a minute, make the assumption that this time he was telling the truth. The Cathedral Egg is a fake. Why would anyone do such a thing? It makes no sense."

"In the history books it says that *compañero* Stalin sold many things to get foreign currency; why not this *huevo grande,* then? It would have been worth a great deal even then. Perhaps he replaced it with this copy so no one would know."

"I don't think Stalin was that subtle. To him selling off czarist treasures would be a patriotic act. Besides, he didn't come to real power until 1922. I don't think he was worrying about Romanov eggs back then." Holliday shook his head. "It's the only question that counts—why switch out the eggs?"

"The eggs of Fabergé, they all had surprises inside—yes?" Eddie asked.

"That's right." Holliday nodded. "The Trans-Siberian Egg had its own little solid gold train; the Rosebud Egg had a tiny diamond crown and a sapphire pendant; the Imperial Yacht Egg had a tiny platinum replica of the yacht *Standart* inside. What's your point?"

"Perhaps the egg of the Cathedral had a secret within it that someone wanted to keep secret."

"A nice theory, but who do we ask about it?"

"If one thing Genrikhovich said was true, maybe something else was true as well," said Eddie.

"Such as?"

"The man *gospodin* Zukov said was one of Genrikhovich's fantasies. The *bastardo* son of this KGB defector."

"Anatoliy Golitsyn's love child. Anatoliy Ivanov."

28

There were eleven A. Ivanov in the Moscow phone book, but only one of them lived on Sivtsev Vrazhek Lane. Number thirty-six was a two-story nineteenth-century granite block of flats with a leaded mansard roof, built to look like the old aristocratic mansions that had once been common on the street.

The building stood on the corner of Sivtsev Vrazhek and Plotnikov Street, a block from the kilometer-long pedestrian-only section of bustling Arbat Street. In the old days the Arbat had been home to top-ranking government apparatchiks, and in the "new" old days, when the *Mafiya* and the gangs ruled in the old historic neighborhoods close to the Garden Ring, the Arbat was a place of purchased sex, expensive vodka and lines of black Escalades lining the streets like a Muscovite's dream of Fifth Avenue in New York.

At the turn of the nineteenth century it was home to writers, artists and young revolutionaries; at the turn of the twentieth century, gentrification had turned like a grinding wheel, and it was turning into Greenwich Village all over again.

Eddie peered anxiously around at the eighteenth- and nineteenth-century buildings that ran up and down the narrow street. It was dusk now, and the Cuban looked apprehensive. Dealing with a few thugs in a St. Petersburg square was one thing in broad daylight, but something else in the dark of a Moscow night.

White racism was alive and well in Russia, and Moscow was its capital. Groups like the banned Slavic Union, Young Russia and Young Moscow were becoming more powerful each day, and Eddie knew that the longer he stayed in Russia the more dangerous it became, no matter how fluent he was in the language. The groups had become so bold they were even posting their immigrant "kills" on YouTube.

"What apartment is he in, again?" Holliday asked.

Eddie glanced at the scrap of paper from the phone book. "*Número tres.* Three," he said. They stepped up to the main door and pulled it open. In the old days a housekeeper would pop out of her single room at the first creaking of the door, but today there was nothing but a corridor stretching the length of the building.

Number three was on the right. Holliday could hear music playing softly. It sounded like Rimsky-Korsakov, the man who wrote "Flight of the Bumblebee." Holliday could also hear low voices, the tone urgent. He knocked. The voices stopped abruptly, but the music played on for a few seconds longer. Then it too fell silent. Holliday knocked again. He heard another sound; slippers swishing on wood floors.

"Kto eto?"

Holliday gave Eddie the nod. *"Druz'ya Viktora Ostrovskogo,"* answered the Cuban. There was a long pause and then the sound of chains being drawn and latches turned. Holliday touched the side pocket of his jacket. The flat Serdyukov pistol he'd taken from the woman on the Trans-Siberian was still there. He kept his hand in his pocket and popped off the trigger safety. Unless Anatoliy Ivanov wore something better than a grade-three Kevlar vest to answer the door, they were covered.

The door opened. Holliday found himself staring at a man in his late forties or early fifties with salt-and-pepper hair and a long graying beard. He was dressed in a plain black suit with a large silver three-banded pectoral cross around his neck, identifying him as a Russian Orthodox priest. The walls behind the man were covered in icons of every size and type. There was a second man sitting on a worn, faded green corduroy couch, eating something that looked suspiciously like a Big Mac. He looked up, his mouth full of food, and adjusted his wire-rimmed spectacles with one hand, the half-eaten burger in the other.

"So, we are friends again, are we?"

It was Victor Genrikhovich.

*   *   *

Although there were certainly doubtful aspects to Anton Pesek's character, morals, personality and perhaps even his sanity, there was no doubt that he was extremely good at his job. Within five minutes of the appearance of Holliday and his black companion at the mausoleum-like exit to the Teatralnaya metro station just off Red Square, he had taken up a loose surveillance, following them at a distance across the cobbled plaza and through the Spassky Gate into the Kremlin.

Pesek, who hated the cold, was dressed in a gray, down-filled nylon ski jacket, an old-fashioned Russian fur hat, jeans and work boots. In a small backpack slung over his shoulder he carried several pieces of potentially useful equipment that had come in handy on other assignments. He looked like everyone else, and he looked like no one in particular, which is the best way to look when you're following someone.

The Czech assassin followed Holliday and his friend as they meandered through the Kremlin, looking at the sights, but he stopped when they entered the Armoury Museum. Father Brennan had briefed him on the egg and its importance, but there was no way Holliday was going to try to steal it from behind the prisonlike walls of the Kremlin. Instead he stepped inside the small gold-domed St. Lazar Church across from the Armoury's main entrance and waited. He picked up a pamphlet beside a donation box and began to read, one eye on the Armoury entrance.

According to the pamphlet, the Kremlin had originally been called Mastera Gornogo, or Wizard's Mountain—a burial place for wizards, witches and magicians whose spirits were restless. A priest had once cursed the place and, according to legend, was martyred on the spot. Pesek smiled. According to the stories Pesek's father had told him, Comrade Stalin had martyred more than priests in this place.

Reading on, Pesek discovered that in 1750 Elizabeth, empress of Russia, had ordered St. Lazar's Church to be built for the indigents and beggars of the city. Twice each year all the dead beggars who had been kept in a giant icehouse to keep them from decomposing were brought to the church and buried in a single grave. There were so many beggars in Moscow, however, that the ritual was ended after only a dozen years for lack of space, but the church still stood, the cemetery paved over hundreds of years ago, its nameless occupants forgotten.

Twenty minutes after they'd entered the Armoury Museum, Pesek saw Holliday and his friend come out. He followed them again, this time to a taxi stand on the far side of the square. Pesek got his own cab and followed them to the Holiday Inn on Lesnaya Ulitsa, a relatively modern hotel a few miles across the Moskva River to the north. They picked up their key from the desk clerk and headed up the elevator. Pesek waited for a moment, then crossed the plain, brightly lit lobby and approached the clerk. Speaking Russian, he booked a room for himself, expressing an interest in getting a room adjoining the one occupied by the two gentlemen who had just come in, describing them and making his interest clearer by putting two folded hundred-euro bills down on the reception desk. The bills disappeared and he was given the key card to a room on the fifth floor. Pesek didn't fret about the expense of two hotel rooms, or the two-hundred-euro bribe; the Catholic Church had plenty more where that came from.

He found his room, rummaged around in his backpack and eventually found his tiny FM wireless microphone and the headset radio he used. He knelt down beside the adjoining door, switched on the microphone and eased it forward under the doorsill, then took the headphones back to the comfortable-looking bed and lay down. He turned on the headphone radio, tuned it to the bottom of the FM dial and slipped the headset over his ears.

Pesek could clearly hear the quick flipping of pages. There was a pause and then the black man's voice came clearly through the headset.

"There are many men with that name here. They are all listed as A. Ivanov."

"No Anatoliy Ivanov?"

"No, but there is only one of the names listed on

Peryeulok Sivtsev Vrazhek—number thirty-six Sivtsev Vrazhek Lane."

"Does it give an apartment number?"

"Three."

"That has to be the one."

"In Russian Vrazhek is meaning *una arroyo*."

"Stream?"

"*Sí.* In the olden days there would have been such a stream there. In Habana there are many places like this—streams covered over and turned to sewers. Do we go and see this man?"

"Yes, but I need a shower and some dinner first. I'm starving."

Pesek smiled. He slipped off the headphones and sat up on the edge of the bed. He had what he needed now, except for one last vital element.

The assassin stood up, removed the listening device, then put it and the headphones back in his knapsack. He slipped on his ski jacket and left the room. Pesek then headed downstairs, picked up a taxi from the rank near the door and told the driver to take him to the Central Bus Terminal near the Shcholkovskaya metro station. He settled back in the comfortable leather seat of the Avtoframos Thalia, a Russian-made Renault, feeling quite pleased with himself. For the present, at least, things seemed to be going quite well.

For being in a profession renowned for its short life spans, Anton Pesek had done quite well for himself over a career covering an astounding four decades. He had a generous retirement fund spread over seven banks and five countries; a beautiful albeit somewhat compulsively murderous wife, Daniella Kay; a condominium in Vancouver, Canada, close to the Southlands so Daniella could ride her beloved Dutch Warmblood, Bohemian Rhapsody; an immense and lavish condominium apartment on Old Town Square in the center of Prague; a villa in Tuscany; and another condominium in the tiny village of Mougins in the Alpes Maritimes, fifteen minutes from Cannes and the slot machines of his favorite casino, La Croisette.

While Pesek had developed few if any real friendships over those four decades, he had accumulated a remarkable number of contacts, acquaintances, people who knew people and people he'd done favors for at one time or another. It was one of those people he was visiting now.

Three days a week Yuri Otrepyev ran a small souvenir booth next to the bus station, mostly selling cheap plastic icons and matryoshka nesting dolls, and T-shirts with the word "Moscow" stenciled on them in Cyrillic writing. His market was almost entirely made up of hayseed country bumpkins on their way home after a visit to the big city.

Each Wednesday afternoon, however, as Pesek knew, Yuri's uncle, Grigory Otrepyev, the real owner of the booth, would leave his last shift at the Izhevsk Mechanical Plant and would take the overnight train to Moscow, arriving at noon on Thursday. He would then take over the booth's operations until Sunday afternoon, when he would ride the train back to Izhevsk and his poorly paid job as an inventory clerk in the huge factory.

On the surface it seemed ludicrous for a man in his sixties who barely had a job at all to travel so far to operate a souvenir booth that rarely did much more than break even most months, but like many things in Russia, things weren't always what they seemed. During his four days in the booth Grigory Otrepyev generally netted the equivalent of between three and five thousand American dollars—roughly six times the net monthly salary of an Aeroflot pilot. Otrepyev was the chief inventory clerk in the largest combat weapons factory in Russia, and the suitcase he carried with him to Moscow each week was filled with the factory's stock-in-trade.

The taxi dropped Pesek off at the Central Bus Terminal, and he made a pretense of going into the big modern terminal. He came out again a moment later and wandered around the cluster of booths to the left of the entrance. Most of them sold souvenirs, but a few sold soft drinks, snacks and sandwiches for travelers about to go on their way. He purchased a plastic bottle of Polustrovo water and sipped it as he meandered among the booths. He finally stopped in front of Otrepyev's establishment, by no means the largest one at the bus terminal.

Grigory Otrepyev bore a remarkable resemblance to

Mr. Toad of *The Wind in the Willows*. He was short and squat, with wide, rubbery lips, a bulbous nose and slightly bulging eyes. The resemblance was heightened by the old curved pipe inevitably clamped between his teeth that constantly sent up a cloud of choking smoke that had long ago given Otrepyev a permanent squint in his right eye. To top things off, the man's complexion was cratered with pockmarks like the surface of an asteroid, and he made only the most basic passes with a razor at the white stubble on his cheeks and chin.

"I'm looking for a matryoshka doll," said Pesek in Russian.

"As you can see, *gospodin*, I have many such dolls," answered Otrepyev, making a sweeping gesture over his stock and grinning around the yellowed stem of his pipe. Even from six feet away behind the counter, the man smelled like an overflowing ashtray. "Do you have any particular size doll in mind?"

"I thought that today I would like a nine-millimeter doll," said Pesek, pitching his voice softly. Otrepyev reached out and picked up a doll. "I have a rather nice Grach in stock. As you can see, it is very nice."

"How heavy?"

"Point nine seven of a kilogram."

"I think I would like something lighter today."

Otrepyev put down the first doll and randomly picked up another. "What about the PMM Makarov. Just point seven six of a kilogram?"

"Out-of-date, and it has a tendency to jam," said Pesek.

"Then perhaps I could interest you in our Baghira doll. Nine-millimeter Parabellum, fifteen-round capacity, the same weight as the Makarov and with a slope return/buffer mechanism to prevent shock and increase accuracy."

"How much?" Pesek asked.

"Eight hundred euros," said the Russian, squinting at Pesek. Eight hundred euros, almost twelve hundred U.S. dollars.

"Expensive," commented Pesek.

"Worth it." The Russian shrugged.

"I'll take it," said Pesek.

"Ammunition?"

"A single magazine." If fifteen rounds wasn't enough he was dead anyway. He took out his wallet, removed four yellow two-hundred-euro notes and folded them into a small rectangle that fit between his index and middle fingers and against his palm. Otrepyev picked up a nesting doll, bent down to get a bag from beneath the counter and rose a few seconds later, handing the plastic bag to Pesek. For his part the Czech assassin reached out and shook the Russian's hand, passing the four folded notes in a single rapid move.

"Good doing business with you again," said Otrepyev.

Pesek nodded, smiling. "And you," he replied. He checked his watch. Forty minutes had passed since he'd left the hotel on Lesnaya Ulitsa. He turned away from the booth, went to the taxi rank in front of the terminal and headed for 36 Sivtsev Vrazhek Lane.

29

Genrikhovich stared at them, chewing on the hamburger. Holliday stared back, feeling the taste of bile rising in his throat along with his anger. Genrikhovich swallowed and smiled.

"You find this amusing?" Holliday asked.

"You are here, aren't you?" Genrikhovich said blithely, taking another bite of his Big Mac, the Russian version of special sauce oozing out of the bun and onto his fingers.

"Not for long, pal," said Holliday, bitterness in his tone. "I went along with your goose chase because you mentioned the name of someone I admired and respected. I neither admire nor respect you, Mr. Genrikhovich; in fact, I have it on good authority that you're something of a pathological liar."

The Orthodox priest who had answered the door stared at Holliday. *"Patologicheskii' lzhets,"* translated Eddie.

"I understand English quite well, thank you. I am just surprised he said it," answered the priest.

Genrikhovich popped the last of the Big Mac into his mouth, chewed briefly, licked his fingers and swallowed noisily. He picked up a napkin from the coffee table in front of the couch, then wiped his mouth with it and cleared his throat. "Father Anatoliy Ivanov, may I introduce you to Colonel John Henry Holliday and his friend Eduardo Vladimir Cabrera Alfonso."

"Edimburgo, not Eduardo," said the Cuban.

"I beg your pardon," Genrikhovich said.

"Why did you leave the train like that?" Holliday asked bluntly.

"I was afraid, of course," said Genrikhovich with a languid shrug. "Why don't you sit down and we'll discuss the situation." He gestured toward a pair of old, worn upholstered chairs.

"I'll stand for now," said Holliday. "What were you afraid of?"

"I live in Russia, Colonel Holliday, and in Russia fear is a way of life."

"Don't feed me that kind of old crap, and don't try to change the subject. What were you afraid of?"

Genrikhovich sighed and then let out a little belch. "I overheard the *provodnitsa* on the train talking to the . . . *poezda,* the conductor, about you and your black friend. She was suspicious. They were going to have the police waiting for you in Perm."

"But not you," said Holliday bitterly.

"I had to save myself," aid Genrikhovich. "I could not allow myself to be taken by the FSB. They would have tortured me, and I know too much."

"About Rasputin and the rest of the crap you were feeding me? Don't make me laugh," said Holliday. "You're a nutcase, plain and simple."

"Would a nutcase, as you call me, have known of your relationship with Rodrigues the monk, or your position within the Templars? I think not, Colonel."

"But you were willing to feed Eddie and me to the dogs," said Holliday.

"It was a question of priorities." The Russian shrugged again. "Besides, it doesn't matter now. You are here, and now we can proceed."

Holliday let out an exasperated sigh and dropped down into one of the upholstered chairs. He kept his hand on the automatic in the pocket of his jacket. Something was still bothering him about the Russian, but he couldn't quite put his finger on it. "Proceed with what?" he asked as Eddie sat down in the chair beside him.

"Our holy quest, of course." Genrikhovich smiled. It occurred to Holliday that perhaps the Russian was more than just a nutcase and a liar; from the crazed look in his eyes he could well be completely, right-out-of-his-mind, barking insane. His expression made him look like a cross between a Bible-thumping evangelical preacher and a greed mad Scrooge McDuck.

There was a soft clicking sound from the front door; somebody was slipping the lock with a credit card. Holliday turned his head sharply but it was too late; the door burst open and Anton Pesek appeared, an automatic pistol held in a two-handed grip, his sharp eyes scanning the living room of the apartment. Without turning, the Czech killer lifted his foot and kicked backward, closing the door behind him. He twitched the weapon toward Father Ivanov, who was still standing to the left of the couch occupied by Genrikhovich.

"Sidet', svyashchennik," the Czech ordered. The priest did as he was told and sat down on the couch beside Genrikhovich.

Genrikhovich looked as though he were about to be sick. "FSB," he whispered, gagging.

"No such luck," said Holliday, recognizing the intruder. "Mr. Pesek here is just a run-of-the-mill contract killer."

"You know this man?" Genrikhovich asked, goggle-eyed. His complexion had turned gray with terror, beads of sweat putting a sheen of moisture on his forehead.

"Of course he knows me," said Pesek, smiling. "I saved his life not too long ago. We are the best of friends. Isn't that right, Colonel?"

"Not anymore." Holliday blindly squeezed the trigger of the Serdyukov in his pocket. The automatic made a sound like a loudly barking dog. A smoldering hole appeared in Holliday's jacket, and the single round gouged a trough like a giant ice-cream scoop in the left side of Anton Pesek's head from his eye socket to the back of his skull.

Blood and brains fountained, spraying the ceiling and the wall behind the assassin, spattering against the mounted icons. Pesek slipped to the floor like a puppet with its strings cut. Once upon a time Holliday had slit this man's throat on a tossing boat in Venice Lagoon, but this time he was dead for good.

There was a long, stunned silence in the room. The only thing left of the gunshot was the ringing in Holliday's ears. Bizarrely, a quote from *The Good, the Bad and the Ugly* popped into his mind: "When you have to shoot, shoot—don't talk."

"You fool! You stupid American fool! You killed him!" Genrikhovich moaned.

"I could have let him kill you," said Holliday. "Would you have liked that better?"

"He was coming for you, not for me!"

"You seem awfully sure of yourself."

"I am sure!"

"Why?"

"Because your . . ." Genrikhovich stopped abruptly.

"Because why?" Holliday asked.

The Russian shook his head. "There is no reason, but you said you knew this man, and I have never seen him before. You must have been his target." Genrikhovich folded his arms across his chest and closed his mouth firmly. The discussion was clearly over.

Ivanov the priest continued to stare at the crumpled corpse on the floor as though it were as hypnotic as a weaving cobra in a basket. Eddie sat in his chair for a moment, then stood and left the room.

Holliday got up from his chair, crossed to the body and squatted down, careful to keep out of the blood-and-muck puddle behind what was left of Pesek's shattered skull. He quickly went through the man's pockets and came up with a passport, a wallet stuffed with euros and a cell phone.

The phone was obviously a throwaway—it had only two numbers in its directory, one with a 420 country code and a 2 area code—Prague. The other had a country code and no area code: 39. There was only one country in the world with that prefix.

"He was working for the Vatican," said Holliday.

"Why would he be doing such a thing?" asked Genrikhovich.

"The Vatican does not employ assassins," said Ivanov, shocked.

"You are very naive if you believe that, Father," said Holliday. "This man has tried to kill me before. The Vatican does whatever it needs to do to protect itself. They also have a long-standing quarrel with me."

"The Vatican does not have people killed," said the

Orthodox priest firmly. "It goes against everything that any Christian faith stands for."

"You have never heard of the Assassini? They date back to Pope Callixtus and the Borgias."

"They are a myth," said the priest.

"The man on your floor is no myth." Holliday grunted, rolling the body over and taking the automatic out of Pesek's hand.

"This is madness," said Genrikhovich.

Eddie reappeared with a towel in one hand and a large plastic garbage bag in the other. "I have emptied the *frío*, the refrigerator," said the Cuban.

"Good thinking." Holliday nodded.

"Why have you emptied my refrigerator?" the priest asked, looking at the Cuban strangely.

Instead of answering, Eddie went and knelt down beside Holliday. He eased the towel around Pesek's ruined head and wrapped the rest of the towel around the face and neck. He then spread out the plastic bag beside him, and together he and Holliday lifted the dead man's shoulders onto it. Without speaking the two men each grabbed one of the dead man's feet and dragged him out of the room, the towel and the plastic bag keeping too much mess from spreading across the old pinewood floor. Genrikhovich and the priest followed them as they dragged the body into the kitchen.

The door to Ivanov's refrigerator was sagging open. Everything had been removed, including the shelves, and had been laid out on the narrow counters. Holliday and Eddie manhandled Pesek's body in front of the refrigerator and then wrestled it into a sitting position.

"What are you doing!?" Ivanov asked, gazing at the piles of food stacked around the small room.

"Putting the body inside." Holliday grunted as they lifted Pesek's shoulders, pushing his ruined, towel-covered head and his upper body into the refrigerator. They pushed a little more until they'd folded the dead man's legs underneath his buttocks and squeezed in the dangling left arm. Panting with the effort, Holliday and Eddie closed the door and leaned on it until the latch clicked.

"What have you done?" Genrikhovich whispered.

"We've bought ourselves some time," said Holliday. There was a tea towel hanging over the bar of the stove and he wiped his hands on it. "It's October. If you keep the heat off in the apartment and the refrigerator on, the body's not going to start to stink for a while. It won't stop decomposition forever, but maybe long enough for us to get away."

"Get away?" Ivanov said. "This is where I live! We must call the police! It was self-defense; I will testify to it."

"Really?" Holliday said. "As I understand it, you're the son of one of the most infamous defectors in KGB history, and there's a corpse with half its head blown off in your apartment. Do you really want to advertise that fact? Your friend Genrikhovich here is already wanted by the FSB, and so are Eddie and I. We're both in this country on fake passports, which, by definition, makes us spies—you really want to call the Moscow police about this? The public prosecutor would hand you over to the ghouls in the Lubyanka within five seconds. Do you really want that, Father Ivanov?"

"I am afraid he's right," said Genrikhovich. "I am very sorry, Anatoliy."

"But I was so close!" the priest said. "I'm sure I have it right this time. The coins prove it!"

"What coins?" Holliday asked.

"Come with me," said the priest. He gave a last long look at the closed refrigerator and then turned back to the living room. There was a large gilt-and-silver icon on tin of the Virgin Mary and the Christ child hanging on the wall next to the couch. Ivanov took it down, revealing a strip coin holder taped to the back. He showed the strip of coins to Holliday and Eddie, his glance occasionally slipping toward the mess on the floor and the wall made by the exploded remains of Anton Pesek's head.

There were ten coins, all gold, all the size of a quarter, all showing the profile of a man with long curling hair. "Who is he?" Holliday asked.

"Constantine the Eleventh, Dragasēs Palaiologos," said the priest.

"Is that supposed to mean something to me?"

"He was the last emperor of the Byzantines," said the priest. "When his daughter Sophia married Ivan the Terrible, Constantine gave him his great library as a gift so it would not fall into the hands of the Vatican."

"And?"

"The great library was Sophia's dowry. It was brought here."

"Here as in Russia?"

"Moscow," said the priest.

"According to experts it was buried in an underground chamber beneath the Kremlin."

"And is hasn't been found?"

"Stalin looked for it, Khrushchev looked for it and so did Yeltsin and Gorbachev. Now Putin searches for it," said Genrikhovich. "If Putin and his cronies find it they will have the power to destroy the Western world."

"Why?"

"It holds the secret of the fifth sword," said the Russian. "Everything we have been looking for."

"And you think you've found it?"

"Not yet," said Genrikhovich. "But we are very close. We have found the final clue."

"We have found the hidden maps of Ignatius Yakovlevich Stelletskii, of course," said Ivanov.

"Oh, God," muttered Holliday, "not another Russian name."

30

"Okay," said Holliday, "I'll bite. Who the hell is Ignatius Yakovlevich Stelletskii?"

"*Father* Ignatius Stelletskii was a priest, like myself and like his father before him. He was born in 1878 in the Ukraine."

"In 1878? Is this going to be a long story?" Holliday asked. "Because if it is, maybe you should tell it somewhere else; somebody may have heard the shot and called the police. We should be on our way out of here pretty soon; there's blood all over the place and a body in the refrigerator."

"Nobody actually *calls* the police in Moscow because they heard a gunshot, Colonel," Genrikhovich said with a grunt. "Nobody wants to get involved in such things, believe me."

"Keep it short anyway," said Holliday.

Ivanov nodded, casting a wary glance at the mess on the floor and walls. "Father Stelletskii went to the Kiev

257

Seminary. He was a brilliant scholar, especially in the subjects of history and scriptural archaeology. In 1906, less than a year after he graduated, he was teaching history and geography at the Russian-Arab Seminary in Nazareth. While he was there he became convinced from his studies that Christ himself had written his own gospel and that it had been secretly taken from Judea by Joseph of Arimathea."

"The Grail myths," said Holliday.

"Yes," said Ivanov, enthusiasm creeping into his tone despite the gore all around him. "Father Stelletskii could never understand why any great significance should be attached to a cup Jesus drank from at the Last Supper. Why not a plate, a bowl, a jug or some other vessel? In Aramaic, the language both spoken and written during the time of Christ, the masculine word for 'cup' is *kas*. In its written form it is often confused with *kat,* or sometimes *ktaa,* meaning 'book.' According to Father Stelletskii, Joseph took the book to Constantinople, where it eventually came into the possession of the Latin patriarch of Constantinople. After the Byzantines recaptured the holy city, the book became part of the hoard of Constantine the Eleventh, the last Byzantine emperor. When the Turk Sultan Mahomet the Second attacked the city in 1481, Constantine packed up his great library, including the book, and dispatched it to Moscow in the care of his niece Sophia—who became the grandmother of Ivan the Terrible." The priest paused. Eddie went to the front window of the apartment and peeled back the heavy velvet curtain slightly. He turned back to Holliday.

"I think we must hurry, *compañero*; I do not like the sound of things in the street."

"What is it?" Holliday asked.

"There is nothing. That is what is making me nervous. I do not like it."

"Hurry it up," said Holliday to the priest.

"When Ivan built the Kremlin he made a special place for the books and treasures from Constantinople. As time went on, more and more rooms and passages were built beneath the Kremlin. The Kremlin itself changed from wood to brick and stone. The great library was lost. It has been lost for more than five hundred years, and everyone has looked for it."

"Including your Father Stelletskii," said Holliday.

"In 1912 Father Stelletskii organized the Commission for the Study of Underground Antiquities, which was built to study the underground tunnels of Moscow. He asked for permission to dig beneath the Kremlin, but he was not permitted to. In 1914 he discovered Dabelov's catalog of the library of Ivan the Terrible, but further work was cut short by World War One and then the Russian Revolution. Father Stelletskii returned to the Ukraine and to Kiev. He continually petitioned the government to dig beneath the Kremlin, and finally in 1929 Stalin gave his permission—the thought of the richness of the hoard spurring his interest. The first dig began in 1933 but nothing was found. The Second World War stopped any further digs at the Kremlin, and Father Stelletskii fell ill. He died shortly after the war, but Stalin had the Moscow Archaeological Institute continue searching up until his death. Khrushchev continued the search, as did Yeltsin, Gorbachev and now Putin."

"And found nothing," said Holliday.

"And found nothing." Ivanov nodded.

"Maybe because there was nothing to find," Holliday said.

"Or maybe because they did not have Father Stelletskii's maps to guide them," said Genrikhovich.

"Señores, por favor," said Eddie, still standing by the window, the anxiety clear in his voice now.

"You have the maps?" Holliday said.

"They were hidden at the seminary in Kiev. I discovered them hidden there when I was a student. I took up the good father's work."

"Where are the maps?"

"Not here." Genrikhovich smiled.

"Show me," said Holliday.

"Señores, ¡os suplico!" Eddie implored.

He could hear, muffled by the distance, the strange warbling of approaching sirens. Ivanov went back into the kitchen and filled a knapsack with bottled water and cans of food, then led them out of the apartment and down a long corridor leading to a rear exit. The exit opened onto Kaloshin Alley, the narrow side street running at right angles to Sivtsev Vrazhek Lane. Ivanov's car, an old Lada, was parked in a small vacant lot behind his building. A few moments later, with the sirens coming closer, they were moving south through the crowded streets of nighttime Moscow, headed toward the Kremlin.

Brinsley Whitman Havers III, deputy assistant to the deputy national security adviser, deplaned at Moscow's Domodedovo International Airport on the afternoon United Airlines flight from Washington Dulles with only his briefcase and an overnight bag. He had spent the entire flight in his first-class seat touching his suit jacket, feeling the weight of his newly minted diplomatic passport in his inside pocket, his brain buzzing with the mental shock and awe of suddenly being thrust into the world of international intrigue, and trying to look cool and detached about his adventure at the same time, and failing miserably.

An embassy marine met him at customs, took him to a waiting Escalade and whisked him off to the walled blockhouse-style embassy in the Presnensky district in the city center. Thirty-five minutes after arriving in Moscow, Whit Havers, seated behind tinted bulletproof glass, was whisked through the gates of Bolshoy Deviatinsky Pereulok No. 8.

A check of his "mailbox" on the National Security Agency's internal computer Web site showed that his contact had requested a face-to-face at some place called Coffee Mania in the Neglinnaya Plaza on Trubnaya Square at nine o'clock that evening. Whit, whose foreign travel outside of Jamaica and the D.C. area consisted of a two-day trip to Toronto for a G8 summit, was beside himself with excitement, but he managed to give the countersignal agreeing to the contact. Whit Havers was going to have a meeting with an "asset" that he was "running." He called the transport pool, arranged for a driver and an unmarked car for later in the evening, and found his way to the embassy cafeteria for a celebratory banana muffin and a nonfat latte.

At seven forty-five the unmarked, a last year's tan-colored Dodge Caravan that stood out like Donald Trump in a Yugo, took Whit across town to Trubnaya Square. Neglinnaya Plaza turned out to be that uniquely European invention, the vertical mall. A perfectly good eighteenth- or nineteenth-century building was demolished and something that was generally an architect's version of a rocket ship or a seven-story twenty-fifth-century blender was raised into the cavity like a glittering tooth, generally created with a lot of brushed steel and glittering glass. Thirty or forty high-end, brand-name boutiques were crammed into the building, and the place began to print money. The real value of the property, of course, was the four levels of underground parking, which the plaza charged an arm and a leg for, parking in Moscow having a street value roughly on a par with high-grade cocaine.

Coffee Mania was half Starbucks, half tapas restaurant, with as many food choices as there were sizes of various coffees. There were at least thirty different sandwiches and twenty-odd desserts listed on the chalkboard menu hanging over the long zinc-and–black marble bar. The clientele were young, rich and dressed like they'd stepped out of an L.A. television show. The music droning through the speakers was some kind of Euro-trance that Whit didn't recognize.

Even though Whit arrived at exactly eight, Bone was there before him, standing out for his drabness of dress as much as his age. He was wearing a gray wool overcoat, corduroy pants that would have looked better on someone weeding his garden and a pair of old brown shoes. There was a black sports bag at his feet. Whit, as usual, was head-to-toe Armani. Except for the dusky color of his skin he fit right into the Coffee Mania crowd. He sat down opposite Bone in the tiny booth at the back of the café.

"Black Tusk," said Whit, giving the recognition code and feeling a little foolish.

"You're the one running me?" Bone said, looking surprised. "A bit young, aren't you, lad?"

"I'm old enough."

"Why are you here? I would have thought they'd use someone local."

"The powers that be decided they want this run closely."

"I thought your people frowned on face-to-face meetings," said Bone.

"They've gone back to old tradecraft; cell phones and computers are too easy to monitor."

"Would you like some coffee?" Bone asked, gesturing toward the cup on the table in front of him. "It's very good. Much better than the weasel's pee we get at home."

Whit had the feeling that the meeting was getting away from him. It was surreal enough for him to be sitting in a Moscow café discussing coffee with a professional assassin without feeling as though he had no business being there and that Bone was secretly laughing up his sleeve at him.

"You ask a lot of questions," he said, trying to make his voice sound crisp and severe. It came out like a whining complaint.

"If you don't ask questions you don't get answers, and for a man in my line of work, not having answers when you need them can be fatal."

"Well, it's my turn to ask them," said Whit.

"Fire away then, lad."

"And I'd appreciate it if you didn't call me 'lad.'"

"All right, then, Agent X, whatever you like."

"We haven't heard from you since Amsterdam."

"I had nothing to say."

"And now?"

"Your intelligence is poor. There was nothing in Yekaterinburg. It was fluff and flummery. The real objective should have been the Russian, Genrikhovich. He got off the train early, leaving Holliday and the other to fend for themselves. I followed Genrikhovich rather than the American."

"That wasn't the protocol we established," said Whit.

"It was the course of action I deemed would get the best results."

"And has it?"

"I believe so." Bone nodded. He took a sip of his coffee.

"Do you have any idea where Holliday is?"

"He should be here within the next half hour or so."

"Here?" Whit asked, bewildered.

"Look over my right shoulder. Across the square. There are the ruins of an old mansion. A few people park their cars there illegally. Once upon a time the mansion was owned by a member of the Russian nobility who was carrying on an affair with the princess who lived in the palace next door, which is now a department store. To facilitate the affair he dug a tunnel from the basement of the mansion to the palace."

"What does this have to do with Holliday?" Whit asked.

"For the last four nights, between eight thirty and nine p.m., Genrikhovich and an Orthodox priest named Anatoliy Ivanov have parked a green 1995 Lada Niva Cossack in the lot of the remains of the mansion. They get out of the car and disappear into the ruins. I have ascertained that they shift a large slab of paving stone that leads down into the old passageway. From there they make their way into one of the original Trubnaya subway maintenance tunnels."

"And why is this important?"

"I have no idea, except that according to my information the priest is also a member of the Moscow Archaeological Institute. More to the point, before I came here I watched Holliday and the black man go into the apartment where the priest lives."

"You think Holliday will come here?"

"I'm almost certain of it. According to you, Holliday is searching for something; clearly so are Genrikhovich and the priest."

Whit was staring over Bone's shoulder. His eyes were on the ruins of the old building on the far side of the square. As he watched, a dark-colored Lada bumped up off the street and onto an empty patch of ground. "The car just pulled in," Whit said, his voice low.

"Excellent," said Bone, smiling pleasantly. He slid out of the booth and bent down to pick up the sports bag. "Care to join me?"

"No. I don't think so," said Whit.

"I thought not," said Bone. "Ta-ta then. I'll give you a ring when it's all over, shall I?"

"Yes," said Whit, suddenly feeling unaccountably ashamed of himself. "Please."

"No bother," said Bone. "No bother at all."

31

"His name was Count Peter Alekseyevich Pahlen, and the princess who spent her summers in the palace next door was named Caroline of Hesse-Darmstadt," said Father Ivanov as they climbed down the rusty iron rungs of the ladder. "The tunnel facilitated their affair and kept them from being discovered by the princess's husband. Not a nice man, by all accounts."

Above them Genrikhovich slid the paving stone over the opening. The only light now came from the big flashlight Ivanov was carrying in his free hand as they went down the ladder.

"Is any of this important?" Holliday asked, directly above the priest.

"Not really."

"Then let's forget about them; I've got enough Russian names floating around in my head."

"I thought you were a historian," answered Ivanov.

"I am," said Holliday. "But not a historian of *everything*."

They reached the bottom of the ladder. Eddie came down the ladder next, followed by Genrikhovich. Ivanov turned on several large portable lanterns and the chamber was flooded with light. Holliday found himself in a low-ceilinged room a little larger than a jail cell. At the far end of the oversize cell there was a very narrow arched brick passageway. The smell emanating from beyond the archway was indescribably foul.

In the chamber there was a bench with a box of leather workman's utility belts, each equipped with a large climber's hammer, coiled rope and a short pry bar. A pile of hip waders stood in one corner, and spikes in a brick wall were hung with a number of Tyvek biological suits, complete with hoods. Each suit had a half-mask respirator with it.

There was a box of hard hats fitted with miner's lamps in a rotting cardboard box on the floor beneath the bench, and several folding spades and small pickaxes.

"You seem well equipped," commented Holliday.

"I have been doing this for six years, on and off." Ivanov shrugged. "I have accumulated some experience." He slipped off the knapsack full of bottled water and food and then began to strip off his outer clothes. "A few of the Diggers have helped me from time to time; that is why I have the extra equipment."

"Diggers?" Holliday asked.

"That is what they call themselves," said the priest fondly. "Diggers of the Underground Planet. Their leader is a man named Vadim Mikhailov; he has been exploring underneath the streets of Moscow for twenty years. He is a devout Orthodox and has helped me greatly, teaching me the 'tricks of the trade,' as he calls them, and warning me of the things to watch out for."

"You might be surprised." Ivanov smiled. He picked up the folding shovel and clipped it to his utility belt, then handed Holliday the short-handled pickax. "Last month the FSB discovered an underground mosque and three hundred illegal aliens in an underground bunker where the Rossiya Hotel used to be."

The priest took a very up-to-date Magellan eXplorist 610 GPS unit out of his knapsack, slung the bag over his shoulder, then took one of the hard hats out of the box.

"Father Stelletskii's maps?" Holliday asked.

"On microchips." Ivanov nodded.

"For an Orthodox priest you have some unorthodox methods."

"Even the Church must keep up with the times, Colonel."

A few moments later, when everyone else was ready, Ivanov flipped on the miner's light, adjusted his respirator mask so that it covered his nose and mouth, and led the way into the narrow, arched brick passageway.

Holliday stayed close behind Ivanov with Eddie and Genrikhovich. Even with the respirator masks the stink of rotting waste was almost overpowering, and Holliday's eyes began to water at the sting of ammonia seeping from the walls. The corridor was barely wide enough to allow a man passage, and every few yards the light on Holliday's hard hat caught ominous bulges in the bricks, as though some terrible pressure were building up behind them.

The bricks making up the wall were covered with a gray-green, mucuslike substance, and thin icicles of dripping lime hung from above them like the brittle bones of gigantic spiders. The floor beneath their feet seemed made of some soft, almost spongy gravel, and where the floor met the walls there was a ridge of brownish, tarry goo.

"It is just *un poco claustrofóbico* in this place, no?"

"Just a little," agreed Holliday.

The passage went straight for what seemed like about two hundred yards and then suddenly dropped down a long slope and narrowed so much they had to turn sideways, their faces no more than a few inches away from the slime on the walls. The spongy footing had gone, replaced now by a gruesomely warm, thick brown semiliquid the consistency of porridge.

"Esto es repugnante." Eddie groaned.

"It's even worse than the sewers in St. Petersburg."

Suddenly something big, muscular and brown struck

Holliday on the shoulder, skittered across his back and dropped down into the stagnant filth at Eddie's feet. The Cuban lashed out hard, bellowing in horror, connecting with the creature and sending it spinning against the wall. It recovered and raced off the way they had come. Holliday shuddered; he could still feel the harsh, bristled fur of the rodent against his face and see the gray, whipping tail lashing as it leaped onto his shoulder. From the feel as it hit him Holliday figured it must have weighed close to ten pounds.

"*¡Carajo!*" Eddie moaned. "*¡Odio las ratas de mierda!*"

"They become very large beneath the streets," called back Ivanov, his voice muffled by the respirator. "Down here there is a great deal to eat."

"Which is why there are no *ratas* in Habana anymore," said Eddie. "There is *nothing* for them to eat."

They continued slipping through the cracklike passageway for another hundred yards or so and then the terrain changed again. The passage widened and the roof above their heads was stone instead of brick. The muck beneath their feet deepened, and every few steps Holliday felt something give beneath his feet. Throughout his career he'd gone through every kind of terrain, from deserts to jungles and rain forests, but he'd never traveled over ground like this before.

The passage ended in a brick wall thickly covered by a hardened carapace of slime that had turned into a greenish yellow solid and dripped down into the swampy sewage muck at their feet like candle wax. There was a narrow hole in the wall, barely large enough for a small man like Ivanov to wriggle through.

"We'll have to make it bigger," said the priest. He unlimbered the spade from his belt, unfolded it and began to strike the wall. Holliday stepped up and hammered the pickax into a spot on the wall where the mortar had long since disappeared and pulled.

"Just so long as there are no more *ratas*," said Eddie, taking the climber's hammer off his belt.

Genrikhovich laughed hollowly behind his mask. "You're standing up to your knees in a thousand years of Russian piss, shit and vomit and you're worried about a few rats?"

It took them twenty minutes. The straw in the bricks had rotted away years before, and the bricks themselves crumbled like old cheese. With each brick the stench became more intense. Pausing for a moment, Holliday heard a faint skittering, whispering sound, like the distant hard patter of raindrops on an iron roof.

"What the hell is that?" Holliday whispered, turning his ear toward the barely discernible sound. It was not only growing louder by the second, but there was something else about the noise—it was getting stronger, a summer shower growing first to a rolling thunderstorm and then to a hurricane of sound; whispering voices raised to chattering conversations and finally to the screams of hell-racked banshees. Something terrible was coming.

"Moi dorogoi Hrista!" Ivanov whispered.

"I do not like this, *compadre*," said Eddie. "Whatever it is, it is very, very bad for us, I think, no?"

"Yes," agreed Holliday. Some sudden intuition of horror shuddered through him. He dropped the pickax. "Get back from the hole!" he ordered. "Keep away from the walls; stand in the center of the crap on the floor! Now!"

Within seconds all four men were gathered in a small, tight group, back-to-back in the muck. Ahead of the sound came a grotesque wave of odor, a filthy, poisonous attar of oily stench.

Horrified, Holliday trained his miner's lamp on the newly enlarged hole in the brick wall and suddenly he saw a foaming, roiling mass of gray and white come pouring through it. The wave began to thicken and spread, a thickening tongue lolling from the hole, then spreading upward as well, slipping up the walls and the roof of the passageway but staying away from the liquefied stream in the middle.

Individually each member of the terrible army was at least four inches long, six legged, with long antennae and pale, almost transparent almond-shaped bodies that pulsed obscenely as they scrambled around beside and even over their fellow warriors. Huge albino cockroaches, their brown color bred out of them over millennia of generations in the dark bowels of the great city.

Thousands, then hundreds of thousands, then millions of the wretched creatures poured through the ragged hole. They became so thick on the ceiling above them that the outer layers began to slip and slide and then rain down on them, landing on their hooded heads and Tyvek-covered shoulders, sliding into and then out of their hip waders in clicking hordes, filling the air and then flailing on the sea of ooze covering the floor, all struggling in the same direction, pushing the weaker beneath them to provide a solid raft for the mindless mass to move over.

Holliday felt his gorge rise with burning acid bile and his recent dinner rising in his throat. He clenched his teeth, knowing that if he began to vomit he would either have to take off the mask or fill it and choke to death. He bent his head down, closed his eyes tight and waited for the nightmare to end.

It seemed to go on for an eternity, but eventually the noise passed and only the reeking stink of their passage was left behind. If not for the filters on their masks the four men would almost certainly have passed out from the fumes. Finally Holliday lifted up his head and opened his eyes. Tens of thousands of the creatures were floating on the surface of the muck, their legs fluttering weakly, but the main army had passed. There was a long silence.

"I have never seen a thing like this before," said Eddie, finally lifting his head and looking around, awestruck and revolted.

"I don't think anyone has ever seen something like this before," said Genrikhovich.

"The bugs are gone, but they left *el olor de cucarachas* behind them," said Eddie. "*Dios mío,* what a smell!"

"The smell is a combination of their feces and an oily waste of regurgitated food they vomit when they are stressed," said Ivanov. "When you consider the number of creatures that went past, you can only imagine what they left behind."

"Just what I needed, a lecture on cockroach puke," muttered Holliday.

"We should go," urged the priest. "The hole is big enough and the batteries on the lamps will not last forever."

"I'm ready," said Holliday. The thought of being in the dark down here made him suddenly nervous. Ivanov went through the gap in the bricks first, followed by Holliday, Eddie and Genrikhovich. On the other side of the brick wall there was a river of shit; there was no other way of describing it.

A high-arched tunnel of brick rose overhead, while below it the broad stream flowed, at least a hundred and fifty feet wide, thick and brownish yellow, with lumps in it, some recognizable, others not. The bloated corpses of dogs, cats and rats, of slaughtered pigs and sheep, plastic bags, their contents weighty enough to pull them halfway into the impenetrable flow. The body of a man drifted by, so bloated and corrupt it was little more than a floating island for the writhing swarms of maggots industriously eating their way to adulthood on its purple decomposing flesh.

The "banks" of the river were two-foot-wide concrete walkways, dangerously slick with a layer of mucuslike slime that seemed to work its way down off the walls like slow-moving lava from a volcano. A climber's piton had been hammered into the concrete, and tied to it was a twelve-foot-long, five-foot-wide inflatable boat, complete with a pair of plastic oars and a five-horsepower Hidea outboard engine screwed onto the transom at the back.

"It really is worse than St. Petersburg," said Holliday, looking out at the broad flow of waste, foaming eddies and pinwheels of gray-yellow muck making slow-motion patterns on the lumpy surface.

"Your black friend in the front, since he is the heaviest, you and Victor in the center, and I will take the controls," said Ivanov.

"We are supposed to go out there in this little boat?" Eddie asked, looking out at the sluggishly moving flow, the light on his hard hat glinting off a bobbing empty bottle of Kubanskaya vodka, its red-and-black label still clearly visible.

"Afraid so, *compañero*," said Holliday, grinning behind his mask. "You first."

"Coño," grumbled the Cuban, but he stepped down into the boat, dropping instantly into a crouch, then making his way carefully forward. Genrikhovich followed, then Holliday, who sat down beside him, and finally Ivanov took his place at the throttle of the outboard. Holliday reached out and undid the line tying them to the concrete, then used one of the plastic oars to push them out into the current.

"Everyone turn off your lamps except your black friend, Colonel Holliday. We must conserve the batteries."

"His name is Eddie," said Holliday, his tone curt.

"Gracias, amigo," muttered Eddie softly. The rest of them turned off their lamps, leaving only the beam of Eddie's lamp to light the way.

Ivanov turned on the electric starter and there was a gruesome burbling sound as the propeller chewed into the muck. The boat headed out into the center of the current, and then Ivanov steered straight ahead and turned the throttle of the outboard. The horrible burbling increased and they moved slowly off down the ghastly river.

32

Cardinal Antonio Niccolo Spada, Vatican secretary of state through three popes, one of them assassinated, sat at his permanently reserved table in the dining room of Capricci Siciliani, the remains of his roulade of baked anchovies with its wonderful citrus-seafood tang on the plate in front of him. He sipped from his glass of pale Verdicchio dei Castelli di Jesi and gave a slightly melodramatic sigh as he set the glass down beside his plate.

"Father Brennan, you are no aid to a man's digestion." The cardinal shook his head. "I have an office, as you well know; I keep regular hours. Why can't we save our discussions for those times?" In the distance the blaring of horns from the nighttime traffic on the Lungotevere Tor di Nona could be heard, and beyond that the never-ending rumble of the city of Rome.

For Spada a meal in the peaceful old section of the city was an escape from the complex responsibilities and intrigues of his occupation in the Vatican, but even now, late in the evening, those responsibilities and intrigues reached out and found him. The fact that they took the form of the disheveled, chain-smoking and foulmouthed head of the Vatican Secret Service just made the intrusion that much more distasteful.

"Sorry to be bothering Your Eminence's evening meal, but some things just won't wait. Even for a man such as yourself and his plate of sardines."

"Anchovies, Father Brennan, cooked in garlic butter with parsley and tomato sauce with the juice of a lemon. It is a classic dish from Sicily, where I had the great fortune to be born."

Brennan frowned. "Anchovies? Salty things they put on pizza pies, aren't they, Your Eminence? Couldn't be good for the blood pressure, could they?" Like most Irish the cardinal had ever met, Brennan never made a statement without making it a question.

"Anchovies aren't born salty, Brennan—these are fresh."

"Is that right? Well, you could knock me over with a feather now, couldn't you?"

Spada had known Brennan long enough to recognize when the Irish priest was needling him. "Get on with it, Father Brennan; what ill wind is it that blew you to my table tonight?"

"Pesek was to call me with a report tonight."

"And?" Spada said, sipping his wine.

"He has not done so."

"Perhaps you should call him then."

"It's not in the way of how he does things, Your Eminence." The priest paused, gauging whether the cardinal's meal was actually over and whether or not it was diplomatic to light a cigarette. It had been almost twenty minutes since his last and he decided to chance it. He took a dark blue flip-top pack of Richmond Superkings and lit one from the store of kitchen matches he kept in his jacket pocket. The cardinal frowned. A busboy appeared and cleared away the dinner plate, and a few seconds later a waiter arrived with Spada's dessert, Cassatella di Sant'Agata, literally the Breasts of Saint Agatha, a delicate layer of shortbread in the shape of a breast, then stuffed with chopped pistachios and custard. Finally it was covered in pink icing and each mound was topped with a maraschino cherry.

Realizing he'd made a mistake, Brennan pinched out the tip of the cigarette with a stained and calloused thumb and forefinger, then dropped the butt in his other pocket.

"Certainly a way to test your vows of celibacy," said Brennan, looking at the mildly obscene dessert.

Spada smiled and plucked one of the cherries from the tip of one of the sugar-icing breasts. He popped it into his mouth. "Saint Agatha was tortured cruelly; the eating of her breasts is an act of fealty to her passionate faith in Jesus Christ."

"Patron saint of bell founders and bakers, too, as I recall, yes?"

"As you know perfectly well, Father Brennan." Spada ate the other cherry. "Now get on with it."

"As I said, Pesek hasn't called and he's long past due."

"Some context for all of this would be nice," said Spada, sticking a fork in the left breast, breaking through to the oozing custard-and-chopped-nut center.

Brennan flinched a little; had the cardinal been in his full red cassock and biretta it would have been something out of an old Fellini movie. He looked up at the ceiling of the dining room and spoke. "Pesek had traced them to their hotel in Moscow. He somehow learned they were to meet with Genrikhovich later that evening. He was going to deal with the situation for us then."

"Does Pesek have any idea who Genrikhovich really is?"

"I doubt it. He would have been in his late teens at the time, and it was not the name by which he was generally known. It was his patronymic, and he generally went by his mother's name, even inside Russia."

"What about Holliday?"

"Almost certainly not; in the first place, if he knew he would have run like an Irishman from a temperance meeting."

"He's a historian."

"He's an *American* historian, Your Eminence. In the

history books of the United States the name Genrikho-vich probably doesn't even rate a footnote. Besides, his specialty is medieval history, not the Cold War."

"All right, assuming that is so, why do you think Pesek has not called?"

"Either he's forgotten, lost them somehow, or Holliday has killed him instead of the other way around."

"Which do you think is the most likely?"

"If Pesek hasn't called me within the next couple of hours I'd put my money on Holliday. He almost killed Pesek in Venice; maybe the bugger succeeded this time. He's got the skills."

"If Pesek is dead, do we have any other options?"

"Do you mean does Mother Church have any more *assassini* up its holy sleeves?"

"Yes, that is exactly what I mean," said the cardinal stiffly, the dessert and the wine in front of him forgotten. Brennan lit the butt of his cigarette and puffed on it gratefully.

"None that I know of, not of Pesek's stature."

"So what do you suggest?"

"I know one of the people who work for Pezzi in the archbishop's office in Moscow; perhaps he knows of a few thugs in the archdiocese."

"Paolo Pezzi is no friend of mine," said Spada, his voice sour. "He wanted my job more than I did, but there were too many rumors about his sexual proclivities. He considers Russia to be a banishment."

"I'm afraid we'll have to take our friends where we find them, Your Eminence. I'll call my connection in Moscow."

"Holliday cannot be allowed to get his hands on the book. It would ruin us," said the cardinal.

Brennan smiled. "The Church has lasted these one thousand, nine hundred and seventy years, Your Eminence. One man isn't about to bring it down."

"I'm afraid that's where you're wrong, Father Brennan; one man is precisely what it would take."

Their ride on the grease-slicked, unholy river of Moscow's sewage was an hour-long nightmare. On the voyage they saw every conceivable type of waste that a city of eleven and a half million people could produce, animal, vegetable and even mineral. To make things worse, the high-arched tunnel was thick with stalactites of lime that had clearly been forming for centuries, and these pendulous horrors hanging from the stone of the ceiling had become roosts for generations of bats, who dropped their guano where they roosted and fed on whatever had the misfortune to float or fly past them. Fortunately the filters in their respirator masks removed the majority of the odors, but the ammonia-fumes emanation from the bat feces was eye-wateringly dense.

"Where are we?" Holliday asked, raising his voice over the glutinous blender sound of the little outboard.

"Close now," called back Ivanov, checking the GPS on the seat beside him. "We are beneath the old Zaryadye district. The same place they found the bunker of illegals. We must move carefully now."

"Why so careful here?" Holliday asked.

"Spetsnaz," said Genrikhovich. "Although we are below the levels of the special Kremlin telecommunications conduits, we are very close."

"We're below them?" Holliday asked.

"Certainly," said Ivanov. "Moscow today is not the Moscow of a thousand years ago. There have been many cities here, one built atop the next, like the ancient city of Troy. Each in its turn had its own way of dealing with its waste. According to Father Stelletskii, there are seventeen distinct levels under Moscow's streets, each with its own secret passages, tunnels, dungeons and bunkers."

Ivanov eased off on the throttle and guided the rubber dinghy to "shore." Holliday twisted around in his seat and saw an outflow channel on their left. A mountain climber's piton had been driven into a crack in the concrete. As they bumped into the walkway Eddie took the forward line and threaded it through the piton's eyelet.

"This like the character Arne Saknussemm," said Eddie, tying them up and stepping up out of the little boat. He held out a hand to Holliday and pulled him up.

"Who?" Holliday asked.

"You have never read this story?" Eddie said, surprised.

"What story?" Holliday asked. Genrikhovich clambered awkwardly out of the dinghy, almost losing his footing, and Ivanov climbed up onto the concrete walkway.

"It is very popular in Cuba, oh, my, yes," said the Cuban. "*Viaje al Centro de la Tierra* by the writer Jules Verne, no?"

"*Journey to the Center of the Earth*," said Holliday.

"Yes." Eddie nodded. "Arne Saknussemm left behind A.K. to guide the people who came after; the *padre* leaves these," said Eddie, nudging the piton.

"Eddie, you never cease to amaze me."

"Thank you . . . I think."

Once again Ivanov led the way up the outfall passage. The effluent in the narrow, downward-sloping channel was different from anything else Holliday had seen so far on their odorous journey beneath the streets of Moscow; it was dark, almost black, and it flowed thickly, like molasses. Even through the respirator Holliday could tell the smell was different, too: richer, a sweet-rotten scent, like potatoes left too long in a root cellar.

After traveling along the outfall for a little more than two hundred yards they stepped out into an enormous circular domed room at least three hundred feet in diameter. The room was made entirely of brick, and very old. At least a hundred broad, troughlike spigots had been inserted into the sloping walls of the dome, one spigot every few yards, and from each one there was a steady trickling flow of the tarry goop.

From the spigots the thick fluid fell over the edge of an iron walkway that surrounded the base of the black, shallow lake that filled the middle of the room like some enormous tar pit. There were a dozen outfall channels ranged around the enclosure, just like the one they came up. The fumes rising off the artificial lake were thick, choking and easily identifiable. In the center of the lake greasy bubbles rose and broke lazily.

"That's alcohol!" Holliday said.

"Indeed," said Ivanov. "As I mentioned, we are traveling underneath the old Zaryadye district. The fruit and vegetable markets have been there for more than three centuries. At market's closing each day the spoiled or rotten fruit and vegetables are tossed into a central refuse area and forgotten. The produce rots further, of course, and over time, the heat created by the rotting began a fermentation process. By the mid-nineteenth century the fumes created became both a health and fire hazard, so this collecting pond was created. Essentially what you see in front of you is a lake of vodka. Poisonous, but vodka nevertheless."

"Good thing the local drunkard population hasn't found it," Holliday commented. His lamp shone out over the glass-smooth surface of the pool.

"They have," said Genrikhovich, laughing behind his

mask. "That's why it's so poisonous; several of them have fallen in and added their decomposing corpses to the brew."

They moved off to the left, following Ivanov's lead. He paused again at the fifth archway and turned into the passage beyond. They left the dark fuming lake behind them in the enclosing darkness. The thought that the only way to get back to the surface was by retracing their steps began to prey on Holliday's thoughts; in the Rangers you always left yourself with at least one line of safe withdrawal, but he saw none here. As they walked along the side corridor leading away from the lake he asked Ivanov about it.

"There are several escape routes, none of them easy, all of them mapped out by Father Stelletskii through the years. They lead upward to sewer grates and storm sewer passageways. Most of them are very dangerous: straight up and terribly narrow. Rungs on ladders rusted through."

A few minutes later they reached another tunnel running at a right angle to theirs. Ivanov stopped just inside the entrance and held up one hand. He listened for what seemed a very long time, then turned and whispered.

"We are within reach of our goal now. This passage leads under the Kremlin Wall but it is guarded by Spetsnaz patrols almost constantly. We must not speak at any time."

The others nodded and Ivanov stepped into the passageway, followed by the others. It was barely wide enough for a man to move through without brushing the sides, and the ceiling was so low that both Eddie and Holliday had to stoop slightly. There was a trough-like channel on either side of the tunnel about three feet wide and about as deep, presumably for runoff during heavy rains.

There were bundles of cable stapled to the side walls above the troughs and even heavier conduits overhead. The wire bundles and conduits were all stamped with Cyrillic lettering. One stenciled notation was clear even to Holliday: ФСБ, FSB, the post-Soviet version of the KGB. They were in one of the telecommunications tunnels Ivanov had mentioned. They had been walking along the corridor for ten minutes when Ivanov suddenly stopped dead and raised his hand. "The lamps! Turn them off!"

They did as Ivanov instructed and they were instantly bound by complete darkness. In the far distance Holliday could faintly hear people speaking. A few seconds later he saw the bobbing of lights flickering off the walls ahead of them.

"Spetsnaz!" Ivanov hissed. "Into the runoff channels, and keep absolutely quiet!"

Holliday dropped down and rolled into the runoff trough on his right. He could hear the equipment rattling on his work belt and prayed that the Spetsnaz patrol was either too far away or talking too loudly to hear it.

They all held their breath as the patrol approached and the voices got louder. Eventually they appeared, five of them walking in file, each with a miner's light like the one Holliday carried, but brighter and attached to simple plastic headbands. In the bobbing illumination of their lights Holliday could see that they were heavily armed.

Each man carried an assault rifle at port arms, and each had a sidearm holstered at his side. Stun grenades were clipped to a bandolier strapped diagonally across each man's chest. Each was protected by a black Kevlar bulletproof vest, and they were all wearing heavy black combat boots. The men were all big, Holliday's height or better. Hell on wheels in any kind of fight.

They finally passed by, the sound of their boots echoing in the distance. Holliday stood and switched on his lamp. All around him the others rose up from the runoff channels and did the same.

"Close call," said Holliday.

"There may be others," said the priest. "We must hurry." He took out the GPS unit, checked it and continued down the passageway. A hundred yards on, he stopped and turned, letting his light sweep over the left-hand wall. There was a narrow archway and another short passage that ended in a concrete wall. At the base of the wall the concrete facing had been chipped away in a rough, two-foot circular patch to reveal a brick wall behind.

"I believe that the way to Ivan the Terrible's library lies behind this wall," said Ivanov.

Together, working in two-man shifts, the four worked away at the wall with their climbing axes and Ivanov's folding spade. Eventually they knocked out enough of the old brickwork for a man to pass through. A wash of pale light came through the hole, which was surprising, but when Holliday wiggled through the small aperture what he found beyond the wall was even more stunning.

"Incredible," he whispered. "The old stories were true!"

"*¿Dónde estamos?*" Eddie asked, looking around.

"Amazing!" Holliday said. "A metro station. This is Stalin's secret subway!"

33

The Leningrad Four—Vladimir Putin, prime minister of Russia; Dmitry Medvedev, the president of Russia; Vladimir Gundyaev, patriarch of Moscow; and Vasilyevich Bortnikov, head of the FSB—sat in their comfortable green leather armchairs drinking fresh tea from the silver samovar at the end of the inlaid oak–and-brass conference table. In the background the four big Ilyushin engines droned on steadily through the night sky over the Ural Mountains. All four men had been at a secret meeting with their "foreign" counterparts at Putin's billion-dollar Black Sea residence near the tiny village of Praskoveyevka, population four hundred and forty-two. They were now an hour out of Moscow on the Russian version of Air Force One, a luxurious gutted version of an Ilyushin II-96, the work done by the English company Diamonite for a reported ten million British pounds sterling. Another few million euros had been spent in Voronezh, the headquarters of the Voronezh Aircraft Production Association, to protect the aircraft from any satellite, EMP or broadband intrusion. VAPA and a variety of other engineers then installed enough electronic equipment in the aircraft to launch every army, navy and air force group to defend Mother Russia from any foe stupid enough to step into the great bear's den. It also had the telemetry to launch all sixteen thousand nuclear warheads left in the Russian arsenal.

"A very nice dacha you have, Vladimir," commented Gundyaev, patriarch of Moscow. "There has been some comment on it in the press lately, foreign and domestic. Very lavish."

"Not nearly as lavish as Buckingham Palace." Putin laughed.

"A billion dollars, Volodya?" Medvedev asked, using his childhood nickname for Putin. "A little much, don't you think, in a worldwide recession, as they call it?"

"And during that same recession the Canadian prime minister, the one with the plastic hair, spends the same amount on a weekend in Toronto for a G8 conference." Putin snorted, then took a long swallow of the fragrant tea. "At least I built something with the government's money."

"The Canadian was reelected with a majority," teased Medvedev.

"Who knows." Putin shrugged. "Maybe Canadians like their leaders to have plastic hair. To me he looks like the man who plays the organ at a funeral. He makes me queasy." Putin laughed. "Not that Canada matters much in the scheme of things."

"They have enormous natural resources," said Medvedev.

"What they have, others own. It was the essence of the meeting we just had," Putin said. "It is no longer a world of governments; we must face that or Russia will fade into history, her best people lost in a diaspora of greed to other nations."

"You really believe that?" Bortnikov said.

"Certainly," replied Putin, nodding. "The future of Russia lies in private equity."

"Do away with government?" Gundyaev said. The patriarch of the Russian Orthodox Church actually looked frightened by the thought.

"Why not?" Putin said. "Effectively the world as we know it is run by half a dozen major corporations and another half dozen secret conglomerates the world has never heard of."

"And the Vatican?" the patriarch asked.

"There have been various audits over the years, rarely placing the value of the Vatican holdings at something just over a billion dollars, which is absurd, of course. In terms of simple real estate they probably have holdings of at least a trillion dollars worldwide, and this doesn't include their corporate investments, like Fiat automobiles and Bank of America."

"What about our corporations?" Bortnikov, the FSB chief, asked.

"Gazprom, Rosneft, LUKOIL, Novatek, Gazprom Neft—the top five companies are all oil and gas producers, and the other five making the top ten are steel companies. Natural resources requiring outside buyers—exactly like the Canadians. An economy like that is always vulnerable to the whims of Wall Street and other stock exchanges. Watch CNN or the BBC—how often is the RTS mentioned? Never. We have one billion dollars in the equity trading market; the Americans have more than a *trillion* dollars in private equity funds. There are individual *companies* in America larger than our entire country's investment in private equity. This is insanity, gentlemen."

"During the Cold War it was an arms race; now it is all about money," said Bortnikov wistfully.

Putin angrily rattled his spoon in his teacup, placing another lump of sugar in it. "During the Cold War the Russian bear was a world power to be feared. The Americans shook in their boots when the bear roared. We were a worthy foe. Now the Americans dance in the streets when their military kills one sick lunatic cowering in his compound in Pakistan, watching himself on television. If the Americans think of us at all it is as a source of immigrant organized crime, the *Mafiya*. We are little more than a joke, and a joke unable to deal with its own domestic squabbles, like Georgia or Chechnya. It must change, and soon."

"What you say is all fine and good, Volodya, but I still don't see how this has anything to do with the Church, Victor Genrikhovich, the American or the Phoenix order."

"It has everything to do with them," answered Putin. A white-jacketed steward who was actually a junior officer in the Kremlin presidential guard appeared carrying a tray of freshly made blinis, Golden Osetra caviar, crème fraîche, a bottle of Georgievskaya vodka and four flare-topped crystal glasses. The guard set down the tray, deftly put a glass and a small plate in front of each of the four men, filled the glasses from the bottle and then withdrew as silently as he appeared. In the background the engines of the big jet thundered quietly through the darkness.

Putin took a blini off the stack on the tray, put a big dollop of the pale yellow caviar in the center of the crepe-thin pancake and topped it with another dollop of the slightly sour crème fraîche. He folded the blini into a little package, then popped the whole thing into his mouth. He closed his eyes for a moment, savoring the wonderful assortment of tastes, then swallowed. He opened his eyes, took a sip of the chilled vodka, then sat back in his armchair with a contented sigh.

"The Church, Victor Genrikhovich and the American," reminded Gundyaev, spooning a heaping mound of caviar onto his own blini. "Not to mention the Phoenix order."

"Ah, yes." Putin nodded. "It's like pieces in a puzzle—each piece has its place in the larger picture. As you are aware, we have consolidated the Church's position inside Russia and are ready to expand to include all the Orthodox churches worldwide. We are already the largest of those churches numerically, and consolidation would give us power equal to that of the Vatican."

"All of which I am well aware, Volodya," said Gundyaev.

"But if our assumptions about Genrikhovich and his theory are correct and he was right about the Bulgarian monk and his long-lost knight, then the Phoenix order's power is permanently broken, and we will have a weapon to hold the Vatican in check forever."

"And if it is a fantasy, like it was for Stalin, Khrushchev and the others who came after . . . including yourself, Volodya?"

"Then we have Holliday, at least." He nodded across the table at Bortnikov, the FSB chief. "Vasily has had him under loose surveillance for quite some time, and his research bureau has developed an extensive dossier. Genrikhovich, the Bulgarian and his friend the priest-archaeologist simply provided a way to lure him into our sphere of influence, so to speak. He hardly would have come to Russia without some major incentive, which we provided."

"And what if Holliday and his vast Templar riches are as much a fantasy as Genrikhovich's Holy Grail or whatever it is? Have you thought about that?" Medvedev said.

"Holliday's treasure is no fantasy. The Vatican has tried to assassinate him on more than one occasion, and that maniac billionaire in the United States tried as well. That is not fantasy, Dmitry; even the financial hierarchy of his own order wants what he has and will not share."

"The elusive notebook," murmured Bortnikov.

"The elusive notebook." Putin nodded. "The key to the greatest fortune in the entire world."

It looked surprisingly like an IRT station on the New York subway—tile walls, narrow platform and low ceilings. There were no benches, however, and the track Holliday found himself looking at as he climbed through the freshly made hole in the old brick had only two rails, not three, which meant that the big green car parked at the platform's edge was probably a self-propelled, gas-operated carriage. At the far end of the platform there was a ragged hole in the ceiling where a section of the roof had collapsed at some point, and a pile of concrete and old bricks that had been swept aside against the wall.

It was a smart idea, when you thought about it: a bunch of Russian bigwigs in the Kremlin fleeing from a barrage of American ICBMs wouldn't want to depend on local electricity sources. Holliday also noticed that while everything looked 1950s old, it also looked well maintained. There was even the faint smell of lubricating oil in the air. This place was still being used.

"It's the D-six," said Holliday, fascinated by seeing something he always thought of as a Cold War urban myth.

"*¿Qué?*" Eddie asked.

"It was called Metro-two," replied Holliday. "The KGB code-named it D-six. An escape route for high-ranking members of the Kremlin. It was supposed to lead to several underground command posts and bunkers and even an underground city. Stalin was even supposed to have used it to get to his dacha in Kuntsevo, which is where he spent most of World War Two."

"We have no time for this," said Ivanov irritably. He checked the GPS. "We are three hundred and eleven meters below the surface; this puts us in the time period of Ivan the Terrible. We must continue."

"Continue where?" Holliday asked.

"There," answered the priest, pointing. Under the broad lip of the platform above, Holliday could see a square of brickwork almost lost in the shadows. When the tunnel was dug for the train they must have simply cut through the passageway he and the others had come though, then sealed it up again when they were finished building the underground station.

"Hurry, please," said Ivanov. "The Spetsnaz must patrol here regularly." He scuttled across the tracks and ducked below the platform, crawling on his hands and knees to reach the rough patch of brickwork. The rest followed quickly behind him. This time it took them less than fifteen minutes to break through to the other side. They were instantly assailed by an odor that even their respirator masks failed to dull. Not the smell of human waste in all its forms, but something much worse, a thick stench of rot and mold and death.

The passageway narrowed almost immediately, and within fifteen yards the four were on their bellies, Ivanov in the lead.

"*Dios mío,* what is that stink?" Eddie groaned. "It is much worse than before, this smell."

They crept forward slowly until Ivanov stopped. "What is it?" Holliday asked, his lamp lighting up the man's boots. There was no brickwork here, only an amalgam of broken stone and dank, dark earth.

"A grating of some kind. Pass me up the pry bar."

Holliday slipped the eighteen-inch crowbar off his workman's belt and passed it up to the priest. A moment later there was a grunt and the sound of metal on metal and then the sound of crumbling masonry.

"How many bars?" Holliday called out.

"Five. I'll have to remove them all, and even then it will be a tight squeeze, especially for someone as large as you and your companion."

The sound of straining metal continued for a long ten minutes and then stopped. There was a series of sounds from Ivanov as he slithered forward, his feet scrabbling for purchase and throwing back dirt into Holliday's face. Finally the boots disappeared altogether and Holliday crawled forward, his lamp illuminating the grate Ivanov had been working on.

Ahead lay a letterbox-shaped opening perhaps four feet wide and two feet high. Holliday could see the ancient cement frame that had held the iron bars in place. The bars were gone, leaving nothing but gaping holes like the sockets of rotting teeth. He could see almost nothing beyond except a wall of pitted, dressed stone, the blocks fitted so tightly together there had been no need for mortar.

Struggling, Holliday dug his feet in and pushed himself forward, eventually reaching the opening. He put his arms above his head and slithered forward, finally pushing his shoulders through and then his hips. Halfway through the opening he rolled over and pushed hard with his heels, finally popping completely out of the rectangular opening.

Standing, Holliday saw that Ivanov was shining his lamp down a long, dark corridor about four feet wide, the arched ceiling not much more than six feet overhead. There were low, riveted iron doors with massive hinges every five feet on both sides of the passage. The doors were solid, each equipped with a heavy iron bar set onto massive iron brackets.

Holliday shone his own light down at the opening

he'd just come through and watched as Eddie struggled to free himself. From the looks of it, the grated opening had been some sort of overflow channel for water. Eddie, cursing resoundingly in Spanish with every inch gained, finally pulled his big muscular frame through the hole and stood up. A few moments later Genrikhovich appeared, coughing and choking and spitting out dirt.

"Do you have any idea where we are?" Holliday asked Ivanov.

The priest nodded. "If I'm not mistaken, these are the dungeons of Ivan Chetvyorty Vasilyevich the Fourth, better known to the world as Ivan the Terrible."

34

They moved off down the dark, stone-walled passage. The silence was something you could almost taste, heavy and oppressive, with a tart tang of blood-soaked earth. History was alive down here in the worst of all possible ways, like writhing worms and ancient nightmares. Holliday stopped at the first door they came to and lifted the heavy wooden bar. He pulled on the rivet-studded door and it eventually moved, groaning as he manhandled it open. He shone his light into the interior of the cell.

The chamber was ten feet on a side, and lying in tumbled heaps were the skeletons of at least a dozen men, tossed like so many broken marionettes into a dark corner of a child's cupboard. There was no obvious facility for hygiene, not even a hole in the floor, which was mostly covered with a thick layer of black earth no doubt made from their own waste. The limbs on some of the skeletons had been torn away, the dead feeding the living for a little while longer.

Holliday shivered; the sounds from this place would have been like the moaning of some hellish choir, the sounds fading with each passing day until there was only silence. There would have been no hope here: no hope of redemption, no hope of food or water, only a slow, hideous death. The cell Holliday stared into was the very definition of horror and evil personified, and the man who ordered its construction had been without compassion and had no love in his cold heart for any living thing on the planet. Reflexively, from an almost forgotten past, Holliday made the sign of the cross and whispered the formulas as he did so.

"In the name of the Father, the Son and the Holy Spirit, Amen." Out of the corner of his eye he noticed that Eddie was doing the same thing.

"En el nombre del Padre, del Hijo y del Espíritu Santo. Amén."

"We have no time for this foolishness, Colonel Holliday; we have much more important things to concern us now," said Genrikhovich, his voice a little petulant. "We have better things to do than mourn the deaths of prisoners five hundred years ago."

"Whatever else they were or might have been, they were men once, and their bones deserve a little respect from the living."

"We won't be living much longer if you insist on dawdling and saying your prayers, Colonel. I can assure you of that."

Eddie dropped a big hand on Holliday's shoulder. "You are a good man, *mi coronel,* no matter what this *idiota* thinks."

Holliday closed the door to the cell but he left the bar off; the dead men had been imprisoned long enough; now at least their spirits could be free. When he'd shut the door he went after the others down the low-ceilinged passageway.

The passage seemed to go on forever, sometimes curving, sometimes dipping down or up, depending on the terrain, but by Holliday's calculation they were always heading in roughly the same direction. Ivanov answered the unspoken question.

"We are traveling south. Most of the research points to the Tainitskaya Tower, or the Secret Tower, as it is sometimes called, since it is the oldest."

"Is that the only reason?" Holliday asked.

"No. It is thought that the Tainitskaya Tower also had two tunnels, one leading to the nearby bank of the Moskva River, the other leading across Red Square to the cathedral."

"Was any such tunnel ever found?"

"They filled in the tunnel to the river in the 1930s, when the tower was completely sealed. They never found the second tunnel," said Ivanov.

It was well past midnight before they reached their objective, at least according to Ivanov's GPS, programmed on the basis of Father Ignatius Stelletskii's eighty-year-old maps of the underground city. They stood in a small circular chamber with a rib-vaulted ceiling and finally stripped off their respirators and stepped out of their Tyvek suits.

At the base of each rib in the chamber's vault there was a carved rosette, and beneath the rosette a pillar reaching to the dressed-stone floor. Twelve ribs, twelve rosettes and twelve pillars arranged in a circle around a raised stone plinth set in the middle of the floor.

Around the plinth a deep circle had been carved into the floor, surrounding it, carved wavering rays of light extending outward from the circle like a great, flaming sun with the raised dais at its center: an altar. On the plinth was a stone sarcophagus of a knight carrying a long shield, and on the shield a carved Templar cross. The fourth Templar, who carried the Sword of the South, Octanis, the last of the swords sent forth from Castle Pelerin. In the knight's mailed fist he clutched a broadsword, and along the blade there was an inscription:

YA OHRANNIK VELICHAI SHIE SOKROVISHCHA MIRA.

"It's Old Russian," said Ivanov. "It says, 'I guard the greatest treasures of the world.'"

"A Templar tomb," murmured Genrikhovich.

"I'm not so sure," said Holliday.

Genrikhovich snorted disdainfully. "Don't be absurd.

The stone effigy is carrying a shield with a Templar cross blazoned on it."

"I'm not disagreeing with you about the stone carving; I'm just disputing the fact that it's a tomb."

"What else could it be?"

Holliday, who'd seen something much like this not too long ago in the middle of Ethiopia's Lake Tana, just smiled. He turned to Eddie. "Lend me a hand, will you?"

"Of course, *compadre*," said the big Cuban. Holliday put both hands about six inches apart on the edge of the plinth closest to the effigy's head. Eddie joined him.

"On three, push as hard as you can," instructed Holliday.

"What on earth are you doing?" Genrikhovich asked.

"Ready, one, two and three!" Holliday heaved and Eddie joined him. At first nothing happened, but finally the whole stone structure began to rotate on its axis, rumbling as it followed the narrow circular track in the floor.

"Chto, chert voz mi?" Genrikhovich whispered.

At forty-five degrees from its original position the plinth and its stone figure of the Templar Knight revealed a stone staircase, its steps disappearing into the darkness.

They went down the stairway, one after another, the beams from their miner's lamps playing over what lay ahead. Twelve steps and then a landing, and twelve more steps before a second landing and another ninety-degree turn. There were four sets of twelve steps, eventually turning through a full three hundred and sixty degrees and exiting into a strange, twelve-sided room, its ceiling an oddly shaped barrel vault high above them. In each of the twelve narrow walls was an equally narrow door.

Ivanov slipped off his backpack and unclipped the big eight-volt light from it. He switched on the powerful lamp and the room was suddenly brilliantly illuminated.

"It's magnificent!" Holliday whispered.

The floor of the room was made of mosaic tile, its colors as brilliant as the day it had been constructed. The design was an arcane circular device surrounding a seven-pointed star that in turn enclosed another circle and another star. In the circular ribbons there were inscribed letters and words in an arcane language that might have been Aramaic or ancient Hebrew. In the center of the second seven-pointed star, a design depicting four swords had been picked out in the mosaic, their points not quite touching, the space between them a perfect cross.

Holliday bent down and ran his fingers over the mosaic. The designs hadn't been done in ceramic, as he'd first thought, but in semiprecious stones. The whole floor was made up of obsidian, jade, agate amethyst and opal, garnet, moonstone and amber. The whole floor glittered and flashed in the light from the big lamp. Holliday stood again and stared.

"*¿Qué es?*" Eddie asked.

"I think it's a pentangle of some sort," answered Holliday. "A magician's symbol."

Genrikhovich shook his head. "Not a magician, but an alchemist—in this case Basilius Valentinus, the canon of the Benedictine Priory of Sankt Peter in Erfurt, Germany, a contemporary of Ivan the Terrible and well-known to him. The design is the Key of Solomon; in this case instead of the Hebrew name of God being in the center it shows the four swords of Pelerin."

"Aos, Hesperios, Polaris and Octanis," supplied Holliday.

"Quite right, Colonel," said Genrikhovich.

"Of which one is missing," put in Ivanov. "Octanis, Sword of the South."

Genrikhovich smiled knowingly. "Octanis is not missing, Father Ivanov. It is here, where it has been hidden for the past five hundred years."

"Where?" Holliday asked flatly.

"Look around you and choose," said the Russian, a faintly condescending and aristocratic tone in his voice.

The walls of the twelve-sided room were painted a deep blue-black, like the great wheel of the night sky, and on each door there was a constellation picked out in bright golden stars. The sky wasn't real, however, but astrological. "I would suggest that Father Ivanov use his GPS to find us south, the door to Octanis."

The priest went and stood in the center of the room.

He took out his GPS unit and switched on its compass function. He turned slowly until he faced the side of the room that had been on their left when they reached the bottom of the stairway. "That way." He pointed. "That is south."

"The constellations Castor and Pollux, the twins, or Gemini, and Alpha Cancri, the claw of Cancer," Genrikhovich said. "Which shall we choose?"

"I wouldn't choose either," said Holliday.

"And why not, Colonel? Do you have some knowledge of alchemy and the works of Basilius Valentinus?"

"Never heard of the man until a minute ago, but I do know that in astrology the poles are counterintuitive—north is south and south is north."

"You hardly seem the type to believe in astrology, Colonel."

"I'm not, but my cousin Peggy is always telling me that it's Mercury in retrograde, or my aspect is wonky or something, and I managed to pick up a few things over the years—the north-south transposition was one of them."

"So we're supposed to believe your cousin then?" Genrikhovich sneered.

Holliday finally reached his boiling point. "I don't care what you do anymore, you arrogant Russian jerk; frankly I'm sick and tired of you and your lies and your bullshit. If it weren't for Brother Rodrigues I wouldn't be here, and you'd be the last person I'd be here with."

"¡Bravo, mi compadre!" Eddie laughed.

"One thing more," said Holliday, still fuming. "I don't know a hell of a lot about alchemy, but I know lots about history, and as I recall Ivan the Terrible was famous for his dungeons and his torture chambers. I wouldn't be so quick to go through *any* doors he designed; you might find yourself playing 'The Lady or the Tiger.'"

"What are you talking about?"

"You never heard of the story 'The Lady or the Tiger'?"

"No."

"You'll find out. Think Indiana Jones," said Holliday.

"Ignore him," said Genrikhovich to Ivanov. "We'll go through the Gemini door."

The priest looked briefly in Holliday's direction, a faint light of uncertainty visible in his eyes. Then he turned away and stepped toward the door with the Gemini constellation on it. The door had a simple old-fashioned wrought-iron latch, which Ivanov pressed down. He pulled open the door and stepped through, Genrikhovich following a few steps behind him.

Eddie turned to Holliday. "What should we do, *amigo?*"

"Follow," said Holliday. "Just keep back a little." The two men went after Genrikhovich through the Gemini door.

The first thing Holliday noticed was that instead of

being made of dressed stone, like the walls and the arched ceiling overhead, the floor of the passageway they found themselves in was made of a firm layer of fine, almost powdery sand. Other than that the corridor was featureless, the beams from their miner's lamps lighting up a second door about a hundred feet ahead. The design on the farther door was unmistakable: the gold double-headed imperial eagle of the original duchy of Moscow adopted by Ivan the Terrible when he became Russia's first czar.

"Why sand?" Holliday wondered aloud.

Genrikhovich half turned, the sneer back on his thin face. "Taurus is an earth sign, Colonel, or didn't your cousin tell you that?" The Russian turned away and hurried after Father Ivanov. Holliday heard a faint clicking and stopped dead. He'd heard a sound like that before—a makeshift pressure trigger hidden along a path in the A Shau Valley on the Laos–South Vietnam border. He'd never forgotten the sound, because a split second later the grunt walking point thirty feet ahead had been flayed into hamburger from the knees down by a makeshift claymore. It was like something out of a *Sgt. Rock* comic book—one second the poor bastard's legs were there; the next they were gone. The clicking sound came again and Genrikhovich stumbled. Faintly Holliday could hear a distant, hollow whirring sound. He held a stiff arm out, stopping Eddie.

"Stand perfectly still." He looked ahead. Ivanov was

twenty feet from the far door when he suddenly stopped and stared down at his feet. A hissing sound filled the air. Bubbles began appearing in the sand, racing back over the floor to where Genrikhovich stood transfixed. Holliday took three steps forward and grabbed the Russian's collar and yanked him backward. Ahead of them Ivanov screamed. He was up to his thighs and sinking deeper with each passing second.

"My God!" Genrikhovich moaned. "What is it?"

Ivanov screamed again, arching his back and twisting back and forth, vainly trying to release himself. It only made things worse. It was incredibly fast. Within twenty seconds the sand had risen to the level of his shoulders, and a few seconds after that his head went below the surface and he disappeared. The hissing sound and the bubbles continued for another half minute and then there was silence.

"Help him!" Genrikhovich yelled, staring horrified at the spot where the priest had vanished.

"Too late—he's gone," said Holliday.

Genrikhovich turned and looked at Holliday, dumbfounded. "What happened to him?" the Russian whispered.

"I wondered about the sand," murmured Holliday. "I knew it wasn't right."

"What are you talking about?" Genrikhovich snapped.

"You can find it naturally in the Qattara Depression

in the Libyan Desert and in some places in the Sahara. It's liquefied sand. Somewhere behind these walls there's a piston that pushed air up through the sand, giving it the properties of a liquid. Stop the air and the sand becomes solid again. He could be twenty feet down, for all we know." He shook his head and gave the Russian a cold look. "You were right, Genrikhovich: Taurus is an earth sign, and the earth just swallowed your friend Father Ivanov whole." He turned away in disgust. "Come on, Eddie; we're getting the hell out of here once and for all."

"I don't think so, Colonel," the Russian said quietly.

"Who's going to stop me?" Holliday said, turning angrily.

"I am," said Genrikhovich, the pearl-handled To-karev semiautomatic pistol held in his fist aimed in the general direction of Holliday's belly.

35

"Nice weapon," said Holliday. "Looks like a presentation piece." He seriously doubted that any pistol made during the Soviet era came stocked with pearl grips.

"Yes, Khrushchev gave it to my father, along with the Order of Lenin and his Hero of the Soviet Union medal in 1962." Genrikhovich sneered. "That and a postage stamp twenty years after his death was just about all he received for his good works. My mother and I lived from hand to mouth on the few rubles he gave us."

"I thought your father was a curator at the Hermitage?" Holliday said.

"My father was probably the most famous and successful KGB agent the Soviet Union ever had," said the Russian. "And they treated him like dirt." Genrikhovich smiled thinly. "Since you are a historian I'm surprised that you don't recognize the name, Colonel Holliday."

"In 1962 I was a kid and chasing girls," said Holliday. "I wasn't paying much attention to what was going on in Moscow except for the Cuban Missile Crisis."

"And if I mentioned a certain U-two spy plane pilot shot down over Soviet territory whose name was Francis Gary Powers?"

Holliday stared at the thin, long-nosed Russian with the wire eyeglasses. Suddenly his memory kicked in and he had it. "My God!" he said softly. "Your father was Rudolf Abel, the atom-bomb spy."

"That was the alias he used when he was arrested after being betrayed by his assistant, the traitor Reino Häyhänen. My father's real name was Vilyam Genrikhovich Fisher. He was born in England but grew up in Russia, which is why I speak English—he thought it might be useful for me." Genrikhovich laughed sourly. "He thought he would get me a job with the KGB, but they would have nothing to do with me. I even failed the physical tests for military service."

"This is all very interesting, but I don't see what it has to do with our present situation," said Holliday.

"Our present situation, Colonel, is that I have my father's pistol aimed at you," said Genrikhovich.

He might not have passed the physical for the army, but his grip on the Tokarev was firm. The safety was off and the knurled hammer was fully cocked. The slim, overpowered pistol could put a hole in Holliday's spine the size of a bowling ball, and at this range Genrikhovich couldn't miss. "You're the boss," said Holliday.

"That is correct, Colonel; I am the boss, so you and your friend will turn around slowly and go back the way we came in."

"Whatever you say," said Holliday. He and Eddie did exactly as they were told, heading slowly back along the sand-floored passageway and back out into the ornately painted antechamber. Holliday had seen the blank, distant look in the Russian's eyes. Here in this strange place beneath the Kremlin the veil of normalcy had been removed once and for all. Holliday realized they were finally seeing the man as he truly was—completely insane, lost in a world of bitterness, anger and utter madness.

"My grandfather would have loved this place," said the Russian. "He had a great belief in the spiritual world. He was also a Chekist; you know what that means?"

"The first version of the KGB."

"Yes, and before that he was with the Okhrana, the czar's secret police. But he was a revolutionary at heart. Lenin himself enlisted my grandfather as a double agent. He reported directly to him on the activities of the czar's henchmen in St. Petersburg. From the palace itself."

"Interesting," said Holliday, wondering where all this was going. Eddie just rolled his eyes and kept his mouth shut.

Genrikhovich looked around the circular chamber

with its complex designs. "You said that astrologically north is south and south is north?"

"According to my cousin Peggy." Holliday shrugged. "But I can't guarantee it."

"You'd better decide, Colonel, because your life depends on it." The Russian turned and faced the two doors that said CAPRICORN and SAGITTARIUS. "Choose," he said.

From Holliday's small store of knowledge about the constellations he vaguely recalled that Sagittarius lay almost exactly between the east and west quadrants of the sky, while Capricorn was very faint. He couldn't imagine Ivan the Terrible choosing *anything* that could be described as faint, and besides, Sagittarius was an archer, a warrior. "Sagittarius," he said.

"Very good," said Genrikhovich. "That was my choice as well." He motioned with the pistol. "Open the door. Your friend goes through first, then you."

Holliday walked across the room and put his hand on the latch. It was stiff and resistant with age. He pressed harder and felt the latch begin to give and he paused. In his mind's eye he saw a reconstruction of a medieval ballista, a huge, spring-operated crossbow that could deliver an immense spearlike projectile at incredible speeds. There were larger models that could fire as many as half a dozen arrows at a time.

"I think the door is rigged," said Holliday. "I suggest that you stand aside."

"You're trying my patience, Colonel. I'll shoot you without a second thought."

"Just a suggestion," said Holliday.

Genrikhovich eyed him thoughtfully, then stepped to the left, the gun never faltering. Eddie did the same. Holliday tugged hard on the latch, then stepped rapidly aside. There was a deep, thrumming resonance from the corridor beyond the open doorway, followed by a groaning metallic whirring, like some sort of mechanical device being released. An instant later four immense arrows, each one at least five feet long, hurtled out of the doorway, their eight-inch-long iron points crashing through the mosaic tile on the floor and embedding themselves into whatever was underneath. The projectiles jutted out of the floor at a forty-five-degree angle about three feet from the open door. If Holliday had been standing in front of the door he would have been skewered like a shish kebab.

"Fascinating," said Genrikhovich. "Do you think that is the last of it?"

"Who knows?" said Holliday.

"There must have been a secret way to open the door, or a hidden mechanism."

"Maybe," said Holliday.

"The czar wouldn't make it impossibly difficult to get at his treasure house," said Genrikhovich.

"Unless he had some other way," said Eddie, looking at the door. *"Una entrada privada."*

319

"A private entrance." Holliday nodded. "Makes sense."

"To me, too," said Eddie.

"Perhaps the *negr* is right," said Genrikhovich.

"Poshel na hui slishkom," said Eddie blandly.

"You mean Mr. Cabrera?" Holliday asked.

Genrikhovich sighed and adjusted his spectacles with his free hand. "You are both becoming tedious," he said.

"And you're being rude."

"I do not have time for your petty liberal sensitivities, Colonel Holliday. My family's search for Ivan the Terrible's secret library was begun in 1916, almost a hundred years ago now. I intend to use the secret my grandfather passed down to me to find what Lenin, Stalin and Khrushchev failed to discover even with all the powers of the Soviet Union at their disposal. My rudeness, as you deem it, is irrelevant to such an epic quest, and once again may I point out that I am the one who has the pistol?" He flicked the barrel of the old automatic to make his point. "Your friend Señor Cabrera first, if you please."

Eddie lifted his shoulders; then without hesitation the tall Cuban sidestepped between two of the heavy spears, ducked his head a little and entered the corridor. Holliday followed right behind him.

The passageway here was covered in mosaics, like the floor of the chamber behind them; even the curved ceiling above them was covered with them, except for the wide, dark slit that was surely the source of the spears from the hidden ballista. The symbols were arcane, designs showing the alchemical triangles signifying air, earth and fire, the lightning bolt for water, snakes curled around staffs like an ancient doctor's caduceus, eyes of Horus, more complex pentagrams and mandalas, a gruesome inlay of a skulled man riding on the back of a goat, even the magical square of abracadabra, the alchemist's palindrome. It was a sorcerer's dream brought to life, or perhaps the nightmare fantasy of a long-dead czar with a penchant for torture and the mass murder of his enemies.

"Rasputin knew of this place, although he never came here," said Genrikhovich from behind them. "He told my grandfather tales of it many times."

"I thought your grandfather was a spy for the Okhrana, a double agent for Lenin and his Cheka?" Holliday said.

"He was. He was Rasputin's bodyguard, in fact, assigned to him by the czarina Alexandra. The czar approved the choice because he knew that my grandfather actually worked for him; he provided the czar with the infamous 'staircase notes' of Rasputin's activities. St. Petersburg was like that in those times before the revolution: a place of lies, deceit, betrayals, each man working for his own selfish ends."

"Like your grandfather?" Holliday asked as they continued down the long passageway.

"Czar Nicholas knew the secret, as did the czarina. The secret that Rasputin stole and took with him onto the Moika Canal the night that he died. The secret my grandfather learned and took from him with his last breath."

"I thought it was the British agent Rayner who was there at the end," said Holliday.

"No, and that was the secret Oswald Rayner took with him to his grave. My grandfather was the last man to see Grigori Rasputin alive, and it was my grandfather who took matters into his own hands and pushed him under the ice."

"Why did Rayner lie?"

"Because my grandfather knew he was *pedik,* a homosexual, and also a double agent acting for both the British and the Okhrana. He threatened Rayner with exposure to both organizations. Either would have had him killed or at least imprisoned."

"And so Rasputin died at your father's hand."

"Using Rayner's Webley pistol for the coup de grâce, and finally drowning him. But not before retrieving the key."

"The key to Ivan the Terrible's treasure house?"

"The key to everything," answered Genrikhovich. He began to hum something that sounded like a hymn of some sort, and then began to sing the words under his breath.

"Can you make out what he's saying?" Holliday

whispered to Eddie as they continued on down the mysterious corridor somewhere deep beneath the Kremlin.

"It is something religious, I think," the Cuban said, listening to the mournful, chanting tune. "It is very old, too." He listened again as Genrikhovich repeated what sounded like a chorus. " 'We who *místicamente* . . . mystically? represent' . . . *¿el bebé angel?*"

"Cherubim?" Holliday suggested.

"*Sí* . . . 'cherubim, and singing to the life-giving Trinity the . . . three-times-holy hymn, let us now lay aside all earthly care that we may . . . receive the king of all, who comes invisibly' . . . *transmitido por* . . . 'carried up . . . borne up by angels. *Aleluya! Aleluya! Aleluya!*' "

Behind them Genrikhovich repeated the chorus over and over again, lost within the hymn and whatever it meant to him. A few moments later the passageway ended in a wrought-iron gate with six rusted bars that was closed, but not locked. Eddie cautiously pushed open the gate and waited.

"Step through into the chamber," said Genrikhovich.

"What do you see?" Holliday asked, standing a couple of feet behind his friend. "Any wires, traps, anything out of place in the doorway?" Eddie scanned the iron frame of the gate, paying particular attention to the hinges, the bottom of the frame and the lintel overhead.

"*Nada,*" said the Cuban.

"What about the room beyond?"

"A circle, a dome in the ceiling. There are two other gates and a door. There is a great deal of dust everywhere. The floor is in mosaic. Circles one inside another, red and black, and there are mosaic pictures over the gates."

"Pictures of what?"

"A saint in one, the Holy Mother above the other."

Holliday smiled faintly. You could spend a lifetime under Fidel, but once a Catholic, always a Catholic. "Anything else?"

"Directly across the room there is *¿un . . . púlpito? ¿Un altar?*"

"An altar?"

"Sí," said Eddie. *"Un altar de oro.* A golden altar."

"A golden altar?" Genrikhovich asked, excitement rising in his voice.

"Yes," replied Holliday.

"The Holy Altar of the Ninth Sanctuary," breathed the Russian. "The old stories were true!"

"What old stories?" Holliday asked.

"Step through!" Genrikhovich demanded. "Step through! I must see for myself!"

"Go through," said Holliday to Eddie, his voice soft. "But stay close to the wall."

"Sí, compadre. I understand," the Cuban replied. He stepped through into the room and shuffled quickly to the left, keeping his back close to the wall. Holliday followed, his eyes scanning the room in the light from his

helmet. Genrikhovich stepped through the gateway, the big lantern in his left hand, the Tokarev still firmly gripped in his right.

"It is true," he whispered. "All true." He walked forward, hypnotized by the gleaming vision of the gold altar on the far side of the room.

"I think you'd better stop," advised Holliday. Genrikhovich ignored him and continued forward toward the altar. "Stop!" Holliday said, speaking like a drill instructor.

Genrikhovich stopped and turned, blinking like a man coming out of sleep. "What did you say?" the Russian asked. Holliday noticed that the hand with the gun had dropped slightly. Not enough to do anything about, not yet, at least.

"Look at the floor," said Holliday. "There are four circles of red, four of black and one red circle in the center. Between the last circle of black and the red one in the center it looks as though the dust has settled into some sort of crack."

"What are you talking about?" Genrikhovich asked, suspicion rising in his tone along with the pistol in his hand.

"It's a tiger trap," said Holliday.

"What?" Genrikhovich asked, looking confused. "What is that?"

"Your weight springs a trapdoor and you fall into a pit with twenty or thirty bamboo stakes jutting up. In

Vietnam they used to cover the sharpened ends of the bamboo with human feces; if the spikes didn't kill you the sepsis would."

"You think those deeper lines in the floor could signify such a thing?" Genrikhovich asked.

"Positive." Holliday turned to Eddie. "Give me the shovel."

Eddie handed him the entrenching tool, and Holliday walked forward until he stood just outside the large crimson center ring. He knelt down, raised the shovel above his head, then brought it down hard. There was a cracking noise, the rusty groan of old hinges, and then the gallows thump of two semicircular doors six feet across dropping downward. Holliday edged forward and looked into the pit. It was twenty feet down, and the stakes were made of what appeared to be the pointed blades of upended broadswords. The entire bottom of the pit was covered with a piled litter of bones. One of the sword stakes had slid between the old sepia-colored bones of an intact rib cage. Holliday counted at least twenty human skulls.

"Looks like your friend Ivan had a few practice runs," said Holliday.

Genrikhovich came cautiously forward and looked down into the pit, keeping one eye on Holliday and Eddie. He stepped back quickly, his lip curled in distaste. "No doubt he had the workmen and artisans who worked here killed to keep his secret."

"No doubt," said Holliday dryly. There was a heavy metallic sound from somewhere under the floor, and the trap snapped shut again, ready for its next victim. "What about the two other gates?"

"Simple," said Genrikhovich. "The czar had many enemies and was a great believer in secrets and escape routes. The stairs and the passageways we used to get here led from the dungeons. That was almost surely how the czar had his treasures from Byzantium carried here." He paused and nodded toward the gate with the mosaic of the saint over it. For the first time Holliday noticed that the vestments the saint was wearing were covered with large red crosses, the same eight pointed crosses that were used by the Templars on their shields and even by Columbus on the sails of his three famous ships. "The saint over the gateway is Saint Basil, or Vasily in Russian. When the czar went to Saint Basil's Cathedral a hundred yards away in what is now called Red Square, he would use that passageway to reach his treasure house unharmed. The other passage leads to the Cathedral of the Assumption in the Kremlin itself. The cathedral is consecrated to the Virgin Mary. As you may know, the Cathedral of the Assumption is also known as the Uspenski Cathedral."

"The Fabergé Kremlin Egg," said Holliday.

"The pieces of the puzzle begin to come together at last." The Russian smiled.

"What about the Templar crosses on Saint Basil's robes?"

"Equally simple," said Genrikhovich. "You may not be aware of this, but Saint Basil's lies at the exact geographical center of Moscow. The tenth church of Saint Basil's was known as the Jerusalem church by its priests, since it was by definition the very center of holy life in the great city; they have worn the crosses for almost a thousand years to honor the knights who guarded Jerusalem the way the priests guarded the church. It is why, in the end, the Sword of the South, Octanis, came here with the rest of Ivan's treasures."

"I don't see it," said Holliday, trying to get the Russian's goat and get him off guard. It didn't work.

"The last secret," said Genrikhovich calmly. "Go to the altar, please," he said, waving the gun a little, but standing aside. "Your friend as well."

Holliday and Eddie did as they were told. Approaching the altar, Holliday saw that it was etched with yet another pentacle, and at the symbol's center was what appeared to be a keyhole.

Genrikhovich put the big lantern on the floor, then reached under his shirt and pulled out a large gold key on a well-worn and sweat-stained leather strip. He slipped it over his head and dangled it in his free hand. "The final key," he said, his face suffused with a glowing brightness that might have been religious passion, or perhaps nothing but consuming greed. "The key taken from Rasputin's pocket by my grandfather that night on the cracking ice of the Moika Canal."

"The key to the Kremlin Egg," said Holliday. "And the fake made by the Finnish jeweler?"

"A copy commissioned by Czar Nicholas himself to cover up the loss of the original," Genrikhovich said. With that he inserted the key into the center of the pentangle on the golden altar and twisted it to the left. Like the groaning of the hinges on the tiger trap behind them, there was the distant dull screeching of gears and the harsh whirring of some massive clockwork mechanism hidden somewhere in the walls. Suddenly the sound of ringing bells could be heard, and Holliday realized that it was the same as the hymn that Genrikhovich had been humming in the corridor. The Russian turned toward Holliday, the faint smile back on his face. The smile of a madman. "The Hymn of the Cherubim, a favorite of Czar Nicholas, and the hymn played at the consecration of Saint Basil's attended by Ivan the Terrible. The hymn that plays on the Kremlin Egg music box."

The music stopped, the sound of the bells fading slowly away to faint echoes. There was the grinding of more hidden gears within the walls. Directly in front of them a section of wall five feet wide began to rumble slowly into the floor until it disappeared. Genrikhovich picked up the lantern and shone it through the newly created gap in the wall.

"Gentlemen," said the Russian ponderously, "I give you the lost treasures of Ivan the Terrible!"

One after another the three men stepped across the threshold and entered the room beyond.

36

Genrikhovich stepped into the treasure house, set the big lantern down and turned it up to its fullest light, revealing a room born from the sweat and blood and hearts and hands of ten thousand toiling artisans from the mountains of the Himalayas to the great Horn of Africa. It was large and domed, and surrounded with Palladian columns, steps of granite leading down to a floor that Plato might have debated on, or where the great Sophocles might have set his *Oedipus Rex,* or his *Antigone.*

But the floor was covered knee-deep in treasures, goblets, coins, bars and bolts of cloth so old they had rotted away to rich dust, and the steps had been turned into shelves full of coins and bullion, silver and gold jewelry crusted with gems of all kinds, from ropes of huge pearls to diamonds the size of ice cubes and emeralds the size of green apples.

There were carved ivory elephant tusks, a life size

pair of black onyx leopards being held in check by golden chains grasped in the fist of a carved Nubian slave that might have come from some ancient Egyptian tomb. On one side a stuffed crocodile with amethyst eyes was in full-scale combat with a full-size Russian bear. On the other side turquoise hummingbirds hung from the silver branches of a plum tree blossoming with pale Ceylonese sapphires.

On the cases set along the walls between the high pillars were scrolls wrapped in gold and capped with chased silver. There were manuscripts bound in inlaid horn and every form of precious metal. There were enormous tomes, their leather spines as worked and carved as the backs of ancient dinosaurs, and some volumes slim enough to be held in a child's hand and bound in the thin, translucent mottled shells of unborn tortoises. This was Ivan the Terrible's great library, saved from the vandal pillaging of Constantinople almost six hundred years ago, marking the end of an empire that had lasted since the time of Christ.

Holliday shivered, hearing the last words of the big, sad-eyed monk Helder Rodrigues as he lay dying in the rain under a dark, troubled sky: *Too many secrets. Too many secrets.*

"Poryodok zhar-ptitsa," whispered Genrikhovich, staring across the high-domed room. He began to walk like a man hypnotized, humming softly under his breath.

"What's he saying?" Holliday whispered.

"The Order of the Firebird. The Phoenix," answered Eddie, keeping his voice low. *"¡Querido Dios! ¡Está cantando el saga Krasny!"* said the Cuban, tears suddenly welling from his big brown eyes and running down his cheeks.

"The what?" Holliday said, stunned at the reaction it was having on his friend.

"My mother sang it to me when I was a little boy," said Eddie. "When my father was dying in the hospital of cancer I held him in my arms and he asked me to sing it to him, and I did, but I could not remember the words and he died." The Cuban was openly sobbing now, as though some long-forgotten dam of emotion had burst.

"I'm sorry, friend, so very sorry," Holliday said. It was as though the man were being ripped apart by the memory of his dying father. His eyes on Genrikhovich, Holliday could now see where he was going: a granite podium like the one outside, this one with a sword sheathed in silver hanging over the stone edge of the plinth from a fine gold mesh belt.

Holliday immediately recognized the sword by the simple, wire-wrapped hilt identical to the sword his uncle Henry had kept hidden in his house in Fredonia, New York, for more than half a century. That sword had previously been owned by Adolf Hitler and kept at his mountain retreat at Berchtesgaden in Bavaria. Now,

Holliday could see, this was the last of the four swords sent out from Castle Pelerin by the dwarf swordsmith Alberic in the Holy Land, warning the Templars of their grisly destiny. This was Octanis, Sword of the South.

The front of the plinth the sword hung on was carved with a great fiery bird rising up out of a bed of flames—the phoenix. On the top of the podium and looking remarkably familiar was a large, ornate box. The box looked familiar because it was identical to every illustration or copy of it Holliday had seen since he was a child in Sunday school, right up to the one hidden away in a Pentagon warehouse in Steven Spielberg's famous film.

It was four feet long and two and a half feet wide, the entire box covered in sheet gold and topped by two angels, wings stretched toward each other, wing tips touching, also in gold. The sides of the box were covered in ornate designs, and two poles were permanently fixed to its base for transport. By most accounts it held the shattered stone tablets Moses had smashed at the foot of Mount Sinai, but occasionally was thought to include Aaron's rod and a jar of manna from heaven, depending on which book and which translation of the Old Testament you were reading. It was, beyond a shadow of a doubt, none other than the Ark of the Covenant.

The original Ark was thought to have been hidden in a variety of places, from a Templar Knight's ancestral home in Warwickshire, England, to a lake in Ethiopia, returned to Mount Sinai, now known as Mount Horeb, hidden inside a hill in Ireland, the Languedoc region of France and even hidden away in a museum in Harare, the capital city of the Republic of Zimbabwe. To Holliday's knowledge no one had even once suggested that it had rested under the Kremlin for the last few hundred years, although it made a certain amount of sense when you considered the origin of most of Czar Ivan's riches.

Genrikhovich reached the podium, grasped the wings of the angels on the peaked cover of the ark and pulled upward with a jerk. The top of the box came up and off without any problem. For a single second some idiot part of Holliday's brain expected a ray-gun beam of brilliant light to zap out of the box and melt Genrikhovich's face like a wax candle, but nothing happened. The Russian simply set the top aside and reached inside.

A moment later he removed a large jeweled slipcase made out of beaten gold. From inside he withdrew a simple leather-bound volume about eighteen inches high, a foot and a half wide and three or four inches thick. He laid it carefully on the surface of the podium, sweeping the top of the box to the floor, where it split into several pieces. He turned back the cover and stared. An instant later he crowed like a rooster at dawn.

"I have it!" he screeched. "I have it now!" The Russian did a gruesome little jig, his lank hair plastered to his temples as trickles of sweat coursed down his face.

He took off his spectacles, peering closely at the text, then put them on again, fumbling as he hooked the arms of the glasses over his ears.

"It is in Aramaic, Holliday. Can you read Aramaic? No, of course you can't, but it doesn't matter. I don't need you anymore—or them, for that matter. Or your silly notebook; they can have it all!" He crowed again, a terrible shriek that dissolved into convulsive giggles.

"You know what it says, you poor fool of an American? You know what the title of this book is? No? Well, I'll tell you. It says, 'The Gospel of Yeshua ben Yusef.' You know who he was, at least, surely."

Holliday knew. He stood stunned beside his weeping friend. Yeshua ben Yusef had been Christ's name as a man. If the book Genrikhovich held in his hands was literally Christ's own words as written by himself in the years before his death—or, Holliday thought, *after* his supposed crucifixion—if they were the words of a man and not a god, then those words would have more real power than anything dreamed up for a Hollywood movie or in the beakers of horrors at the Almaty Biological Weapons Facility in Kazakhstan, so short of money now that they kept their supplies of anthrax in old coffee cans.

"Come!" Genrikhovich offered generously, waving his hand in Holliday's direction. "Leave the crying nigger and I'll show you."

"*¡Basta ya!*" *Enough!* Eddie roared. "*¡Es suficiente, pedazo de mierda inútil ruso!*"

Holliday didn't have any time at all to react.

Tears still streamed down Eddie's cheeks, but his sorrow had turned to rage. He came out of his crouching position on the floor like a sprinter leaving his blocks, a deep guttural groan growing in his throat like some enraged animal finally, at long last, unleashed. He vaulted over the chests of treasure, heading for the Russian, who now stood frozen, wide eyed with fear as the big Cuban thundered toward him, blood in his eyes.

"Eddie! No!" Holliday yelled, taking off after his friend. Genrikhovich suddenly remembered the Tokarev and fumbled for it on the podium, horrified when he couldn't find it. Eddie was getting closer by the second, the growl had now grown to a full-fledged bellow of sustained demonic fury.

"*¡Basta ya!*" he yelled again.

Genrikhovich dropped to his knees and scrabbled through the broken pieces of the Ark on the floor. He found the pistol and stumbled to his feet just as Eddie reached him. He pulled the trigger but nothing happened.

No round in the chamber; amateur's mistake, thought Holliday as he charged after Eddie. Lucky.

Eddie tackled the man shoulder-high and they went down, bringing the rest of the Ark with them in a cascade of splintering wood and thin gold sheeting. The Russian made a screeching sound and then the pistol went off with a muffled roar.

"Eddie!" Holliday yelled hoarsely.

Genrickovich clambered to his feet, the Tokarev held shakily in one hand. A lens of his glasses was shattered, and there was blood all over the front of his shirt. He aimed the gun downward and hauled back on the hammer. "Die, you black bastard!"

Holliday didn't hesitate for a second. He slid Octanis from its golden sheath, raised it above his head and brought it down in a single deadly blow. The brilliantly worked Damascus blade did exactly as it was meant to do, slicing down through skin, flesh, muscle sinew and bone, taking off the Russian's arm at the shoulder. Genrikhovich's arm, Tokarev still clenched in the fist, cartwheeled up and away in a fountain spray of arterial blood that drenched everything, including the book open on the podium. The arm finally landed somewhere in the middle of the chamber with a thump and a clatter.

"My arm," said Genrikhovich almost calmly, staring at the end of his shoulder. The spray was now a pumping mass of veins and arteries that squirmed like trapped snakes with their heads lopped off. "My arm is gone," said the Russian, his voice sounding a little surprised and confused. "You'll have to put it back on."

Genrikhovich took two steps forward and tried to

grip the podium with both hands to support himself. Unfortunately one of the hands was no longer there.

"Please?" Genrikhovich said, and then fell down hard. Holliday had seen wounds like this in Vietnam and Afghanistan—men whose nervous systems continued on for a few seconds when by rights they should have been dead. Holliday looked down at the body on the floor. He was dead now. His arm had pretty much stopped bleeding.

Holliday crouched down, attending to Eddie. He rolled the man over on his back and saw a large red stain on the lower left quadrant of his chest. It wasn't sucking and there was no bloody froth on his lips, so it wasn't a lung. Spleen or kidney, maybe. Not as bad as a lung but bad enough.

"Can you walk?"

"I think so." Eddie nodded weakly.

"Hang on for a second." He turned, slipped off Genrikhovich's gory backpack, then stuffed the book inside it. He shrugged on the backpack and eased himself upward, one arm around Eddie's armpit, the other holding his elbow. After a few seconds the Cuban stood, a little unsteadily.

"Okay?" Holliday asked.

"Okay." Eddie nodded and they headed for the door. They reached it and stepped into the outer chamber. In the distance above them Holliday could hear the sound of boot heels on stone steps.

"Great," he muttered. It was probably the Spetsnaz team they'd almost run into earlier. Not that it made much difference now; going back the way they'd come was too long and too difficult anyway, and he had to get Eddie into a doctor's care as quickly as possible. He helped the Cuban across the chamber to the iron gate leading into the Saint Basil's tunnel and booted it in. The gate tore away easily on rusted-out hinges and the two men stepped into the dark passage.

37

Holliday and Eddie stumbled down the brick-lined tunnel, the way ahead lit only by the dimming lights of their helmet lamps. Each time they hit a crumbling brick on the floor and tripped, Eddie groaned with pain. There was almost no blood on the makeshift compress Holliday had applied to the wound, but Eddie seemed to be getting weaker with every step, and Holliday was beginning to worry about internal bleeding.

He also worried about their immediate future. Arrest by the Spetsnaz squad would be a death sentence. He'd had a brief encounter with one of their teams in Afghanistan back in the days when the United States was backing the Taliban as "freedom fighters," and they were definitely of the "shoot first and don't bother to ask questions at all" school of warfare.

A Russian hospital would be almost as bad. A Cuban with a bullet in his belly brought into one of their emergency wards by an American ex military would have the FSB sniffing around within an hour, and then all hell would break loose. The book or whatever it was he was hauling around on his back only made things worse.

If the volume really was Christ's own gospel and not an interpretation and transliteration of his words written years and perhaps centuries after his death, then it would be the equivalent of a hydrogen bomb going off in the world of religion. Evangelical churches whose entire existence was based on "decoding" and interpreting the words of Christ would collapse overnight. The fundamental tenets and faith of the Catholic Church would almost certainly be called into question, and the "deconstruction" of a figure seen as a god or even as "the Son of God" could send shock waves through all of Christendom. The actual content of the gospel would eventually tell the tale.

Were the gospels the considered, thoughtful religious philosophy of an enlightened, brilliantly intelligent mind, or the rants and raves of a roving holy man with wild delusions of grandeur, a revolutionary turn of phrase and an innate ability to irritate and anger the rich and powerful? Not that it mattered, really; right now the last thing anyone needed was more fuel to feed an already violent mistrust among the great religions of the world.

From somewhere behind them Holliday heard a distant, drawn-out scream and he smiled. At least one of the Spetsnaz team had been impaled on Ivan the Terrible's tiger trap. One less for him to deal with.

As they moved on down the corridor, Eddie seemed to be leaning more and more heavily on him.

"What's wrong, *compadre?*" Holliday asked.

"Muy cansado, mi amigo, muy cansado," answered Eddie in a mumble.

"*Cansado,* tired?"

"*Sí,* very tired."

"We can rest for a minute," offered Holliday.

"Just a little minute." Eddie sighed, sinking down to the dusty brick floor. Seated, Holliday crouched down beside him and gently peeled back the rear of his jacket. There was no blood on the back of his shirt. No exit wound, which meant he was almost surely bleeding internally. Holliday grimaced. How far from the chamber to the Saint Boris cathedral? Two hundred yards, three. They'd gone less than half that in almost fifteen minutes, and he could hear footsteps echoing in the tunnel behind them now. Maybe it was time to stop and fight. What? Bricks against AK-47s?

"We gotta go, Eddie boy," said Holliday, putting on his worst Irish accent.

"Leave me, *tío,*" muttered Eddie.

"*¿Tío?* I'm not your uncle, and this isn't some stupid Audie Murphy film where that round-faced little Mr. Perfect stays back to zap a hundred crazy Japs with his machine gun and when he runs out of bullets he starts whipping them over the head with the red-hot barrel. You're coming with me and you're coming right now, goddamn it!"

"¿*Qué?* Who is this Audie Murphy?" Eddie asked. Holliday dragged him to his feet, got his arm under his shoulder and stumbled forward. A few yards later the tunnel turned sharply to the left and then ended. Holliday would have fallen over the edge if his headlamp beam hadn't dipped out of sight first.

"Shit," said Holliday. He played the light from his lamp over the edge and realized where they were. A foot beneath him the pile of broken rubble drifted down to the old metro station with its waiting self-powered car. He suddenly realized he could see a faint light coming from the driver's cab in the front of the car. There was someone inside. As calmly as he could he reached up, switched off his own lamp and eased Eddie downward until his legs were dangling over the edge of the opening.

"Remember the old metro station we saw with Genrikhovich and Ivanov, the priest?"

"*Sí,*" said Eddie, his voice quavering with fatigue.

"It's right under us. There's somebody on the train. Some kind of guard, I think. I'm going to take him out, but I'm going to have to leave you here for a minute or two. You okay with that?"

"*Sí, Popo Tío.*" Eddie smiled. He was in some kind of shock-driven la-la land now.

"Okay," said Holliday.

"Okay." Eddie nodded, his eyes half-closed in sleep. The footsteps behind them were much louder now.

"Shit," said Holliday.

"Sí, mierda." Eddie grinned.

Holliday eased Eddie to one side, then lowered himself carefully down onto the pile of rubble. He made his way blindly down the pile, concentrating on the little square of weak light coming out of the front of the subway car. He finally reached the platform. The doors of the car were still open. He stepped quietly inside, gripped the door handle of the driver's compartment tightly with one hand and rapped on the door with the knuckles of his other hand.

The door burst open and a belligerent bullet-headed figure appeared, iPod buds dangling from his ears. Holliday could distinctly hear Slayer's "Angel of Death" playing at earsplitting volume.

"Kto yebat' ty?!" Bullet Head grunted angrily. Holliday slammed the door in the man's face as hard as he possibly could. Bullet Head dropped like a stone, heavy metal still pounding out of his ears.

"It's me, the angel of death," said Holliday, and began stripping the man of his weapons.

38

It took Holliday at least five minutes to ease Eddie down onto the pile of rubble below the open floor of the tunnel and another three or four to get him down to the platform and settled into one of the seats on the train. By the time he actually sat down at the driver's seat of the self-propelled subway car he could actually hear the raised, echoing voices of the Spetsnaz team coming after them. They kept on calling out for Boris Byka, presumably their name for Bullet Head, who was still out cold on the rear of the platform where Holliday had dragged him.

Boris had been armed with a folding-stock AK-103 assault rifle, an OC-23 Drotik twenty-four-round automatic pistol, half a dozen RGD-5 fragmentation grenades and a very nasty-looking Kizlyar Scorpion bowie knife. Plenty of killing power, but the seven or eight guys coming down the tunnel would be at least as well armed, and with Eddie down the odds were pretty bad.

Holliday stared at the control panel. Lot of gauges, a big chrome steel T-throttle in the middle of the dashboard and a single pedal on the floor. The T-bar had black plastic inserts at the ends of the T.

There were five big buttons on the right. One red, one green, one yellow with a black lightbulb printed on it and two white ones. The white ones had arrows on them, the arrow on the top button pointing up, the arrow on the bottom button pointing down.

The one with the lightbulb seemed reasonably self-explanatory, so he pushed it down with his thumb. The lights in the car flickered on, then off, then on again, and there was the sudden sound of a generator kicking in. He pressed the button with the downward-pointing arrow. There was a pneumatic hiss and the doors thumped shut.

"So far so good," he muttered. If he assumed the throttle was just that, a throttle, that meant the pedal on the floor was probably the brake. That left the small problem of motive power. In his world, red meant stop and green meant go, but this was a subway from Stalin-era Soviet Russia, so he pressed red instead. There was a mechanical moan like a car started up in freezing-cold weather and then a stuttering roar, and the whole car began to vibrate.

The throttle was resting in a notch, which Holliday assumed was the idle position. He gently slipped the T-bar out of the notch and gave it a tiny nudge, then let it go; the car moved forward a few feet before some sort of automatic device cut in and the car stopped dead. Holliday frowned, confused, and then realized that by letting go of the right-side black plastic insert on the throttle he'd initialized an automated dead man's switch. His father had been a locomotive driver for one of the old unconsolidated New York railroads and had talked about dead man's switches, but this was the first time Holliday had seen one in action.

He pulled the throttle handle back and into the notch, feeling something definitely disengage as he did so. The clutch. He looked out the open doorway of the driver's cab. Eddie was slumped against the nearest seat across the aisle, his eyes half-closed.

"Eddie?"

"Sí."

"Stay awake, *amigo*. I've almost got us out of here."

"Bueno," mumbled the Cuban.

"Here we go." Holliday eased the throttle out of the notch, keeping his right thumb down on the plastic insert. He pushed the throttle forward little by little; the car groaned and clanked but began to rumble out of the old station.

As he pushed the throttle farther the Spetsnaz team in the tunnel began to fire blindly, catching the back end of the car as it moved out of the station, shattering glass and puncturing the cracked plastic covers on the seats. One of the team even managed to toss down one of his RGD-5 grenades onto the platform. Unfortunately it was all a bit too late. The bullets did no real damage to the train, and the grenade only blew out a few tiles on the walls and ceiling and put a few white-hot pieces of shrapnel into the unconscious Bullet Head's brain. By the time the first man reached the platform, the rear lights of the self-propelled car were already vanishing around a curve in the tunnel and Bullet Head was as dead as a doornail.

On that uneventful night in his equally uneventful life, Felix Fyodor Fosdikov sat in the toasty warm cab of his big GS-18.05 motor grader and watched the first snow begin to fall in the Kuntsevo district a few miles south of the Moscow Ring Road. As he watched the heavy snow begin to turn the world a uniform, featureless white, he bit into his wife's black bread–sauerkraut-sausage-and–goat cheese sandwich and chewed. He took a sip of the hot, vodka-laced coffee his wife had prepared for him in his old battered thermos. During the spring, summer and fall Felix Fyodor drove a garbage truck for the Central Moscow district, which he preferred to snow removal.

When you worked garbage you found all sorts of useful and potentially valuable things you could sell at the big tailgate markets in Mozhaysk and other places outside the city. In his forty-six years on the job he'd found everything from a perfectly good gold watch to a pink-enameled artificial leg. Even if what you found wasn't worth anything, there wasn't a day that went by working garbage that wasn't interesting.

Still, driving the big motor grader had its good points. He was alone in the high, glassed-in cab, so there was no one to answer to when the sauerkraut, cheese and sausage produced their inevitably pungent brand of oily farts, and no one to complain when he filled the cab with smoke from the cheap bulk cigarettes he favored.

He finished the first sandwich and started on the second. At sixty-two, with all those years on the job, he was getting far too old for the work, but he couldn't see himself sitting around watching television or growing tomatoes in their little allotment, and his small pension wasn't going to let him do much more than that. It didn't matter, really; one way or the other his wife's sandwiches and the vodka and the cigarettes would get him eventually, either from a heart attack on the road or straining on the toilet fighting to pass the rock-hard bowel movements the sandwiches caused.

Felix Fyodor glanced out of the side door of the cab. The blade of the grader was marked with reflective tape at five-centimeter intervals, like a ruler. When the snow reached the first strip of tape he would begin his route. The route took him east along the perimeter road of the big forest plot with the double razor-wire fence, then south and west and north until he got back to where he was right now. When he finished the big square around the forest plot, he'd put the grader onto the closest on-ramp of the highway into the city, then grade the snow all the way to the Ring Road and back again. Then he'd take a piss break, have a snack and do it all over again. On a night with a predicted heavy snowfall like tonight he'd probably do the run seven or eight times before his shift was over.

Once, years ago, he'd asked about the property be-hind the wire and he'd been told to mind his own busi-ness, but eventually he'd heard enough whispered stories to figure out that the land had been Stalin's Mos-cow dacha—the place where he'd spent most of the great patriotic war and the place he'd died in on March 5, 1953, supposedly full of Alzheimer's or syphilis or something and poisoned by the KGB chief Beria to keep him from signing death warrants for just about every-one in the government, including Beria. Someone had wanted to make a museum out of the place, but how did you make a museum for a mass murderer? Khrushchev had stopped the idea and the place had been empty and abandoned ever since. Felix Fyodor took a bite out of the second sandwich, trying not to think of the heart-burn already climbing up his chest. It would be a long night and he needed nourishment. He looked down at the markers on the plow and wished the snow would fall a little faster. He was parked within a few yards of the entrance to the whole estate, and it spooked him more than a little.

They traveled along the almost arrow-straight tunnel, the only illumination coming from the broad beam of the self-propelled car's headlight. Holliday kept the throttle pushed about halfway forward, and according to the speedometer they were going ninety kilometers per, which translated into roughly fifty-five miles per hour. At the forty-five-minute mark that meant they'd gone about forty miles from the original station beneath the Kremlin. On the seat outside the operator's compartment Eddie had fallen into a half-conscious doze, rocking gently with the motion of the train, his big head lolling, his eyes closed.

As they rolled onward Holliday tried to assess the chaos they had left behind them in the subway station. By now the Spetsnaz team would have reported to their bosses and the word would have gone up the chain of command—someone had hijacked Stalin's secret subway from more than half a century ago and was hightailing it up the line to wherever it ended up. Personally Holliday didn't care. At the first opportunity he wanted to get off the damn thing and figure out some way to get himself and Eddie safely behind the walls of the American embassy.

There was a heavy clanking from the tracks beneath

the wheels and suddenly the throttle moved under Holliday's hand, dropping halfway back to the neutral notch. The car slowed. A minute later there was a second sound from the tracks and the throttle smoothly moved back under his hand. The car slowed to a walk, and ahead Holliday could see that they were coming into a station. As they moved up to the platform Holliday released his hand from the throttle. The car rolled on for a few yards and then stopped. The doors hissed open. Wherever they were going, this was it. The platform was dark.

Holliday switched on his miner's lamp, then stepped out of the driver's compartment and helped Eddie to his feet. They stepped off the train. The platform was completely barren—no signs, no gates, no nothing, just an arch of dark-glazed brick and a single exit. There were half a dozen lights in the ceiling behind wire screens, all of them dark. The place felt like a tomb.

He and Eddie made their slow way to the exit, the light on Holliday's helmet painting the way. Eddie's breathing was ragged, but at least he was still conscious. The exit was in the exact center of the platform—an alcove and four steps leading to a small vestibule. The vestibule was square with a low ceiling, and was completely without decoration. There were two doors, one obviously for an elevator, the other more like a hatchway, with a large round locking wheel in the center. There were faded Cyrillic letters above the wheel.

"Can you read what it says?" Holliday asked.

"Bomboubezhishche," read Eddie, not hesitating at all over the mouthful of a word. "Bomb shelter."

Holliday pressed the single button beside the elevator doors and remarkably they creaked open. He helped Eddie inside the plain gray steel compartment. There were two buttons on the wall. He pressed the top one. The doors closed and the elevator began to rise.

The United States Embassy in Moscow consists of a ten-story office block, a connecting, windowless security block, a series of low barracks-style offices, all surrounding a central courtyard and further surrounded by a tall brick wall. There is only one means of access and egress to the complex—the front gate, which in turn has several well-hidden anti–suicide bombing measures as well as a SWAT team on twenty-four-hour duty. To get into the main building, any guest or official must first pass through a sally port, which allows movement of only a single individual at a time and in one direction.

The bachelor and guest quarters at the embassy were located at the far end of the complex and offered only the most basic amenities—bathroom, shower, bedroom with a single narrow bed, a desk and a telephone. The decor was resolutely beige. The telephone in the room being occupied by Brinsley Whitman Havers rang at three twenty-five in the morning. Whit had been having trouble sleeping, knowing that his man was in play, and he picked up on the second ring. It was the security office, a man named Tapsinger.

"Yes?" Whit said.

"You'd better get over here pronto, sir; there's a lot of back chatter in the air about your boy."

"Which one?"

"The target, as I understand it, Holliday."

"What kind of back chatter?"

"FSB back chatter, sir, and it's coming out of the Kremlin itself. Scary stuff, sir. Seems he's hijacked Stalin's old private subway train. There're bodies everywhere. This stuff is going all the way back to Washington. Somebody's in it up to his eyeballs. It's starting to sound like a first-class international incident."

"Shit," said Brinsley Whitman Havers. What was it Kokum had said about the real reason they had case officers? To have someone to flush down the shithole when the whole thing came apart? Something like that. "I'll be right there." He sighed, already seeing the water swirling around the bowl, and him along with it.

39

The elevator opened up into someone's pantry. Holliday could tell it was a pantry because the walls were lined with shelves, and the shelves were lined with cans and jars and boxes. The cans all had black-and-white illustrations of their contents on paper labels, as did the boxes. It was hard to tell about the jars, because over the years most of them had burst, their contents long turned to mold, the mold vanished into the air, leaving nothing but shriven remains behind, like mummified human organs in an Egyptian tomb. Everything in the little room was covered in a thick coat of gray dust. It had been a long time since anyone had taken food from here.

The only exit from the pantry led into a good-size kitchen equipped with thirties- or forties-era gas appliances. There was a wooden table and four straight chairs in the center of the room. Like everything else, the table and chairs were thick with dust. The floor was gray linoleum, the ceiling raw-pine beams and rafters. The windows above the big dry sinks were small, the plain dark curtains pulled.

The kitchen led in turn to a broad carpeted hallway with a set of stairs going up on the right. There were two doors beyond the stairs, one leading to a plainly furnished living room, the furniture old, upholstered and dreary. The other door led to a study. A velvet-upholstered banquette stood at the end of the hall beneath a row of wooden pegs still hung with heavy winter coats. Holliday eased Eddie down onto the banquette, his back against the patterned wallpaper.

"You rest here for a minute," said Holliday. "I want to look around a bit and then we'll be on our way."

"*Lo que usted diga, mi amigo*—whatever you say," the Cuban answered weakly.

Holliday turned back and went into the study. There were windows on two walls and here the curtains were pulled back. It had snowed since they'd gone underground hours before, a thick, soft blanket of it at least six inches deep, the scattered birch trees throwing long, skeletal shadows. The study was filled with the strange blue light that comes when moonlight reflects off newly fallen snow, and the room had a surreal, almost sinister quality.

The study was large, with open beams like the kitchen and a pine plank floor covered in carpets of various sizes. There was a fireplace, a huge wooden desk, a high-backed leather chair and two straight chairs in front of it. Dust coated everything.

He went to the desk and stood behind the tall leather office chair. There was a circular brass pie rack complete with a sandpaper striker and a handful of wax-headed phosphorous matches, a photograph of an elderly woman and the most telling object of them all, one that Holliday had seen a thousand times before: a photograph of a bald-headed man wearing a white shirt, loosened multicolored tie and mirrored sunglasses sitting on a garden chair with a dark-haired young girl in ponytails, perhaps ten years old, sitting on his lap. The man had his arm possessively wrapped around her midsection. Behind him a secretary wearing headphones was transcribing dictation, and at a round rattan table a man in a gray uniform complete with Cossack boots was smoking a curved pipe and poring over a sheaf of papers spread out on the table in front of him.

The man in the mirrored sunglasses was Lavrenti Beria, head of the NKVD, later to become the KGB; the young girl was Svetlana Stalin, Joseph Stalin's only legitimate child; the secretary with the headphones was Otto Kuusinen, Stalin's private secretary and one of the very few people to survive the vast Stalinist purges; and the man in the uniform smoking the pipe—the same tooth-scarred pipe sitting in the rack in front of him— was Joseph Stalin himself.

Holliday breathed deeply. This was Stalin's study in

the "nearer dacha" at Kuntsevo, about thirty miles out-side Moscow. Stalin had spent his last years here, and he had died here.

Holliday dropped the machine gun and the knapsack on the desk. He pulled out the big leather chair and dropped down into it, giving in to his fatigue for a few precious seconds.

He realized just how desperately tired he was, not only physically but mentally. The last years had taken their toll. Once upon a time he'd been a historian and a teacher, both roles that suited him well. Sometimes he yearned for the fresh faces of his kids at West Point, but he could see no way back along that path now. Ever since making his promise to the dying monk Rodrigues on that tiny volcanic island in the Azores, he'd gone down a rabbit hole of intrigue and conspiracy and into a dark world he'd never even suspected existed.

He opened the bloodstained knapsack and took out the manuscript that Genrikhovich had removed from the ornate Ark of the Covenant in the treasure chamber. It was bound in some dark animal skin, probably goat, the cover stiff with age. He opened it. The first page had a single line of script in ancient Aramaic, the language most likely to have been spoken by Christ.

Did it say what the Russian had read out so trium-phantly—the Gospel of Yeshua ben Yusef, Jesus, son of Joseph? Holliday flipped through the long pages of small, neat script, the ink faded to a pale sepia. The upper and lower edges of the pages were roughly cut, which made sense if you assumed that such a document had originally been written on scrolls, then cut into pages sometime in the future.

Were they really the words of Christ, perhaps written in his own hand? Unlikely. Holliday had never heard a discussion of the topic, but Jesus was almost certainly functionally illiterate—he most probably could neither read nor write; such a level of education wouldn't have been available to the son of a carpenter, and there was no documentation in any of the other gospels about Christ attending any kind of school. The gospel could have been physically written by one or more of his disciples, several of whom were known to be quite well educated.

Genuine, a fake, a fairy tale? And did it matter? One way or the other it was a time bomb and a document of immense power. Holliday traced a line of script with his finger. Was he touching the word of God?

It was the same with all religions: Jesus, Mohammed, Buddha, Confucius, the Dalai Lama, the gods of popularity cults, like Mao, Che, even Eddie's aging Fidel—before they were revered they were men, and one way or the other, over time the ideas of these men were taken, misused, abused and eternally reinterpreted for reasons of power and personal gain. The Gospel of Yeshua ben Yusef would be no different; it would be used for other people's ends and to satisfy other people's needs.

Once more Holliday heard the dying words of Helder Rodrigues: *Too many secrets, too many secrets.* In that moment, with that memory clear and present in his mind, Holliday came to his decision, a decision that went against all the tenets of truth he'd ever been taught. A secret revealed was a secret that could never be made secret again, and some secrets were better left alone.

He flipped the manuscript over and tented it on the desk. He pulled open all the drawers on both pedestals of the desk and pulled out reams of old paper, brittle and yellow and tinder dry. The irony of what he was about to do and where did not escape him. He was keeping the bright secret of a holy man by destroying it in a place once occupied by one of the most unholy men ever to have walked the earth.

He reached out, took one of the wax-preserved phosphorous matches out of its holder and dragged it down the sandpaper strip. It sputtered for only a second, but then it burst into flame. Holliday gently touched the match to the brittle pages of the manuscript, watching them ignite, and in turn light the pile of papers he'd built up around it.

He picked up the machine gun and stood up, stepping back. Soon the entire top of the desk was alight, pages and sheets of paper carried up into the roof beams on the hot air currents, more pages whirling and twisting over to the curtains. Within less than a minute the entire room was ablaze.

Holliday went back to the hallway. He roused Eddie, stood him up, then managed to get one of the overcoats on the pegs onto him—a gray double-breasted thing with brass buttons and a fur collar. He chose another coat for himself, shrugged into it and guided Eddie toward the front door.

"Something is burning, I think," said Eddie blearily.

"It sure is." Holliday smiled. Holding Eddie under the arms, he managed to open the front door, where they were met by a blast of cold air. It was snowing again. "Let's go find a ride, *amigo*."

40

Unfortunately for Felix Fyodor Fosdikov, the sandwich he had eaten combined with the vodka and the over-heated cabin of his big power grader had conspired to put him into a troubled sleep, his head tucked down to his belly, his snores rumbling like cannon fire. Had he stayed awake he would have seen the snow reach the ten-centimeter tape on the blade of his plow and would have gone off on his route. As it was he slept through the ten-centimeter mark, the twenty and the thirty before he woke up.

At first he thought his heartburn dream had become some kind of hideous nightmare in which Stalin had come back to life as a black man and was sitting beside him in the cab. Beyond the black Stalin was another man with a patch over one eye like a pirate and a very nasty-looking machine pistol.

The man with the patch over his eye said something unintelligible to the black Stalin, who appeared to be very sick and perspiring. Felix Fyodor Fosdikov was perspiring, too, and the heartburn was spreading everywhere now, turning his throat into molten lava. He fought to hold back the vomit while simultaneously clamping down on his bowels. This was no dream. The black Stalin turned to him and spoke.

"Vy znaete sposob amerikanskogo poso'stva?"

"Konechno." Felix Fyodor nodded. Under the circumstances, telling the truth seemed like the best option. Out of the corner of his eye he could see a fiery glow somewhere behind the high fence that surrounded the dacha. Bad things were happening tonight. His heartburn cranked up another notch.

"He knows," said Eddie, turning to Holliday, crammed in beside him in the small, overheated cab.

"Then tell him to go there now," Holliday said, gesturing with his weapon.

"Tuda, v nastoyashchyee vremya," translated Eddie.

Felix Fyodor didn't need to be told twice.

"Da," he said, and threw the big power grader into one of its many forward gears. The tall, insectlike machine lurched forward into the snowy night. Behind it, in the birch woods beyond the fence, the dacha burned and the first sirens could be heard.

The first alarm from the Kremlin had gone out at two fifteen after a forty-minute discussion between members of the special Kremlin Spetsnaz unit about the loss of face that would occur if they asked for help. But help was clearly needed, and the first calls were broadcast. The first went out to the Moscow Metropolitan Police, who, recognizing a political hot potato when they saw one, immediately passed responsibility over to the FSB. The FSB, in the way of all large bureaucracies, spent a great deal of time calling people and playing pass-the-buck for a full ninety minutes. It wasn't until three thirty that a request was made to the army for several of its attack helicopters, which then joined the four Kremlin Spetsnaz choppers, all of which spent a further forty-five minutes coordinating their approach and attack on the dacha in Kuntsevo. A unit of special Kremlin guards was dispatched along the subway line, and a further forty local police vehicles were also roped into the party. When a fire was reported on the old abandoned estate, four local fire stations sent their various vehicles to Kuntsevo as well. At four ten in the morning the first FSB unit arrived at the scene, almost half an hour after Felix Fyodor and his passengers had joined the ubiquitous scores of snowplows and graders out on the Moscow streets and highways. Any trace of the power grader's presence at the Kuntsevo property was long since covered by the freshly fallen snow. At four thirty-five Vladimir Vladimirovich Putin, Dmitry Anatolyevich Medvedev, the patriarch of Moscow, and Vasilyevich Bortnikov, head of the

FSB, had all been individually woken from their beds and advised of the situation. Putin, standing by the phone in his silk dressing gown, summed it up succinctly for the others.

"Ebanatyi pidaraz!"

"Vladimir!" said his wife, Lyudmila. "Such language!"

It was two hours earlier by Vatican time when Cardinal Spada's sleep was interrupted by a knock on the bedroom door of his lavish apartment. The Vatican secretary of state came fully awake to the smell of freshly brewed espresso. He rolled over and saw the bland face of his servant, Brother Timothy, a smart, extremely pretty and well-connected young man who hoped for better things through his attachment to the great Cardinal Spada.

Spada took a sip of the scalding coffee, then set it down on the night table beside the enormous four-poster bed that was said to have belonged to one of the Borgias. He pulled himself up against the scrolled headboard while Timothy adjusted his pillows. The young man offered Spada his wire-rimmed spectacles, and the cardinal slipped them on.

"Presumably there is good reason to interrupt my sleep, Timothy. The pope isn't dead, is he?"

"No, Your Eminence, it's Father Brennan."

"*That* old bugger's dead?" Spada said hopefully.

"No, Your Eminence, he's outside, and he'd like to speak to you on a matter of some urgency."

Spada gave a heartfelt sigh and picked up his coffee from the bedside table. "I suppose you'd better send him in."

"Yes, Your Eminence." The monk shimmered away, closing the door behind him. Spada sipped his coffee.

The Irish priest who was also the head of Spada's intelligence network appeared a few seconds later dressed in a rumpled suit with a stained clerical collar and smoking what was probably his tenth cigarette of the day. He didn't beat around the bush.

"They've found bloody Pesek with a bullet in his eye stuffed into a refrigerator in an apartment off the Arbat. The apartment was rented by a Russian Orthodox priest named Ivanov who was somehow connected to Genri-khovich."

"Dear me," said Spada.

"There're also several unconfirmed reports of some sort of attack on the Kremlin. Bodies and such."

"Holliday and his friend?"

"Yes."

"The book?"

"No."

Porca troia! Spada said, reminding himself almost instantly to say ten Our Fathers and twenty Hail Marys for his use of foul language.

*   *   *

At roughly the same time Cardinal Spada was uttering blasphemous oaths in Rome, Pat Philpot, national counterterrorism liaison at the Moscow embassy, was sitting at his desk in the secure cube, with Whit Havers standing on the other side of it. Pat Philpot, inevitably known by friends and enemies alike as Potsy, was not a happy man. He liked his sleep, for one thing, and his banishment to the Moscow boonies after the catastrophe of eighteen months before at least had the benefit that he could basically do nothing through his working days and still collect a salary. It also took him eight thousand miles away from his nagging ex-wife and his children, who were always asking him for money. Four thirty in the morning was not his idea of a good start to the day. He was also hungry, which was why he was now working his way steadily through four McDonald's Big Breakfasts from the Red Square outlet. Some people would have said Philpot had an eating disorder; Pat would have told you he was a big man who wanted to get bigger. Brinsley Whitman Havers, who hadn't had so much as a roti in fifteen years, was simply disgusted.

"All right, kid," said Philpot, chewing his way through his third wedge of hash browns. "You've managed to get every security officer in the embassy in a tizzy, so spill. I need to know it all—start to finish. You're the case officer; who the hell are you running that's causing all this shit to hit the fan?"

"I'm afraid that's impossible, sir," said Whit as Philpot wiped his fingers on the hash brown bag and started in on some scrambled eggs. "I'm afraid it's the national security adviser's operation."

Philpot belched and took a sip of black coffee. He grimaced. "Don't give me that White House West Wing crap, son; it doesn't cut any ice with me. Besides, I know the kind of crap your boss Kokum gets up to, and I also know where *all* his bodies are buried. Spit it out or you're on the next flight out."

"It's a blue operation . . . sir," said Whit stiffly.

"An assassination?"

"Yes, sir."

"Who's the target?"

Whit hesitated. "A man named Holliday, sir," he said finally.

Whit had heard the phrase "he turned white as a sheet" before, but he'd never actually seen it. The blood seemed to drain out of the fat man's neck. It was amazing; he looked like he was going to have a stroke, which wouldn't have been surprising, all things considered.

"Lieutenant Colonel John Holliday? He's the one responsible for all this crap?"

"Yes, sir," said Whit.

"Oh, shit," said Philpot, his appetite gone with almost a complete Big Breakfast to go.

*   *   *

Twenty-five minutes after Eddie and Doc had left the burning dacha, an alert policeman noted the strange behavior of a snowplow in the middle of a snowstorm that wasn't plowing any snow. When he reported to his superiors, it was discovered that the plow in question was well off its normal route, which began close to the gates of the dacha. Fifteen minutes later somebody put two and two together, and within another ten minutes there was a trail of police cars behind the power grader, sirens wailing. There was very little a one-ton police car could do to stop a massive grader like the one piloted by Felix Fyodor Fosdikov, and eventually air support was called in. One of the attack helicopters that had gone to the dacha headed for the location of the errant snowplow with orders to fire at will.

At four fifty-one a.m. Moscow time, Felix Fyodor Fosdikov turned the big power grader off the Ulitsa Novy Arbat and onto Novinsky Perulok, the trail of police cars following behind, the distant thunder of the helicopter getting louder by the second, its giant searchlight swinging back and forth less than half a mile away, searching for its target in the driving snow.

A hundred yards ahead at the bottom of the hill was Deviations Boulevard. On the far side of Deviations at the intersection of the two streets and lined up right in the crosshairs of a gun sight were the front gates of the United States Embassy.

"Tell him he'll be fine as long as he does exactly as he's told," said Holliday.

Eddie told him.

"Tell him to drive slowly down the hill and stop in front of the gates; as soon as we're outside and on the street he's free to go."

Eddie told him that as well.

"Does he understand?"

"Vy ponimaete?"

"Da," answered Felix Fyodor. He threw the grader into a lower gear, eased his foot off the brake and pushed the throttle forward slightly. He felt terrible, and he didn't believe his two passengers for a second. They were clearly terrorists, and he was going to be involved no matter what he said or did. To make things worse, his heartburn had reached levels of pain he never thought could come from sauerkraut. He was sweating rivers, his bladder was close to voiding and he suddenly had a terrible pain in the back of his neck. And his right eye started to have black spots dancing in front of it. He blinked, gritted his teeth and tried to concentrate on what he was doing. Suddenly his right hand spasmed and jerked the throttle forward. The grader began to speed up, its monstrous transmission growling.

"Tell him to slow down!" Holliday yelled.

And then it was all irrelevant to Felix Fyodor Fosdikov. A dozen or so hibernating arteries in the Russian's head all conspired to blossom into bright flower, while at the same time his already elevated heart rate went into full-on tachycardia. Felix Fyodor's brain and heart both stopped functioning at the same instant. He dropped dead over the controls, his hand pushing the throttle forward to its limit and his jerking knee hitting the blade control, dropping both plows into the snow. By the time the grader reached the bottom of the hill it was going its full forty-two miles per hour. The attack helicopter, finally in range, saw where the grader was headed and instantly sheered away, not wanting to be the root cause of World War Three by firing at the American embassy.

"Holy crap," whispered Holliday.

All eighteen tons of the grader smashed into the gate, broke through the chain behind it, then jumped the steel poles that slid up automatically, while its big solid wheels went over the double strip of six-inch spikes as though they were thumbtacks. It finally struck the main entrance and the sally port before it came to a stop. For a few seconds there was a wintry absolute silence.

And then all hell broke loose.

All hell broke loose, but hell, especially during a Moscow winter, inevitably freezes over. Two weeks passed. Eddie was given an emergency splenectomy in the embassy's clinic and was recovering by leaps and bounds. Holliday was debriefed by everyone at the embassy with clearance to do so, as well as two CIA types from Langley, three more from the NSA, Kokum from the national security adviser's office and a humorless man from something called the Osmond Institute. Holliday's joke about puppy love didn't even make him crack a smile. Brinsley Whitman Havers was sent home on the first flight out the day after the snowplow crashed through the gates, doing an estimated three and a half million dollars' damage.

For his part Holliday told them the truth, right from the beginning. He was relatively sure no one would believe him, and he was right. The only thing he left out was the Jesus gospel; that secret would remain with him until he died.

Privately furious but publicly contrite, the Kremlin apologized to the U.S. ambassador for the damage done by the snowplow by the unfortunate city employee who had dropped dead at the controls of his machine, and promised full restitution. The Kremlin separately and very privately demanded that Holliday be removed from the Russian Federation at the earliest opportunity, and further advised the ambassador that if Lieutenant Colonel Holliday ever set foot on Russian soil again he would be shot on sight.

"The powers that be have reached a consensus," said Pat Philpot, reaching for a Werther's Original from the full fishbowl on his desk. He undid the wrapper and popped it into his mouth.

"And that would be?" Holliday asked.

"You're going home to a closed congressional hearing, and now that your friend is better we're shipping him across town to the Cuban embassy."

"If you give Eddie to the Cubans they'll kill him. In the first place he's a dissident, and in the second place he deserted from their forces in Angola."

"Not my problem," said Philpot, sucking on the candy.

"No, it's my problem, Potsy, but that makes it your problem, too. I testify before a congressional committee, I'll take you down, and a few dozen others with you. I know that you were a mole for the company at the National Counterterrorism Center, and I know that you're a mole here—and that's just the beginning. This is what's going to happen, Potsy: you're going to get a diplomatic flight from Sheremetyevo out of Russia and you're going to put me and Eddie on it. Take us to Ramstein AFB in Germany and we'll make our way from there. I promise you'll never hear from us again."

There was a long pause. Potsy swallowed what was left of the caramel candy and cleared his throat. He stared at the man seated across from him. He'd known Holliday for the better part of thirty years. Twice he'd saved his life. If nothing else Potsy was a good judge of character; he knew that regardless of any past relationship, the one-eyed man would be true to his word. And he knew more than where the bodies were buried—he knew who'd dug the graves. Finally he spoke.

"I'll see what I can do."

Moscow's Sheremetyevo airport is enormous; the passenger terminal is the size of a dozen football fields, and although it has been given a rudimentary face-lift since the fall of the Soviet Union, it still has the low-ceilinged, brightly lit, concrete-columned and utilitarian look that was dominant in that era, although the bare concrete columns had now been plastered with liquor company advertisements. On an average afternoon in early November there can be up to fifty thousand people milling around in the enormous space, some arriving, some departing. After several Chechen terrorist attacks the security presence has been increased, and heavily armed police are a common sight. There are hundreds of cameras, and metal detectors have been installed in all the entrance doorways.

Holliday and Eddie arrived at the airport at three fifteen in the afternoon, each of them handcuffed to a U.S. Marine guard from the embassy and flanked by two black-uniformed and helmeted "special" officers. An unmarked U.S. Army VIP Gulfstream V had been arranged to take them to Ramstein Air Force Base, with a flight time of two and a half hours. Both Holliday and

Eddie had already been cleared by Russian customs and immigration by special arrangement with Prime Minister Putin's office in the Kremlin.

John Bone, seated on a plastic bench with his overcoat over his arm, saw the man first. He looked either extremely ill or worse, drunk, and his weaponry was wrong. He wasn't carrying the standard Czech-made Skorpion submachine gun. His handgun looked like a twenty-year-old Makarov rather than the proper Stechkin APS blowback pistol. On top of that the man's uniform was dirty and ill fitting, hanging on him like a clown's outfit. John Bone was a man of many talents, and one of them was knowing when the kill site had been prejudiced. He stood up, walking crosswise across the terminal and out of harm's way. Maybe some other time.

As Holliday and Eddie headed for the special boarding gate that had been arranged, a uniformed security policeman came out of the crowd almost directly in front of them. His name was Yakov Semenov, and the uniform, weapons and identification allowing him entrance to the airport had been provided by his boss, Yevgeni Ivanovich Barsukov, imprisoned head of the Tambov Gang of St. Petersburg, the assignment done at the request of Pierre Ducos and the other Apostles. Semenov, suffering from metastasized fourth-stage lung cancer, knew there was very little likelihood that he would survive the next thirty seconds—he had been promised that his family in St. Petersburg would be amply rewarded for his sacrifice.

Eddie was the first to see Semenov draw his weapon and he acted instinctively; yanking his marine guard bodily to the right he shouldered Holliday out of the line of fire. He was too late; the assassin had already fired. Falling, Holliday saw rather than felt an enormous white-hot blur of pain in the corner of his right eye, and then there was nothing but the perfect certain blackness of death.

EPILOGUE

The eyewitness statements provided by the two marine escorts agreed that the assassin was definitely aiming for center mass when he fired. If it hadn't been for Eddie's quick thinking there was no doubt that had the home-made dumdum round connected it would have blown Holliday's heart out through his spinal cord. As it was the shot struck Holliday in the empty socket of his right eye, exiting the skull two inches above his ear.

It was decided that the surgeons at the trauma center at Ramstein AFB could do a better job, and he arrived there two hours later. The surgeons put him into an induced coma for three days until his brain swelling subsided, and then he was awakened, not much the worse for wear but suffering from the mother of all concussions and the grandmother of all headaches.

Holliday woke from his first good night's sleep since arriving at Ramstein and opened his eyes. Eddie, sitting in the big visitor's chair by the window, looked up.

"You are awake, *compadre*. You still have the head-ache?"

"It's starting to fade."

Eddie brought the rolling table and pushed it so it was across Holliday's lap. Holliday used the control on the bed and raised it into a sitting position, and Eddie brought him his breakfast tray. He sat down at the edge of the bed.

Holliday looked at his friend; something was clearly bothering him. "What's the matter?"

Eddie sighed. "I spoke with my mother in Habana last night. My brother Domingo, who works for the Ministry of the Interior, has vanished, disappeared. She is very worried . . . how do you say it in English . . . frantic?"

Holliday could see from his expression that Eddie wasn't too far from being frantic himself. He thought about Eddie and what they had been through, both in Africa and in Russia. Holliday had never had a brother and rarely a close friend, but he had one now, and the kind of friendship he and Eddie had together had obligations and responsibilities.

"Okay," said Holliday quietly. "As soon as they let me out of here let's go find him."

Read on for a special preview of
Paul Christopher's next thriller,

VALLEY OF THE TEMPLARS

Coming from Signet in June 2012.

Room 212 Hart Senate Building,
Washington, D.C.
Committee Investigating the Use of Paramilitary
Corporations, Private Armies and Private Police Forces
Both Within and Without the Continental United
States, Senator Fulton J. Abernathy (Dem.),
Wisconsin, Chairman

February 19, 2012

Room 212 in the Hart Senate Building was a multimillion-dollar interrogation chamber, where people from
Enron executives to possible appointees to high positions in government testified. A massive wall of marble
stood behind the central section of the senators' dais.
The other two sections on either side stretched before
walls of exotic wood paneling, with cutouts for press
boxes like some political baseball game. A single long

table faced the senators, with room for two hundred or so spectators behind. The carpeted floor featured plenty of room for press photographers to kneel or squat beneath the senators' dais, and a large United States Senate seal hung on the marble wall, with a convenient swing door beneath it to allow for a television camera to get reaction shots.

The two men and their several lawyers being spitted that particular day were Major General Atwood Swann, president of Blackhawk Special Forces Corporation, and his second in command, Colonel Paul Axeworthy. Swann was dressed in the uniform of a U.S. Marine major general, his chest resplendent with medals from Vietnam, both Iraq wars and Afghanistan. Swann was a big man, square-faced, his Marine buzz cut going from blond to grey. Axworthy was wearing Blackhawk battle dress uniform, or BDUs, consisting of a green-on-green camouflage blouse and trousers tucked into spit-shined combat boots, a bright blue scarf at his throat and a dark green beret bearing the Blackhawk logo: a black bird on a gold background. The beret was tucked into the left epaulette of his blouse. He wore an identical gold-and-black patch on both shoulders. The two men's five lawyers were dressed like lawyers.

Senator Fulton J. Abernathy, the committer chair, wore a dusty suit twenty years out-of-date and a psychedelic tie that wouldn't have looked out of place on the *Sgt. Pepper's* album cover. He had a face like a wrinkled apple. His eyes were bright blue and extremely alert behind a pair of bright green half-framed bifocals. The grilling had already been going on for two hours but Abernathy was still in top form and Swann hadn't flinched once.

AB: What is your annual salary at Blackhawk, General Swann?

SW: I was informed that there would be no questions regarding personal matters.

AB: Well, I'm telling you otherwise and I'm the boss here, so answer the question.

SW: One million seven hundred eighty-five thousand plus bonuses.

AB: What kind of bonuses?

SW: Bonuses for successful missions.

AB: Such as.

SW: Katrina, for one.

AB: Katrina, as in the hurricane?

SW: Yes.

AB: What, pray tell, was your mission there?

SW: We were hired as an adjunct to local forces to maintain order.

AB: What about your mission in El Salvador?

SW: I'm not sure I understand the question.

AB: Were you not hired by the government of El Salvador to "relocate" several villages and their occupants in the interior for the purposes of a major gold mining corporation owned by the same person who controls the multinational corporation that in turns owns both Blackhawk Security as well as Blackhawk Special Forces—one Kate Sinclair, mother of the late Senator William Pierce Sinclair, who recently took his own life?

SW: That's a complicated question, Senator.

AB: I'll try to pay attention when you answer it. El Salvador, in particular the villages of San Diego de Tripicano and the village of Cuscatleon, which according to my information simply do not exist anymore. In fact, the only things left of both places are a scattering of burned-out ruins and a few charred bones. How did you manage that little trick, General, and what kind of bonus where you paid for slaughtering two hundred thirty people, men, women and children?

SW: I'm afraid the El Salvador mission is a matter of national security, Senator.

AB: El Salvador's national security? Ask me if I give a tinker's fart about El Salvador's national security.

[Pause]

SW: My counsel advises me to plead the Fifth Amendment.

AB. I'll just bet they do. One more question before we break for lunch, General Swann. Have you ever been hired by any U.S. government agency to invade the territory of a sovereign nation?

SW: My counsel advises me—

AB: We get the picture. . . . General. Let's break for lunch.

Four miles off Cayo Coco Cuba
Phase of the Moon: New
April 21, 2012

It was midnight, and it was raining. The four ancient rusting fishing trawlers puttered slowly northwest along the coast, offshore from the long archipelago of cays and islands that stretched along Cuba's Atlantic shoreline. Most were uninhabited strips of sand and coral occupied by windblown palms. A few, like Cayo Coco, had been turned into resorts to entice tourists, but it was the end of the season and even the resorts were almost empty. If anyone was listening that night, he would have assumed that the engine sound came from the rock lobster and shrimp fleet that plied the banks of the Bahía de Buena Vista farther south and that the boats were now heading for one of the main fishing terminals, such as Matanzas.

At ten past twelve, the engine of one of the four old boats in the group sputtered and died, and the three others stopped their own engines to see what thay could do to help. Some wit in the head office had decided to name one of the boats *Bahía* and another *Cochinos*—

Bay of Pigs, but under the rust and the filth and the piles of empty nets hanging over the derrick and the mast, it was unlikely that anyone was going to notice the names on a dark, rainy night four miles out to sea. Even if Cuban radar was in good enough repair to be working that night, the four boats were wooden and so low in the water, they would likely have been invisible.

As soon as the engines stopped, the crews of all four boats surged into action. Instead of shrimp and lobster, the trawlers carried ten five-by-six bags, each containing a seven-meter inflatable Zodiac boat and another set of bags holding the vessel's silenced electric motors, hardly neccessary tonight because the tide was rushing ashore. Each trawler also carried 120 men, all fully equipped with weapons bags and LAR V Draegar bubble-free rebreathing apparatus, suitable for the shallow depths and warm waters ashore and with a ninty-minute useful breathing time. Within twenty minutes the boats and all 480 men had been offloaded and were headeding toward a GPS point between two uninhabited cays sixteen miles northwest of Cayo Coco. The four trawlers continued their journey, their course slowly changing to a more northeasterly one and their staging point on the southern tip of Andros Island in theBahamas group.

Ninety minutes later, their Zodiacs sunk in seventy feet of water, the 408-man unit landed on a rocky abandoned beach twenty miles west of the town of Yaguajay. They stripped off their rebreathing gear and stowed in the waterproof knapsacks, where their camo gear had been kept. The weapons bags were unsealed, each man armed himself according to his role in the mission.

At three fifteen in the morning, almost five hundred handpicked men from the Blackhawk Special Forces elite Special Boat Unit moved off the beach in double time, and within another hour, they had vanished into the deep jungles covering the slopes of the Escambray Hills. They were the sixth such unit to have been landed successfully on the empty beaches of Sancti Spíritus Sancti province, and there were four more to come over the next six weeks. Operation Cuba Libre was in full swing.

New York Times bestselling author

Paul Christopher

THE TEMPLAR LEGION

Retired Army Ranger Lt. Col. John Holliday is swept into an adventure as deadly as it is secretive when an archaeologist friend makes a bizarre find in Ethiopia. But when he follows a trail of clues through the chaotic and lawless horn of Africa, he finds himself hunted as he comes closer to a priceless treasure that can only be found by those who can solve a riddle from the past.

New York Times bestselling author

Paul Christopher

THE TEMPLAR CONSPIRACY

In Rome, the assassination of the Pope on Christmas Day sets off a massive investigation that stretches across the globe. But behind the veil of Rex Deus—the Templar cabal that silently wields power in the twenty-first century—the plot has only just begun.

When retired Army Ranger Lt. Col. John Holliday uncovers the true motive behind the pontiff's murder, he must unravel a deadly design to extend the Templar influence to the highest levels of power.

Available wherever books are sold or at penguin.com